Stars

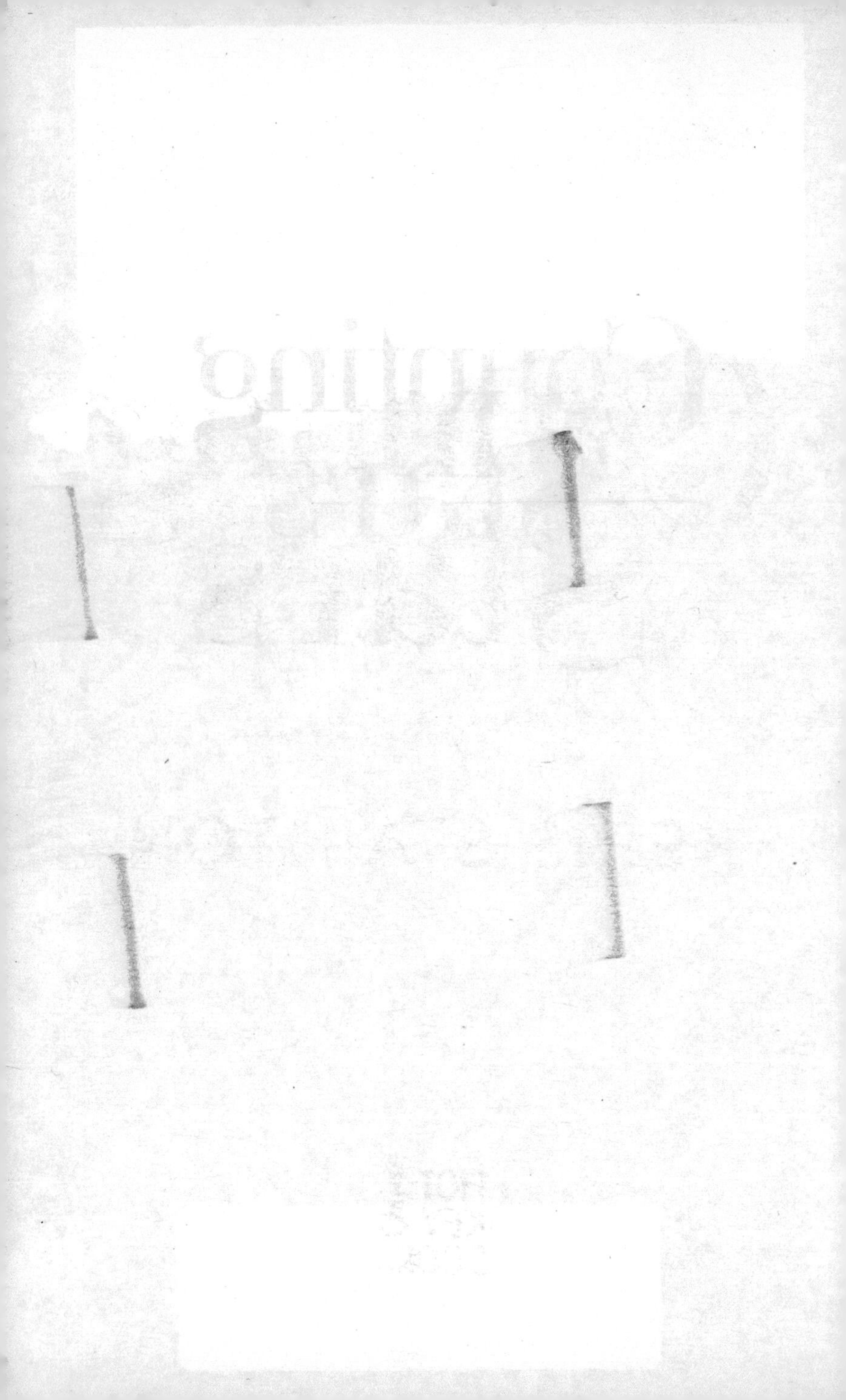

KERIS STAINTON

First published in Great Britain in 2015 by Hot Key Books
Northburgh House, 10 Northburgh Street, London EC1V 0AT

A CIP catalogue record for this book is available from the British Library.

ISBN: 978-1-4714-0463-4

1

This book is typeset in 10.5 Berling LT Std using Atomik ePublisher

Printed and bound by Clays Ltd, St Ives Plc

www.hotkeybooks.com

Hot Key Books is part of the Bonnier Publishing Group
www.bonnierpublishing.com

For everyone who's ever made a bad decision

SPARKSLIFE: Moving

by AnnaSparks 8,021 views
Published on 4 September

[Transcript of Anna's vlog]

So. It looks like I'm moving to Liverpool. I know. I can't believe it either. My parents have agreed to let me give it a go. I've been offered a fantastic job at the theatre where I did my work experience and the brother of the woman I worked with – Hi, Lola! – has a house where I can rent a room. I can't quite believe it's all come together so brilliantly, but I think it has . . .

The only thing that could go wrong is that my mum could see the house and say no. So please can you all cross your fingers for me and say a little prayer, light a candle or whatever you like to do. I really want to go and start my new life.

I will miss my old life though, especially my friends and my room, which I've finally managed to get almost exactly as I want it. Remember the saga of the colour for the walls? All those little paint pots? Big argument in the comments about whether I should paint it Misty Heather or Luscious Blush? And my bed is finally perfectly comfy. But I suppose

I could take my own mattress? I don't know. I can take my own pillows, can't I? And I can even paint the room Pretty Petal or something, if I don't like it.

So that's my news for now. Me and Mum are going to see the house tomorrow so I'll know by the next video. Fingers crossed!

Chapter 1

Anna wondered if she could maybe give her mum the slip. Tell her she needed something from Boots or M&S and then when her mum went to 'just have a quick look' at tweezers or tins of biscuits, do a runner. An hour on the train with her had been more than enough. She couldn't believe she was going to meet the people she would share the flat with with her mum in tow.

'Is it that door?' her mum said, pointing across the busy concourse.

'The one that says "EXIT"?' Anna said.

'There's no need for that, madam. There's another exit over there. Do you know which one we need?'

Rolling her eyes at being called 'madam', Anna shook her head. They went through the nearest door, which took them out to the front of the station, where stone steps led down to face an enormous neon advertising screen.

'Why does there have to be advertising everywhere?' her mum said.

Anna didn't bother responding. She'd heard her mum's opinions on advertising – on everything – over and over again. When she was little she thought her mum was right about everything. Now she was pretty confident her mum was wrong about everything. Except about letting her move to Liverpool. She was right about that. But why did she have to come with her?

'Can you wait for me in a cafe or something?' Anna asked as they stood at the lights to cross the busy main road.

'How many times?' her mum said through her teeth. 'I need to see where you're going to live. I need to meet the people you'll be living with. I'm not sending you off to a city without even being able to picture where you are.'

'I could Skype you,' Anna muttered.

Her mum didn't even acknowledge it. They both knew Anna wouldn't Skype her. As they walked, Anna could feel her mum bristling about the boarded-up shops, the casinos and 'gentlemen's clubs', even the litter. But Anna didn't care. Just the thought of working at the theatre made excitement bubble up inside. And she was leaving home. She was moving away. She was going to do the job of her dreams. On her own.

Her life was finally about to start.

As long as her mum approved.

Anna had always been a good girl. She'd always done exactly what her parents had expected of her and never given them any trouble. She'd never even really *wanted* to give them any trouble. When she heard – or sometimes witnessed – the kind of stuff her friends got up to: going out and getting ridiculously, humiliatingly drunk; lying about staying at friends' houses (sometimes Anna's house) so they could sneak around with their boyfriends; bunking off school and shoplifting, she thought it sounded like too much effort. And somehow inauthentic – like they were going through the motions of how they thought teenagers should behave. Anna just wasn't into it. She wanted to work hard and do well and move out of home and get on with her life. She felt like being a teenager was the bit you had to get through before your life could really start.

But then over the summer she'd got an internship at the Phoenix Theatre and it had changed everything. Lola had been Anna's supervisor. She'd met her in the foyer when Anna, pale and shaking with fear, had first arrived. She knew what a fantastic opportunity the internship was, knew she'd be getting experience and making contacts that could help her in her future career, and so she needed it to go well. She needed to impress. And she'd been nervous as hell.

Even getting the train on her own and then walking through the city had been exciting and nerve-racking. She hadn't been able to imagine doing it every single day, but by the end of the six weeks she had a routine that included getting a hot chocolate at the station and a muffin for the homeless guy who sat at the bottom of the ramp to the shopping centre. (He called her 'smiley face'. No one had ever called her anything like that before. She liked it.)

Much like the homeless guy, Lola had made Anna feel welcome immediately. Instead of taking her up to the office to start work, she'd taken her out to Patisserie Valerie about five minutes away and bought her a cup of tea and a slice of apple tart, which she'd said was fine for breakfast because it was fruit. Dressed like a secretary from *Mad Men* in a fitted bottle-green dress and what looked to Anna like plastic shoes with a huge red heart on the toe, her hair piled high on her head and her black-rimmed glasses continually sliding down her nose, she'd chatted away, telling Anna the history of the theatre, what her role would be, what Lola needed help with and what Anna would be doing. By the time Anna had finished her second cup of tea, all her nerves had gone.

They walked back to the theatre and, upstairs in the office, Lola showed Anna around and introduced her to everyone. By the end of the day, Anna felt like she could stay for ever. The place even smelled exciting.

She couldn't help comparing it with the universities she'd been to see – all within about sixty miles of home since she hadn't felt ready to move too far away from Meadowvale. At every campus they'd visited – her mum asking questions and collecting leaflets and making notes – Anna had waited for one to feel 'right'. But none of them had. There was one that she thought she might get to like, but she hadn't been sure at all. She wondered if it was just that she didn't feel ready, but once she'd started on the work experience, she realised she *was* ready – she just didn't want to go to university.

And it turned out she was actually good at the job. It wasn't exactly what Anna wanted to do – it was admin – but it was interesting because it was admin for a theatre and she was learning a lot. Anna had to check copy for the programs, contact people about props, take proofs to the printers. She even got to go and hang out in the prop room for a little while. She loved it all. She didn't want to go home at night and couldn't wait to get back there in the mornings.

When the six weeks were up, Anna wasn't ready to leave. She'd got loads done while she was there – she'd spotted a mistake in one of the programmes that everyone had been incredibly relieved to catch and couldn't stop going on about. It made Anna feel more worthwhile than she ever had in school. She'd always done well at school, most of it had come pretty easily to her, but she'd never actually thought about what she enjoyed. She'd just kept moving on to the next achievement – from the class prize to her GCSE results to getting a great work placement.

And even when the placement was over, there was still stuff she needed to do – she'd started setting up a database for sub-contractors and related businesses, and it wasn't finished. The other girls were pleased with what she'd done so far, but she'd really wanted to see it right through to the end.

On Anna's last day, Lola had bought a huge chocolate cake that looked like a flower, and a bottle of Bucks Fizz – joking about how Anna wasn't actually eighteen until the following week, the last day of August. Anna relished the feeling of the bubbles going up her nose and tried to take a mental photo – she wanted to remember everything about it. Forever.

Lola made a toast, saying Anna was the best intern they'd ever had and that there would be a job waiting for her as soon as she was ready. Anna had blushed and laughed and thanked everyone and then cried all the way home on the train.

When she'd first told her parents that she wanted to forget about university and go and work at the Phoenix, they'd been appalled. And then confused. One of the many questions they'd asked was if it was because of Lola. Had Lola pressured her into the idea of giving up university? Anna had talked constantly about Lola while she'd been working there. Did Anna have a crush on her? Was something going on between them? Did they need to report Lola for inappropriate behaviour? Anna had been horrified. And embarrassed. Not at the idea of her and Lola together, but because that's what her parents thought her motivation might have been. She did have a crush on Lola, she knew she did. But it wasn't sexual. It was because Lola was the kindest, most confident, smartest person Anna had ever met. She was pretty much Anna's opposite in every single way and so much closer to the person Anna wanted to be. The person Anna was determined to become.

Anna could feel her mum's disapproval as soon as they turned into the street. To be fair, it couldn't have made a worse first impression – on the corner was a knock-off Kentucky Fried Chicken ('Clucky Fried Chicken') and next to that was a Thai massage parlour, its windows painted over in black.

'You lost, girls?' a man said from the doorway opposite.

'No, thank you,' Anna's mum said without even looking at him.

So rude. But then when Anna looked at him, she was glad: he was wearing short shorts and no top or shoes – his feet and legs up to his knees were black with dirt. He grinned at Anna – his two front teeth were missing. She gave him a half-hearted smile back.

'Are you sure this is the right street?' Anna's mother said. 'It looks industrial.'

It looked, to Anna, like the kind of edgy New York street she'd seen in fashion shoots in magazines in the hairdressers.

The street itself was cobbled and the buildings on the right-hand side were mostly red brick and dotted with graffiti. The left side was dominated by new-looking apartment blocks.

'I assume we're looking for one of those,' Anna's mum said, pointing up at the flats.

'No, I don't think so,' Anna said. 'It's a house.'

'Down here?' Her mum's expression reminded Anna of the time she'd accidentally walked dog shit into their home.

'Yes,' Anna said, deciding to ignore her mum's face and just look out for the house. 'It's opposite a cafe, Lola said.'

Even without looking at her mum, Anna could feel her judgement radiating from her tasteful beige mac.

'It's there,' Anna said. 'I think.'

The cafe opposite had its shutters down – they were spray-painted with a silhouette of a unicorn in a crossed red circle – like a danger traffic sign. Something was written across the red line, but Anna couldn't see what it was, and she wasn't going to go and look while her mum was there. She just wanted to get her into the house as quickly as possible. At least, she thought she did. She didn't really know what to expect from the house or her housemates. Lola had told her the house was great, that the people living there were great, and she thought she could trust Lola's judgement, but the fact of it was that she didn't really know Lola at all. She had only recently met her, after all. What if the house was a total mess and the housemates were dodgy too? She'd be frog-marched back to the station and the whole Liverpool idea would never be spoken of again.

Anna closed her eyes and muttered a little prayer to herself: 'Please let the house be nice. Please let the people be nice.

Please let Mum be nice.' Anna wasn't religious, but she still couldn't resist asking for help when she really needed it. And she really needed it now.

'Are you sure it's this one?' her mum said, stepping back into the road and looking up at the three-storey building. 'It looks abandoned.'

It didn't look abandoned to Anna, but it didn't exactly look well-loved either. The semi-circle of window panels over the door had been covered with brown paper, the drainpipe had come away from the wall and was tied up with blue twine, and the small downstairs window was protected with black iron bars. Anna couldn't see a bell, so she knocked on the door. While they waited, she did a bit more praying, but no one came, so she knocked on the door again.

'Do they know you're coming?' her mum said.

Anna gritted her teeth. 'Yes. Lola's brother's meeting us here.'

'And do you know anything about him? Except for the fact that he's Lola's brother?'

'He's a business student,' Anna said. 'At Liverpool Uni. And he works part-time in a coffee shop on Bold Street.'

They waited a bit longer. Anna couldn't believe no one was answering the door. This kind of thing was right up her mother's street. She loved complaining about people not keeping their promises and how irresponsible young people were these days. Anna couldn't bear it. She knocked again.

'I don't think anyone's home,' her mum said.

'Maybe they're upstairs and can't hear the knocking.'

'In that case, a bell might be a wise investment.'

Anna rolled her eyes and prayed a bit more.

Chapter 2

'Shouldn't you have left by now?' Sharda asked Alfie.

He glanced up at the oversized wall clock and nodded. Where the hell was Molly? She'd promised to be there fifteen minutes ago so he could get back to the house to let the new girl – the potential new girl – in.

'Yup,' Alfie said. He grabbed a cloth and wiped the milk off the frother, then dropped the cloth in the tupperware box under the counter.

'I don't know why you still ask her,' Sharda said. 'She lets you down every time.'

Alfie shook his head. 'She had a class. It probably ran over or something.'

As Alfie turned back to the counter, he saw Sharda roll her eyes. He was rolling his eyes at himself too. Sort of. He just couldn't say no to Molly. She needed the money and so he gave her shifts whenever he could. Even though she was totally unreliable and the last time she'd covered for him the till had been down. Only a few quid, but he still had to make it up from his wages. But it was worth it to make her happy. And he knew she needed the money.

By the time Alfie had served the next customer – a tall Scottish woman who couldn't choose between Ethiopian and Sumatran blend coffee, and wanted to chat about how much Liverpool had changed since she'd been there as a student – Alfie really did need to leave.

'Just go,' Sharda said. 'I'll be fine.'

Alfie frowned. He wasn't supposed to leave Sharda on her own. There was supposed to be two members of staff in the cafe at all times.

'Don't worry,' Sharda said. 'Molly'll probably be here in a minute and if not you can come back, can't you?'

'Yeah,' Alfie said, undoing his apron and pulling it off over his head. 'Shouldn't imagine it'll take more than half an hour or so. They're just having a look.'

'I'll ring you in half an hour if she's still not here,' Sharda said, flapping a tea towel at him. 'Go on. Go.'

'OK!' Alfie said, walking around from behind the counter. 'I can be here in two minutes.'

'I know. Don't worry.'

'Thanks.' Alfie weaved between the tables on his way to the door. 'I owe you one!'

'More than one,' Sharda muttered, smiling, but he'd already left.

'Anna?'

Anna turned towards the shout and saw a man running towards them. He had cropped hair, brown skin and a huge smile. Anna almost groaned with relief.

'I'm so sorry I'm late,' he said, skidding to a stop in front of them.

Now that he was closer, Anna could see he was definitely Lola's brother. He looked just like her – the same bright smile and eyes that looked like he was about to laugh. And where Lola was striking – as Anna's mother would say – rather than pretty, Alfie was really handsome.

'I'm Alfie,' he said, holding his hand out to Anna's mum. 'You must be . . .' He frowned. 'Anna's mum.'

'I am indeed,' her mum said. 'Good of you to make it back to let us in.'

Anna felt hot at her mum's rudeness, but it didn't seem to bother Alfie at all.

'No problem. Like I said, sorry I'm late. I was waiting for Molly to come and take over at work and she was late. As usual. She lives here too,' he told Anna. 'She's really great.'

'But not at punctuality,' Anna's mum said.

Alfie laughed. 'No. Definitely not at punctuality.'

As Alfie opened the door, Anna marvelled at his ability to just laugh off her mum's comments. Maybe they annoyed Anna so much because her mum was, well, her mum. Maybe she wasn't actually as rude as Anna thought. Or maybe Alfie's method for dealing with rudeness was just to ignore it. He probably had to do that a lot working with the public. Anna had done a Saturday job in a bakery for a while and it made her hate people.

The first thing Anna noticed when Alfie opened the door was a rainbow on the floor. At first she couldn't quite think how it could possibly be there, but then she thought to look behind her. What she'd thought was brown paper over the semi-circular windows was actually a different colour of tissue paper on each pane, the light shining through them making the rainbow.

'Carpet rainbow,' Alfie said, seeing Anna looking. 'Molly's work. She said the hall needed cheering up and what's more cheerful than a rainbow?'

Anna felt rather than heard her mum snort, but she ignored her. She loved the rainbow, no matter what her mum thought.

The rest of the hallway was fairly dark with plain walls and one of those scratchy rope carpets.

'The house is sort of upside-down,' Alfie said. 'Except the kitchen.' He gestured through to the right, and Anna and her mum followed him into a huge kitchen with white units, an overstuffed sofa piled with cushions, a breakfast bar and, on a shelf around the top of the wall, dozens of empty bottles. At least, Anna assumed they were empty. It smelled a bit like the bin needed to be cleaned, but Anna could also smell something lemony – washing up liquid or some other cleaning product. She wondered if they had a cleaner. Or a cleaning rota.

'Are the bars warranted?' Anna's mum asked Alfie, pointing at the window. The glass was frosted, but they could see the outline of the bars anyway.

'Sometimes. But we've never really had to deal with anything bad. It's generally a pretty friendly area.'

Anna couldn't help wishing he'd just said 'no' but her mum hadn't dragged her out of there yet, so she couldn't be too horrified.

'There was a man at the end of the road,' her mum said, her eyes scanning the room. 'He was practically naked. And filthy.'

So she had seen him. Anna hadn't even seen her look.

'Oh, yeah,' Alfie said. 'That's Orville. He's a sort of local character. He used to be a roadie for loads of bands . . . or so he says. He's harmless.'

'Right,' her mum said. 'Shall we have a look at Anna's room?'

They followed Alfie up the stairs in silence.

'I just need to warn you . . . it's pretty small,' Alfie told Anna once they'd reached the landing.

'I know,' Anna said. 'Lola told me.'

She wasn't worried. She didn't need much.

When Alfie opened the door it banged against something and he had to step out of the room to let Anna and her mum go in. It really was small. Smaller even than Anna had expected. The door had banged against the foot of the single bed that took up the whole of the left wall. Next to it, in front of a radiator under the window, was a bedside table. And that was it. No wardrobe, no chest of drawers, nothing else.

'Well—' Anna's mum started.

'I like it,' Anna said.

Her mum scoffed. 'Where would you even put your clothes?'

'Yeah,' Alfie said. 'Sorry about that. Harry, who had the room before? He had a small clothes rail, but he took it with him.'

Anna frowned, but then noticed the large drawers under the bed. 'They'll be fine in there. I haven't got much.' One of the things that she hoped would change when she moved here was that she would find some sense of her own style rather than just buying whatever was easiest.

'You'll need curtains,' her mum said.

Anna shook her head. The window was large – taking up most of the far wall – and a venetian blind split the light against the opposite wall into strips. Anna crossed the room and looked out at the brick and windows opposite, then down at the road. It wasn't the best view, not unless you liked industrial dustbins and graffiti, but Anna found that she did. For years she'd looked out of her bedroom window over her parents' perfectly manicured garden and felt stifled. This was perfect.

'I love it,' Anna said, grinning.

'Fine,' her mum said. 'Can I give you the first month's rent now?' she asked Alfie.

Anna opened her mouth to speak but closed it again. She hadn't expected it to be so easy. They hadn't even seen the living room yet.

'You haven't even seen the living room yet!' Alfie said. 'That's the best bit.'

Anna's mum tucked her bag more firmly under her arm and followed Alfie up another flight of stairs.

'Wow,' Anna said, as soon as Alfie opened the door.

The room was huge. It took up the whole of the top floor of the house. A battered-looking wooden table surrounded by mismatched chairs and piled high with books and papers and dishes and cups stood over to the right-hand side. In the middle were two huge squashy sofas angled towards the flat-screen TV in the far corner. The left wall was lined with bookshelves, crammed with books, magazines and DVDs. But the most incredible thing was the far wall. It was almost entirely glass and opened out onto a roof terrace.

'This is very nice,' her mum admitted.

'Great, isn't it?' Alfie said. 'It's why my parents bought the place.'

'I wanted to ask you about that,' Anna's mum said. 'When did they buy it?'

Anna was quite interested to know the answer, but she was more interested in the terrace.

'Can I go outside?' she said, interrupting her mum, who tutted.

'Course,' Alfie said. 'The doors are probably open.'

Anna flicked a quick look at her mum to see if she was bristling at that revelation, but she was still gazing about the room. Anna swerved around the sofas and grabbed the handle on the centre door, sliding it. It was obviously double glazed because as soon as she opened it the sounds of the city hit her: sirens and traffic and people shouting. It made her want to laugh out loud. The only sounds she ever heard at home were the birds and occasionally the milkman if he got a bit slapdash putting the bottles on the step.

Anna stepped out onto the terrace. The floor was wooden decking. On the left was a picnic table with bench seats – someone had left a cushion on one of the seats; it looked wet and a bit mouldy – and on the right, a white metal table and two metal chairs were pushed up against the wall. Anna noticed a wine bottle on the floor behind it. Under the front wall were a few planters but the plants inside looked mostly dead. Anna crossed over to the edge and looked down at Bold Street. Bright bunting stretched across to the old building directly opposite. The higher floors were pretty with carved stone lintels and tiny windows encased with iron balconies, but the bottom floor held a takeaway pizza place and a newsagent.

Anna took a deep breath. She was actually going to live here. She couldn't believe it.

When she turned back to the room, her mum was leaning on the dining table and writing a cheque.

'I've paid the deposit and the first month's rent,' her mum told her when Anna joined them at the table. 'After that you're on your own.'

'Thank you,' Anna said.

'When can she move in?' her mum asked Alfie.

'Can't wait to get rid of her, eh?' Alfie said, smiling at Anna.

'She can't wait to leave, I'm afraid,' her mum said.

Anna felt a pang of guilt and looked at her mum. It was true, she couldn't wait to get away, but she didn't think she'd been quite that obvious about it.

'It's OK,' her mum said. 'We'd got used to the idea of you going. We just thought it would be to university.'

Anna hadn't really thought about her leaving home as something her parents would have to get used to. She'd been more focussed on actually going than what she was leaving behind. But she knew they'd be fine without her. They had very full lives. And she knew her mum wanted to spend more time on their business. They'd be fine.

'I'll be coming home,' Anna said. 'It's not like you'll never see me.'

Her mum smiled. 'I know. But it's a big step.'

'Should I make a cup of tea?' Alfie said.

Anna smiled at him.

'No, no,' her mum said. 'That won't be necessary.'

'It's OK,' Alfie said. 'I'm a barista. It's what I do.'

'No, we need to go and get the train. Thank you though.'

She picked her handbag up off the table and pulled her mac tighter. Anna's heart sank at the thought of the hour journey home. Her mum was relatively positive now, but she knew she'd spend the entire journey enumerating everything that was wrong with the house, Anna's room, the area and, probably, Alfie. She felt exhausted at the thought.

'It's a shame you can't stay, actually,' Alfie said. 'We're having a group dinner tonight. It's not that often we're all at home at the same time lately. Everyone is pretty busy now college has gone back.'

Anna almost said 'Oh, can I?' to her mum but then realised she was leaving home. She was leaving home to come and live here. What difference did it make if she left today rather than next week?

'That sounds good,' she said, trying to sound casual. 'I'd love to.'

'But you don't have a change of clothes or anything,' her mum said. 'You haven't even got a toothbrush!'

'I'm sure I can buy a toothbrush,' Anna said. 'We're in the centre of Liverpool.'

'We've got spare bedding somewhere,' Alfie said. 'I'll hunt it out.'

Anna had forgotten there was no bedding on her bed. Her mum's nostrils flared, which Anna knew meant she wasn't at all impressed with this plan, but she said, 'Fine. You'll come home tomorrow for your stuff?'

'Dad said he was going to bring it over for me,' Anna said. 'He can still do that, can't he? Maybe on Saturday? It's only a couple of days.'

'I imagine so,' her mum said. She suddenly looked tired and Anna was relieved she wouldn't be getting the train home with her. She was always at her most negative when she was tired.

'OK then,' Anna said. 'Thanks.'

'We'll take good care of her,' Alfie said.

Anna glanced at him and smiled. He was just like his sister – she'd made Anna feel immediately welcome at work too.

'I'm sure you will,' her mum said. 'So. I'd better go and get that train.'

'Do you know the way back?' Anna said.

'Of course,' her mum said.

'If you take the first left when you leave the house, you can walk up Bold Street,' Alfie said. 'It's a bit nicer than the way you came in.'

Anna knew he meant it was the way to avoid passing Orville and she was grateful to him. She walked down to the front door with her mum and stood on the rainbow to say goodbye.

'So we'll see you at the weekend then,' her mum said, opening the front door.

'Yes,' Anna said. 'Thanks. And thanks for paying the—'

'You have to thank your father for that,' she said. 'It was his idea.'

'Oh. Right,' Anna said. She should have known. 'Well, thank him then.'

'Maybe you could phone him later?'

'Yes. I will. Thanks.'

For a second her mum looked like she was going to step back inside and hug her or something, but she obviously thought better of it. She just pulled her handbag up on her shoulder again and said, 'Bye then.'

Anna closed the door behind her and, for a moment, rested her head against it. She'd left home. She was living in Liverpool. In a shared house on an amazing street with a fabulous roof terrace. No, she didn't have a change of clothes or a pillow or any of her stuff, but that was only for a couple of days.

It was an adventure. Her first ever.

Chapter 3

'Hey!' Sean shouted. He was halfway up the curving staircase when he saw Molly fast-walking across the black and white tiled foyer.

'I can't stop!' Molly waved at him. 'I'll see you later.'

'No, I need to talk to you now.' Sean ran down the stairs and met Molly at the main door.

'Seriously, I can't stop. I'm taking Alfie's shift and I'm really late.'

'I'll walk with you,' Sean said. He opened the door and Molly ducked under his arm and out into the street.

'Haven't you got a class?' Molly asked as she headed down the stone steps.

Sean shrugged. 'Don't worry about it. I need to talk to you.'

'This is about Charlie, right?'

'Of course it's about Charlie,' Sean said. 'Are you seriously going to scurry all the way?'

Molly stopped and looked at him. 'I told you! I'm late!'

'But we're only five minutes away. You doing your mum-run thing isn't going to make that much difference. It just means you'll arrive all sweaty and unattractive.'

'Fast walking!' Molly said, setting off again. 'Also, "mum-run" is totally sexist.'

'Yeah, OK. So. I saw him this morning in the canteen. He was sitting with that guy from Community Theatre. You know, the one that looks like a Viking? Blond hair, red cheeks, cheap jeans?'

'Were Vikings known for their cheap jeans?'

'You know what I mean. They were having breakfast together.'

Molly grabbed Sean's arm to stop him crossing the road. 'They were having breakfast together or they were sitting together and having breakfast?'

'They were talking.'

'Did they look intimate or were they just having a conversation?' The lights changed and Molly linked her arm through Sean's as they crossed the road.

'They weren't licking each other or anything, but, you know? I think they were together. So, what do I do?'

'Ask him about it?'

'Who? The Viking?'

'No, you idiot – Charlie.'

Sean stopped walking and stared at Molly.

'Fast walking!' Molly said, pulling him forward.

'You seriously want me to ask him?'

'God, Sean, I don't know. You like him, don't you? Wouldn't it be easier to tell him you like him?'

Sean shook his head. 'Sometimes I think you don't understand men at all.'

Molly laughed. 'Sometimes? Sean, if I understood men, my life would be a hell of a lot easier.'

'If you just picked one instead of trying to shag them all at once . . .'

'Not all at once,' Molly said. 'Just one at a time.'

'Yeah,' Sean said. 'All of them. One at a time.'

'What can I say?' Molly said, pulling her phone out of her pocket and then shoving it back in without even looking at it. 'I'm a collector.'

'Men aren't Pokémon,' Sean said, grinning.

'I can't believe you're lecturing me about this,' Molly said as they turned into Berry Street. 'You're supposed to be sowing your oats too. We're meant to be going out on the pull together, occasionally finding we've shagged the same bloke—'

'Shoe shopping, drinking cocktails . . .' Sean said. 'You've watched too much *Sex and the City*.'

Molly looked up at the clock on the bombed-out church and groaned. 'How am I so late? Again?'

'Oh, I can't imagine,' Sean said.

'Worst gay best friend ever.'

They turned into Bold Street and Molly said, 'I'm going to run. See you later.'

'Wait,' Sean said, grabbing her arm. 'Tell me what to do about Charlie.'

'Oh, for God's sake. You know what to do. Ask him out for a drink! Tell him you like him!'

'To his face?!' Sean looked appalled.

Molly laughed. 'I'm not going to do it for you, if that's what you're thinking. Just do it.' She ticked a Nike swoosh in the air and Sean laughed.

'Ugh. Go to work. There's no use talking to you.'

Molly grabbed him by the shoulders and planted a kiss right on his mouth. 'See you at dinner.'

'See you,' Sean said, watching her run down the street. 'You mad cow.'

Sean took out his phone. No messages. He didn't know why he was expecting any. He was sort of half hoping that Charlie would have noticed him. Would somehow have intuited that he liked him. Would have found his number. And would text to ask him out. It hadn't happened yet, but Sean lived in hope.

He started walking down Bold Street towards home, but remembered Molly said the potential new girl was coming round and he really didn't feel in the mood to make polite conversation with someone new. Especially since she was taking Harry's old room. And she'd probably have her mum or someone with her. And he'd get roped in to helping build a wardrobe or, because he was gay, help choose curtain fabric.

He turned round and walked back up towards the church, pulling his sunglasses out of his jacket pocket to protect against the September sun. It's not like he didn't have stuff to do at college. It's not like he was only going back there to see if he could find Charlie and maybe try to work out if there was anything going on with him and the Viking.

He was wondering whether he was hungry or thirsty or neither when his phone buzzed in his pocket. He felt a little thrill before realising it really wasn't going to be Charlie. It was his dad. He thought about ignoring it, but he couldn't remember when he'd last spoken to him, so he pressed answer and tried to make his voice sound cheerful.

'Everything all right?' his dad said. He actually sounded

quite cheerful too. Better than he'd sounded for a while.

'Great!' Sean said. 'What's up?'

'Nothing much,' his dad said. 'Working a bit.'

'Oh, yeah? On the house?' Sean crossed the road to turn into Rodney Street.

'No. You know. At work.'

'What do you mean?' he asked, frowning. 'You got a job?'

His dad laughed. 'You knew that.'

'I didn't. When did you get a job?'

'I've had it for years. At the paper.'

Sean stopped walking and shook his head. He felt like he'd missed something vital. Or he'd got the wrong end of the stick. Or . . . something.

'You haven't worked at the paper for years,' he said. 'You mean the Hebden Times?'

'Of course. They came crawling back. I knew they would.'

'When did this happen?'

'Just recently. Didn't I tell you?'

'No. You didn't.' Sean started walking again. 'So . . . what are you doing there?'

'Now? Just watching a film on Channel Five. Some old black-and-white thing.'

'No, I meant at work.'

'What work?'

Sean stopped again and actually held out the phone and looked at it. 'You were just telling me about being back at work,' he said.

'Oh, don't worry about that,' his dad said. 'Listen. Do you need some money?'

Sean laughed. 'I always need money.'

'I'll send you a cheque,' his dad said. 'Same address?'

'Um,' Sean said. 'Yeah.' His dad was the only person he knew who still even used cheques.

'Great. I'll do it now.'

'OK, that's really . . . kind. Thank you.'

'Least I can do for my favourite son, isn't it?' his dad said.

Sean laughed. 'You're not wrong.'

He was just about to thank his dad again, when he realised he'd already hung up. So, Sean thought, that was weird. But by the time he'd got up the steps and back inside the old stone building, he'd put it out of his mind.

Chapter 4

'What are you doing?' Nina hissed.

Jack looked up at her from under the delivery ramp at the back of the hotel. 'Bloody hell, Nina! I nearly shat myself!'

'Are you smoking?'

He grinned and she wanted to punch him. Right in his beautiful face.

'If you get caught, you'll get sacked,' she said.

'Yep. And it'll stunt my growth. Listen to yourself.' He put the cigarette behind his back and smiled up at her. 'Come down here for a bit. Give your nag muscles a rest.'

Nina looked behind her, back into the hotel. There was no one around. She scurried down the ramp and joined Jack underneath. The ground was covered with damp leaves and empty fast food packaging. It smelled like autumn even though it was only early September.

Jack put one arm around her and squeezed. 'That's more like it,' he said.

Nina relaxed against him for just a second, before straightening up again.

'I'm serious though,' Nina said, looking out at the bins, the graffiti-covered back wall, the patch of bright blue sky above. 'You're on your last warning.'

'Don't worry. The old bag's not here. She's gone to a conference.'

'I know,' Nina said. 'But here's an idea. Get your work done – do more than you have to – and then she'll be impressed when she gets back.'

'I could do that,' Jack said, pretending to think about it. 'Or I could just go and watch porn on her computer.'

'You don't!' Nina said, her voice coming out at a higher pitch than usual.

Jack laughed out loud and Nina's stomach clenched again at the sound. She loved his laugh. She thought about that laugh when she was in bed at night. She always heard it right between her legs.

'Nah, I don't,' Jack said. 'I watch it on my phone.'

'You don't!' Nina said.

Jack turned towards Nina and stared intently at her face.

'What?' she said. She hated the way her stomach flipped when he looked at her like that. 'What?!'

'I was just thinking . . . you look nineteen, but you're obviously actually much, much older.'

'Oh, shut up.'

He grinned. 'Haven't you heard the expression "live a little"?'

Nina rolled her eyes. 'I didn't know that included getting the sack, having no money . . .'

'I'd get another job.'

'Yeah, cos it's that easy.'

'Did I miss the part where you told your parents you'd dropped out of college?'

Nina groaned. 'Ugh, God. I just worry about you, that's all.'

Jack smiled at her. A real smile, not one of his supercilious or annoying ones. Her stomach fluttered again.

'You worry too much,' Jack said, giving her another squeeze. 'This job sucks. I'm just having a break. And now you are too. Are you nearly finished?'

'Yeah. Just got one room left.'

'I'll wait for you then,' Jack said.

Nina knew that only really meant that he wanted to come home with her and have sex, but still. It was something. She reached round, took the cigarette out of his hand and put it in her mouth.

'That's my girl,' Jack said.

Nina inhaled so sharply she had a coughing fit.

Nina had met Jack on her first day at The Campbell hotel the previous year. Janice – their boss, the 'old bag' – had given Nina a long lecture about hotel security, which had culminated in a visit to the security office. It was a small room with a desk and a wall of TVs showing film from the various CCTV cameras dotted about inside and outside the hotel, and Jack, who looked about Nina's age, and an older guy called Ali, had been sitting side by side, staring up at the screens.

Jack had been cheeky to Janice – who had rolled her eyes and huffed – and charming to Nina and she'd fancied him straight away, but within a couple of weeks of working there, she realised he was like that with almost everyone, so she didn't think he was particularly interested.

And then at the hotel's Christmas party – which had actually taken place at another, cheaper, less fancy hotel, tucked away in a side street off Church Street – Nina had mixed her drinks so disastrously that she figured making a move on Jack wouldn't hurt. What was the worst that could happen? For a while, she hadn't been able to find him, but she had found Ali who told her Jack was looking for her, so she got another drink and kept looking.

She had found him in the hotel's second bar, lounging in an oversized armchair, holding court with a bunch of the younger lads from the hotel. She'd headed straight over and dropped down on his lap, the cigarette he really shouldn't have been smoking indoors catching the base of her thumb. Nina still remembered the other lads laughing and telling Jack he was 'in there', but she'd been fine with that. He absolutely was. She'd kissed his neck and felt his hand slide up her leg and under her dress and then her next memory was up in one of the rooms – she still didn't know whose room it had been.

They'd both been too drunk to properly take advantage of the room situation. Nina remembered going down on Jack and then being really surprised when he'd reciprocated. She remembered that he couldn't stay hard, which had turned out to be a good thing since neither of them had condoms and Nina had been too drunk to care. She remembered Jack telling her how hot she was, how much he wanted her and she'd felt hot; she'd felt like she'd got exactly what she wanted. Until the next day when she just felt like shit. And she had thrush.

Jack took the cigarette back from her now, took one last drag and dropped it on the floor, stamping it out with his boot.

'Back to work?' Nina said, looking up at the hotel door.

'Not just yet, eh?' Jack said and pushed her back up against the wall.

Nina needed to get back to work. But Janice wasn't in. And Jack was right: she was young, she needed to relax. She hooked her fingers into the waistband of Jack's jeans and pulled his hips against hers.

Chapter 5

'I can't find the spare duvet,' Alfie said when Anna got back upstairs. 'I've got a pillow though. And there's a blanket on the sofa in the kitchen. Maybe one of the others'll know where it is.'

'It's fine,' Anna said. 'Thanks.' She wasn't concerned. She'd happily sleep on the mattress in her clothes as long as she got to stay.

'Do you want that cup of tea now?' Alfie said. 'You look a bit freaked out.'

Anna smiled at him. 'It's all a bit overwhelming. I can't believe I've actually left home. I'm going to be working and living here. And, more importantly, I'm not going to be living at home and with my parents.'

Alfie smiled. 'Your mum was nice.'

'You were great with her, actually,' Anna said. 'Thank you.'

'No, I mean it,' Alfie said. 'She was nice.'

'She was polite,' Anna said. 'Mostly. I don't think anyone has ever really called her nice.'

'She'll miss you,' Alfie said. 'Even if you don't think she will. My parents converted my room into a gym when I moved out, but whenever she's had a few drinks my mum phones to say she's proud of me.'

Anna laughed. 'Mum's not a big drinker. And she's never told me she's proud of me. They'll be fine. It was nice of them to pay the first month's rent though – that means I've got a month's money spare. Should I go and buy something for the dinner tonight? When I get my toothbrush and stuff?

'No, it's fine,' Alfie said. 'We've got everything we need, I think. Just go and have an explore. There are some pretty cool shops.'

'Right,' Anna said, looking around. 'I can't remember where I left my bag.'

'In the kitchen, I think. And I'll have another look for the duvet while you're out.'

Anna crossed the road to read what was written on the unicorn graffiti. It said: 'Please don't feed the hipsters'. Grinning, she did what Alfie had suggested to her mum, and turned left to take her straight into Bold Street. It definitely had a different atmosphere to the street she was living on. Cooler, more lively, less grungy. It was surprisingly busy too, considering it was the middle of a week day. Anna found herself dodging out of people's way and stepping on and off the kerb to let people pass. About halfway down the road, she stopped and stepped up into the doorway of an empty shop – she just wanted to look around and take it all in. But then she realised she was thirsty and spotted a cafe back the way she'd come. She walked up to it and got herself an iced mint tea, wondering if it was the same coffee shop Alfie worked in. Once she had her drink, she walked down into town and got on with shopping for the few things she needed.

She was back at the house less than an hour later, and she hadn't gone far, but she already felt madly in love with Liverpool. She loved the atmosphere; everyone had been friendly in every shop she'd been in. There was a ferris wheel on the main street and a busker singing 'Here Comes the Sun' in front of Boots. Since Alfie had said they didn't need any food, Anna had bought a big bunch of flowers from a stall on the corner. It was only when she got back that she realised she didn't have a key yet.

She knocked and waited and knocked again, but no one came. She was glad her mum wasn't with her – she'd be tutting and rolling her eyes. She knocked again, wondering if maybe Alfie had realised they didn't have everything they needed after all and popped out. She didn't even have the phone number. She'd just decided to go back to the cafe and sit down with another drink when the door opened and Alfie said, 'Sorry, sorry. I was in the shower.'

He'd obviously just got out when she'd knocked the last time because he was still glistening with water and he had a towel wrapped around his waist. Anna felt her face flame. She didn't know where to look.

'Sorry,' Alfie said again.

'No, I'm sorry,' Anna said, looking down at the rainbow. 'Sorry for getting you out of the shower.'

'It's OK,' Alfie said. 'I was done. I need to get a dressing gown or something. I just didn't want you to be standing out here on your own. I'll have to find you the spare key.'

Rather than heading straight up the stairs as Anna expected, Alfie turned into the kitchen and started rummaging through a drawer just under the kettle. She tried not to look at him, but it was hard to tear her eyes away from the muscles in his arms and shoulders. Eventually she crossed the room and stood looking out through the barred window. She could hear herself breathing.

'A-ha!' Alfie said. 'I think this is the one. Do you want to go and try it?'

He met her halfway across the kitchen and handed her the key, his fingers grazing the side of her hand. She felt a fluttering low in her stomach and her face burned again.

'Thanks,' she said, but it came out as a squeak. 'I'll go and . . . try it. Now.'

She mentally kicked herself as she left the kitchen. Why couldn't she even form a half-decent sentence? He'd think she'd never spoken to a boy before. Though she'd never actually spoken to a half-naked boy as good-looking as Alfie. A few of the boys at school were nice enough, but she'd never really fancied any of them. And they hadn't been even slightly interested in her.

She opened the front door ready to try the key and instead was faced with a girl with cropped hair, dyed bright red, like the Little Mermaid.

'Oh!' the girl said.

Anna realised she had her hand out, a key clutched in her fist.

'Sorry!' Anna said. 'I was just coming out to—'

She saw the girl looking over her shoulder inside the house, her eyes widening and the corner of her mouth quirking up.

Anna turned to see Alfie – still in just a towel – standing behind her.

'Oh,' the girl said again. 'Sorry! I didn't mean to interrupt! Should I go and get a coffee and come back?'

Anna wasn't sure what she meant at first, but as soon as she realised she felt her face burning again. 'Oh, no! Nothing like that! I'm Anna!'

She sounded ridiculous. Hysterical and prim and . . . like her mother.

'Anna's taken Harry's room,' Alfie said. 'Anna, this is Molly. She's the one I mentioned earlier. The one who made me late for meeting you.'

Molly rolled her eyes dramatically and said, 'I wasn't that late!'

Anna glanced back to see that Alfie was smiling. She wondered if he smiled all the time.

'So are you leaving already?' Molly asked Anna. 'Had enough of Alfie wandering around semi-nude?'

'No, no,' Anna said. 'I mean . . . I was just—'

'She was just going to try the key,' Alfie said. 'Come inside and let her get on with it, eh?'

Anna stepped to one side to let Molly pass and then went out onto the street to try the key.

It worked fine.

'Do you all take turns cooking?' Anna asked Alfie, who was now dressed and standing in front of the stove, stirring something fantastic-smelling in a huge blue pan.

'Not really. We generally just sort ourselves out cos we're all in and out at different times.' He smiled at her over his shoulder.

'And do you all get on OK?'

'Yeah, most of the time,' Alfie said. 'We've all had fights, of course, but nothing too major. Always gets sorted out after a bit of sulking and some plate smashing.'

'Really?' Anna said.

Alfie laughed. 'No. Well, yes to the sulking – people go and stew in their rooms until they've calmed down.'

'I think plate smashing would be quite good,' Anna said, absent-mindedly flicking through a pile of papers on the breakfast bar before realising everything was addressed to someone called Sean and stopping. 'My parents never fight, they just stop speaking to each other. Sometimes for weeks. Even though they run a business together.'

'Oh, God,' Alfie said, turning and leaning back against a cupboard to look at her. 'I'd hate that. My parents have full-on screaming rows and then everything's fine. Mostly.'

'I think that's better, yeah,' Anna said. 'I don't think my parents ever resolve anything. One of them just eventually forgets they weren't speaking to the other. But they never discuss what they were upset about, they just bury it deep inside. Where it festers.' She smiled.

'How did they feel about you moving here?' Alfie said. 'Your mum seemed OK about it. They weren't expecting you to go to uni?'

Anna winced. 'They were, yeah. I looked at a few places, but I don't know . . . They never felt right. And I felt like I was doing it because it was expected of me rather than something I actually wanted to do, you know?'

Alfie nodded. 'I do, yeah.'

'But now I feel like I . . .' Anna wrinkled her nose in thought. 'I feel like I found a better option. Something that's more me.'

'Working with Lola?'

Anna nodded. 'I know I was only there for a few weeks, but it was the first time that I really felt like myself. And then I started preparing for uni – I accepted a place at Nottingham – but I just . . . I couldn't stand the thought of it. I can't stand the thought of it.' She shook her head. 'I know it sounds mad.'

'It doesn't at all,' Alfie said. 'I think when you find the thing you love to do you just want to start doing it straight away.'

'Have you found it?' Anna asked.

Alfie frowned. 'I think so. Maybe. But . . .'

'You don't have to tell me!' Anna said. 'Sorry, I was just being nosy.'

'No, it's fine. It's just something I've been sort of brewing over.' He smiled, more to himself than at Anna. 'We'll see how it goes.'

Anna heard laughter from the street outside and then the front door opening. Her stomach clenched with nerves. More housemates to meet. What if she hated them? What if they hated her? She really should have made sure she met everyone first. But then maybe she wouldn't even be here now and she was so glad to be here.

The girl walked into the kitchen first. She was very pretty with bobbed brown hair and the most perfect eyebrows Anna had seen outside a magazine.

'Hey!' she said, smiling at Alfie. 'What'cha makin'?'

'Veggie curry,' Alfie said. 'And this is Anna. Anna – Nina.'

'Hi,' Anna said. 'Nice to meet you.'

Nina said hey and then, 'I'll be back in a minute, just going to get changed.'

As Nina headed upstairs, Anna caught a glimpse of a boy passing the door and heading upstairs too, but he didn't come into the room.

'That was Jack,' Alfie said. 'Nina's sort-of boyfriend.'

'Does he live here too?' Anna asked.

Alfie pulled a sceptical face. 'No, he's got his own place, but he stays over fairly often.'

'Right,' Anna said. She couldn't think of a response to that, so instead said, 'Is there anything I can help with?'

Alfie shook his head. 'Nope. Thanks. It's all under control.'

'Let me do something!'

Alfie laughed. 'OK. You can do the bread.'

He passed her a fresh unsliced loaf and a knife and pushed the wooden breadboard across the breakfast bar to her.

By the time Anna had cut and buttered the entire loaf, Nina had come back downstairs on her own. She looked flushed and was all giggly, poking Alfie in the ribs and making him laugh and humming to herself. Anna wondered if she and Jack had just had sex. Had they had time? She glanced up at the clock and was surprised to see it was almost seven. No wonder she was hungry – at home they'd have finished eating by now.

'Red or white?' Nina said to Anna. 'Or beer?'

'Red, please,' Anna said.

She couldn't quite believe that this was her house and these were her housemates and they were offering her wine. Not just wine, but a choice of wine. She felt like she was playing at being a grown-up.

Nina handed her the huge glass and Anna took a sip. It was nice. It tasted warm.

'Where's Jack?' Alfie asked Nina as she emptied the last of the red into her own glass.

'Just having a shower,' Nina said.

So they probably had had sex then, Anna thought. She wondered which room was Nina's.

'Is he staying for dinner?' Alfie asked. 'There's plenty of food.'

'I doubt it,' Nina said. Then she looked at the breakfast bar and laughed. 'Have you done enough bread, do you think?'

Anna looked at the plate. There was a huge mound of bread. It looked ridiculous. She probably only should have done a few slices or something. She felt her cheeks reddening and drank some more wine to take her mind off it.

Chapter 6

They moved upstairs to the dining table in the corner of the lounge, which was lit with fairy lights wound around the bookshelves and out on the terrace. It looked magical, Anna thought.

Molly joined them and then another boy came in who turned out to be Sean. He was really cute, but he and Molly immediately started talking about some guy called Charlie who Sean seemed to be obsessed with, so Anna assumed he was gay.

Alfie dished out the food. Anna thought it was one of the most delicious things she'd ever tasted and the bread was fabulous too. And it had all disappeared quickly.

'So we sort of have an initiation,' Nina said, as Anna was taking a second helping of curry.

Anna groaned.

'No, no,' Nina said. 'It's not bad, honest. It's just, first time, last time, strangest place.'

'First time . . .' Anna repeated, even though she knew exactly what it was. She drank some more wine. She should probably go and get some water at some point, she realised.

'First time, last time, strangest place,' Nina repeated. 'I'll tell you my first time, OK?'

The others groaned then and Nina, laughing, told them to shut up.

Anna nodded. And drank.

'I was fifteen. He was a friend of my brother's. I'd fancied him for ages. He was round our house all the time and this night he'd been playing some computer game thing with Chris – my brother – and then Chris fell asleep on the sofa. I went up to the loo and when I came out he was waiting for me on the landing. And he kissed me. And the next thing I knew we were in my room – I don't remember moving there, it was mad – and he was trying to put a condom on and I was laughing and then we did it. Or I thought we did. He was so small, I wasn't sure. He kept saying, "It's in, it's in . . . Oh, no, it's out".'

She clinked her glass against Anna's.

Anna drank some more wine and poked at a piece of potato on her plate. 'I . . .'

'Sean!' Nina said. 'Tell Anna about your last time!'

'Oh, God,' Sean said, leaning back in his chair. 'It was shit. It was a guy I'd just met, that night. I fell asleep after, and then I woke up and I could hear him whispering, so I pretended to still be asleep. And I heard him whisper "I love you".'

He opened his eyes wide as Anna said, 'Oh, my God!'

'I know, right? So I waited until he was asleep. Snoring like a bastard. And I sneaked out. So that was nice.'

'Didn't he phone you or anything?' Anna asked. If that had happened to her, she'd live the rest of her life in fear of bumping into him. She still worried about seeing a girl from primary school who'd witnessed her wetting herself in the Year 3 loos.

'He didn't have my details,' Sean said. 'I still worry about bumping into him though. I mean, what would I say?'

'Surely he'd leg it at the sight of you,' Alfie said.

'Thanks very much!' Sean said and then grinned. 'You'd hope so, wouldn't you? But, I dunno . . . If you tell a virtual stranger you love them, what won't you do?'

'You were lucky he didn't boil your bunny,' Molly said.

'Oh, he boiled my bunny, all right,' Sean said, raising one eyebrow.

Everyone laughed and Nina leaned over and poured more wine into Anna's glass. Anna thought for a second that it probably wasn't a good idea. She was sure if she asked for water someone would rush off and get it, but she didn't want to be the noob; she wanted to fit in.

'Who is going to tell us their strangest place?' Nina said. 'Molly? Alfie?'

'I haven't even got a strangest place,' Alfie said. 'All my places have been totally ordinary.'

Anna leaned forward to see him better. She wasn't sure if he was serious. He was smiling, but she got the impression he was telling the truth.

'OK, I'll do mine,' Molly said.

'Go on . . .' Sean said, pretending to put his face in his hands.

'The canteen. At college,' Molly said.

'Piss off,' Sean said, grinning.

Molly shook her head. 'It was with Joel – the guy who got chucked off the course for basically being a total slacker. I was pretty drunk. It was empty. Even the dinner ladies had gone. Those tables are sturdier than they look.'

They all stared at her for a second.

'It's not that bad!' Molly said.

'It's pretty bad,' Sean said.

'Come on, Anna, your turn,' Nina said. 'First time, last time, strangest place.'

Anna drained the last of her second glass of wine – or was it her third? – and, before she could change her mind, blurted, 'I can't. I'm a virgin.'

As soon as the words were out of her mouth she regretted it. No one said anything. They all just stared at her, their mouths slightly open.

'I mean . . . I had a boyfriend,' Anna said, her voice trembling. 'For a while. But it wasn't really serious. And there just wasn't . . . I didn't . . . No one . . .'

'Oh, my God!' Sean said, putting his arm around her shoulder and squeezing her against him. 'You don't need to explain or apologise! You're a virgin! Be out and proud!'

'It's embarrassing, I know,' Anna said.

'It's not,' Molly said. 'Or it shouldn't be. God, you're young. It's fine. And I don't get why it's such a big deal anyway. It's just sex. Why does there need to be a word that means "hasn't had sex"? It's really fucking weird, if you think about it!'

They all stared at Molly.

'Well, it is!' Molly said.

'So is there a strange place you've done it on your own?' Nina asked Anna. 'Or is it a religious thing?'

Anna blushed.

'Leave her alone,' Molly said, reaching across the table and taking the wine bottle from Nina. She tipped it over her glass but it was empty.

'No, it's . . . I'm not religious,' Anna said. 'I just haven't . . . met anyone. How old were all of you when you . . . ?' She couldn't even say it. She just waved her hand. How could she *do* it when she couldn't even say it?

'I was sixteen,' Molly said.

'Oh, God, Mol,' Sean said. 'Tell her your blow job story. That'll make her feel better.'

Alfie stood up, his chair making a screeching noise on the wooden floor. 'Back in a sec.'

'So I had this boyfriend at school,' Molly said. 'We'd been going out for a while and he wanted to have sex, but I didn't really so then he asked if I'd give him a blow job. And I didn't really want to do that either, but I thought if I did he'd stop going on about sex so much.'

Sean clutched his heart. 'It's so romantic!'

'So we bunked off school one afternoon and went back to his house. His bedroom was really messy and it stank of trainers – you know that sort of sweaty cheese smell?'

Anna nodded even though she wasn't sure she did. She hadn't spent much time in boys' bedrooms.

'And he lay down on his bed and just . . . got it out. And I really didn't know what I was doing so I sort of . . . licked it like an ice lolly—'

Sean snorted.

'But then he said I needed to suck it and he grabbed my head and pushed me down on it and he came straight away and it hit me right in the back of the throat and I threw up. On him.'

'Oh, my God,' Anna said.

'I know, right?' Molly grinned.

'Best story ever,' Sean said and held his hand up to high-five her.

'I'm not high fiving you for that,' Molly laughed.

'What did he do?' Anna asked.

'He was disgusted,' Molly said. 'Served him right for pushing my head.'

'Did you keep going out?' Anna asked.

Molly laughed. 'God, no.'

'So you just never spoke to each other again?' Sean said.

Molly shook her head. 'Nope. I don't even think we ever met each other's eyes again.'

'Yep, that is my favourite story ever,' Sean said.

When Alfie came back, he'd brought a jug of water and a stack of plastic cups. He put them in the middle of the table and poured some water for Anna.

She smiled up at him. 'Thank you.'

'No problem,' he said. 'The curry was a bit spicy, I know.'

It wasn't at all. Anna knew he was just being sweet. She looked at his mouth. He hadn't told a story, had he? Maybe he was a virgin too. She frowned. No. Of course he wasn't. She downed the glass of water almost in one.

Chapter 7

Once everyone had finished eating, they moved outside onto the terrace. Alfie and Molly joined Anna at the picnic table, while Sean and Nina sat on sofa cushions on the floor, leaning back against the low wall. Molly lit a citronella candle to keep the gnats at bay and turned on more fairy lights that were twisted through the railings.

'It's like being on holiday,' Anna said and the others all cheered.

'What?' she said, embarrassed.

'Someone always says that,' Molly told her. 'Every time we come out here.'

Anna grinned. 'Well . . . it is.'

She tipped her head back, expecting to see a sky full of stars, like at home, but of course it was too bright in the city. She couldn't really see anything at all.

'So . . . can I ask you about this virgin thing?' Nina said.

'Nooo!' Molly said. 'Leave her alone!'

'It's OK,' Anna said.

'What I want to know,' Nina says, 'is what you have done?'

'Nothing,' Anna said, cheerfully.

'You've kissed a boy though, right?' Molly said.

'Or a girl!' Sean chipped in, holding up his glass.

'I have kissed a boy, yes,' Anna said. 'But not a girl.'

'Not yet,' Sean said.

Anna giggled. 'No. Not yet.'

'The night is young,' Nina said.

'Neen always gets a bit lesbionic when she's pissed,' Sean said.

'Boobs,' Nina said, dreamily. 'I just love boobs.'

'So, anything other than kissing?' Sean asked. 'Boob action. Finger pie?'

Molly snorted so hard that wine dribbled out onto the table. 'Oh, my God,' she said. 'I'm sorry, that's disgusting. But finger pie!'

'No,' Anna said. 'No finger pie. No pie of any kind.'

'What other kinds of pie are there?' Molly said, swiping at the puddle of wine with her sleeve.

'Penis pie?' Anna suggested and then felt proud when everyone howled with laugher.

'I've always said the one thing that would improve a penis is putting pastry around it,' Sean said.

Anna laughed so hard she bent double and banged her head on the edge of the table. 'Ow. God. I think I'm drunk.'

'You think?' Molly said, giggling. 'Me too. I just wiped up wine with my sleeve. MY SLEEVE!'

'I'm so happy to be living here,' Anna burbled.

'We're happy to have you,' Sean said. He stood up and joined them on the other side of the table.

Anna leaned round to look at Nina, but she was curled up on the bench, her head on the biggest cushion, her eyes closed.

'She always does that,' Sean said. 'She peaks too soon and then passes out.'

'She works hard though,' Alfie says. 'She's always knackered.'

'Where does she work?' Anna asked.

'A hotel near Lime Street,' Sean said. 'But if anyone asks, she's at college with me and Mol.'

Anna frowned. She couldn't quite grasp what he meant. She didn't really work, she was at college?

'She dropped out of college,' Molly said.

'To work in a hotel?' Anna asked.

Molly shook her head. 'That wasn't the plan exactly. She just didn't get on with college so well. We keep trying to talk her into coming back, but . . .'

'Jack's there so she won't leave unless he does,' Sean said.

Molly shook her head and put her finger to her lips.

'It's nothing to do with Jack,' Nina said without opening her eyes or sitting up. 'I just wasn't good enough.'

'That's not true though,' Sean said.

'And I don't want to talk about it,' Nina sing-songed.

'OK then!' Sean sang back and topped up Anna's glass.

'I've never drunk this much before,' Anna said.

'Anna, you're a teenager, living away from home for the first time!' Sean said. 'You need to build up your tolerance to alcohol.'

'I don't think she needs to build it all up in the one night,' Alfie said, smiling.

'Alfie!' Sean said, turning to look at him. 'You didn't tell us any sordid sex secrets!'

'I haven't got any,' Alfie said.

'Fucking hell, you're not a virgin too, are you?' Sean said.

Alfie grinned. 'No. Not a virgin. Just boring.'

'Nope,' Sean said. 'Don't believe you. Tell us something.'

'I told you mine when you moved in,' Alfie said. He'd brought a bottle of water out with him and he unscrewed the cap and swigged it.

'I don't remember,' Sean said. 'Tell us again.'

'You don't remember cos it was boring,' Alfie said.

'Tell us about . . . your first wank,' Sean said.

'Or your last wank!' Nina said, from the bench.

Anna looked over. Nina hadn't opened her eyes.

Alfie laughed, shaking his head. 'I'm not telling you anything.'

'But I told you mine,' Anna said. 'It's only fair.'

'She's not wrong,' Molly said, clinking her glass against Anna's.

Alfie groaned and ran a hand through his cropped afro. 'OK. When I was about fifteen, I found a porn mag.'

'You found it?' Sean said, faux-sincerely. 'Up on a shelf? In a shop?'

'No, smart arse. I didn't buy it. Someone had left it in the changing rooms at school.'

'Ugh.' Sean shuddered. 'Nothing worse than a second-hand wank mag.'

'It was fine,' Alfie said. 'It was new. I think. I took it home – obviously – and hid it in a pile of magazines I already had in my room.'

'What kind of mags?' Molly asked.

'Gaming mags, mostly,' Alfie said. 'Couple of music mags, I think. I didn't look at it straight away—'

'Why not?!' Sean said.

'I just felt . . . It creeped me out a bit. Especially cos I found it at school, you know?'

'No,' Sean said.

'Yeah, OK. So I think I'd probably had it for a couple of weeks when I finally thought I'd have a look.'

'Bloody hell,' Sean said. 'This is tragic.'

'And when I took it out of the pile, there was a Post-it note on top of it.'

Molly and Anna both leaned towards Alfie, rapt.

'What the fuck?' Sean said.

'From my mum,' Alfie said. 'It said: *Experimentation and masturbation are natural, but respect for women is important too.*'

'Oh, my God,' Anna said. The thought of her mum finding porn in her room . . . and leaving it there, note or not, made her feel dizzy with humiliation.

'Your mum is hardcore,' Sean said. 'No pun intended.'

'I know,' Alfie said. 'I couldn't even open it after that. I put it in the recycling. Hidden inside a newspaper.'

'Did you ever talk to her about it?' Molly said.

Alfie shook his head.

'Is that why you keep your door closed?' Sean asked. 'You've wallpapered your room with porn?'

Alfie laughed. 'No. I've never seen another porn mag, actually. So it kind of worked.'

'And there's the internet . . .' Sean said.

'Yeah, there's that too,' Alfie said, grinning.

'I've never seen any porn,' Anna said.

'Of course you haven't,' Sean said.

'I'm not totally naive!' Anna said and grabbed for her wine, but just succeeded in knocking it over. 'Shit.'

'Don't worry,' Molly said. 'One of us always does that.'

Anna could feel the wine dripping between the planks of the table onto her jeans. She thought she should get up and go and get a cloth or something, but the thought of it was too much. It didn't matter. It would just dry up on its own.

Anna's eyes were doing something really weird. She turned to look at Molly – who was talking about some awful temp job she'd had where someone had hit her on the head with . . . something – but it took a few seconds for her eyes to catch up with her head. Weird. She turned back the other way and it happened again.

'Do I look weird?' she said.

Alfie peered at her and she stared back at him. He had really lovely eyes. Brown. Brown eyes. Lovely.

'Weird how?' Alfie asked.

'My eyes aren't working properly. Everything's in slow motion.'

Alfie grinned. He had a lovely smile. Anna thought about telling him, but then she thought she probably shouldn't. They'd only just met. She tried to focus on the fairy lights along the edge of the railing. They were different colours: red and yellow and blue and green. And they were jumping up and down. Why were they jumping up and down? That was a bit weird. Anna tried to focus hard and make them stop, but they wouldn't. She started to feel a bit sick.

'I feel a bit sick,' she said.

Alfie pushed his water bottle across the table towards her and she swigged some.

'When I was younger I thought this was like kissing,' she said.

'What?' Sean said. 'Swigging from a water bottle? Who'd you been kissing, armadillos?'

Anna stared at him. She didn't get it.

'Armadillos?' Molly said. 'Why would swigging from a water bottle be like kissing an armadillo?'

'I don't know,' Sean said, as if responding to a joke. 'Why *would* swigging from a water bottle be like kissing an armadillo?'

'What?' Anna said. 'No, I mean it's like kissing Alfie.'

'What?' Alfie said.

'Alfie isn't an armadillo!' Sean said. He picked up his wine glass and tipped it back. It was empty. He put it back on the table in disappointment.

'No,' Anna said, holding on to the edge of the table, which was bouncing a bit now too. 'Alfie drank from the bottle and then I drank from the bottle. So it's like kissing Alfie!'

'Bloody hell,' Sean said. 'We need to get you laid.'

'I thought that when I was *little*!' Anna said. 'I don't think that *now*!'

'Anteater!' Sean said. 'Not armadillo!'

'What?' Molly said again.

'The bottle,' Sean said. 'It's like an anteater shape. But I said armadillo.'

'What are you talking about?' Molly said.

Sean was laughing too hard to answer.

Anna swigged some more water and thought for a second that her head had started to clear, but then her mouth filled with saliva and she realised she was going to be sick.

She tried to stand up, forgetting she was sitting on a bench attached to a picnic table. Her legs smashed into the table, the remaining glasses fell over and Alfie's bottle rolled off the table onto the floor. Anna could feel the vomit building and she really didn't want to throw up on the table in front of everyone. She managed to get one leg over the bench. Her other foot got caught and she teetered for a second, panicking that she was about to fall smack on the floor, but Molly grabbed her arm and helped her out.

'It's OK,' Molly said. 'You're OK.'

'No,' Anna said. 'I'm going to be sick.'

She staggered across the roof towards the living room, already worrying she wouldn't make it, and she wasn't even sure she could remember where the bathroom was. But it was too late anyway. She clamped both hands across her mouth, but it didn't make any difference. The vomit sprayed out sideways from behind her hands, splattering the sliding glass doors.

Chapter 8

Anna woke up with her tongue stuck to the roof of her mouth and her head banging like . . . she had no idea what. Like nothing she'd ever experienced.

'Oh, God,' she groaned.

She tried to turn over, but it was just too painful. Everything ached. Had she been run over? She couldn't even remember. She raised her arm to shield her eyes from the morning light and was overwhelmed with the smell of vomit. Her stomach contracted violently. She barely had time to roll onto her side before she was throwing up.

Once she'd finished, she realised there was a bucket next to her bed. Who'd put that there? Obviously that wasn't the first time she'd been sick. Was that where the smell had come from? She pushed her hair back from her sweaty face. No. It was coming from her. Where? She tried to shift herself up to a sitting position, but she couldn't do it. She closed her eyes and drifted off to sleep.

She woke up with a jolt and was immediately covered with an overwhelming sense of shame. She wanted to curl into the foetal position. She wanted to climb out of her body. She wanted to get up, pack up, and leave. But she couldn't even sit up. What had she done? God, she'd literally just met these people, why did she have to get so drunk? Why couldn't she just have had a couple of drinks like an adult? Why did she have to be so . . . pathetic?

She spent the morning – she assumed it was morning; she couldn't find her phone so she had no idea what time it was – drifting in and out of consciousness. And every single time she came to was accompanied with the shame. What was she going to do? She couldn't go downstairs: too humiliating. But she could hardly stay in her room like a child. And anyway, she needed the loo. Eventually she managed to almost crawl out of bed and pull herself up to standing. Once she was upright, she had to stay still for a few moments, until the room stopped spinning. Then she opened the door and – eyes only half-open – tiptoed to the bathroom.

She tried the door handle, but it was locked. She tried to take the few steps back to her own room, but she just couldn't manage it. She thought she'd be sick again if she moved at all. She closed her eyes, but the spinning started back up, so she opened them and focussed on the corner of the carpet where some loose threads were sticking up. Breathe in. Breathe out. Try not to smell. Try not to think.

She had never felt so bad in all her life. When she was younger and she'd first started going out with girls from school, her mum had warned her about getting drunk, but she'd never thought it would be as bad as this. But she was glad she'd never had more than a bottle of lager or a bit of vodka Red Bull with the girls from school. How much worse would it be to feel this bad *and* have to deal with her mum saying 'I told you so' and being totally unsympathetic.

Anna winced as the loo flushed then the door opened.

'Morning.'

Anna wasn't sure if it was Alfie or Sean. She half-opened one eye. It wasn't either of them. Presumably it was Jack. She tried to say good morning back, but when she opened her mouth all that came out was a sort of creaking from the back of her throat.

'So you're Anna?' he said.

She squinted at him. He was incredibly good-looking. Like, stupidly, ridiculously good-looking. Anna tried to nod, but she felt things moving inside her head so instead she just lifted one hand as if she was waving.

'Welcome to the house,' he said. And then he grinned.

And Anna pushed past the most gorgeous boy she'd ever seen in real life and threw up violently in the sink.

She'd actually felt marginally better after the last round of vomit. She'd managed to have a shower – she'd had to sit in the shower tray and she wasn't sure she'd managed to rinse all the shampoo out of her hair – but at least the vomit smell had gone. Gone from her body anyway, her room still reeked. She hadn't been able to bring herself to look in a mirror, but if she looked even a tenth as bad as she felt, it must be horrific. She got dressed – or half dressed – in her new pyjama bottoms and her hoodie pulled very gently over her still-pounding head – and tentatively made her way downstairs. She'd been listening for a while and it didn't sound like anyone else was up, so she figured she was safe. She just really, really needed a cup of tea.

'Morning,' Sean said, from his seat at the breakfast bar. 'You look rough as.'

Anna groaned. 'Oh, God. I didn't think anyone was up.'

'We're not really,' Molly said.

Anna turned in the direction of her voice. She was lying on the sofa and she was also wearing a hoodie, but she had the hood up and the cord pulled so only her nose and mouth were visible.

'We're waiting for Alfie,' Sean said. 'He's going to make a fry-up.'

Anna clutched the edge of the breakfast bar and her stomach lurched. 'No. Can't eat.'

'You have to,' Molly said. 'It's the best thing.'

'Isn't Alfie hungover?' Anna asked.

Sean shook his head and then clasped it in both hands. 'Ow. Shit. No, he doesn't drink properly. Too much of a control freak. Which is a total win for us.'

'I've never been that drunk before,' Anna said.

She tried to perch on one of the stools, but it felt too precarious. She leaned back against the cupboards instead.

'We know,' Sean said. 'You told us once or twenty times.'

'Oh, God,' Anna said again.

'Don't be embarrassed,' Molly said. 'Everyone talks shit when they're drunk. Didn't you hear Nina?'

Anna couldn't remember whether she had or not. 'Is she OK?'

'No idea,' Sean said. 'She's not up yet.'

'But Jack's here?' Anna said. 'I saw him coming out of the bathroom.'

'Yep. That's what woke me up,' Molly said. 'The door slamming, I mean. Not shagging. Nina's probably too hungover.'

Anna had a flashback to something someone had said last night. Nina? Something about a blow job and throwing up on someone? And Nina was lying down on the floor outside. And did she spill something?

She heard the front door open and close and then Alfie joined them, smelling like fresh air and clean clothes. Anna moved carefully around the breakfast bar next to Sean.

Alfie grinned at her. 'Morning! It's like *The Walking Dead* in here.'

Anna groaned.

'Bacon? Egg? Sausage?'

Anna groaned again.

'Honest, Anna, it's the best thing,' Sean said. 'You'll feel much better.'

'Fried bread?' Alfie said.

'She'll have everything,' Sean said. 'And so will I.'

Alfie put the kettle on and Anna rested her head on her crossed arms. But she could feel her pulse in her face, so she sat back up again.

'I don't know how people do it,' she said.

'You get used to it,' Sean said. 'You'll be better next time.'

'There won't be a next time,' Anna said.

Everyone laughed.

SPARKSLIFE: Moved

by AnnaSparks 8,211 views
Published on 6 September

[Transcript of Anna's vlog]

So. I'm here! I moved in a bit earlier than planned because I came to see the house and I loved it and I didn't want to go home, so I stayed. And my new housemates are awesome. Really awesome. I'll tell you a bit more about them at some point, but I can't do that right now because my brain isn't working properly. Because last night I got horrifically, embarrassingly drunk.

I know. [Drops her head into her hands and then looks back up slowly.] I didn't mean to. Obviously. But they were all so nice and so much fun and they kept topping up my glass . . . I know. Excuses, excuses. There was one guy who was trying to look after me and kept bringing me water, but I'd already had too much wine so I didn't have the sense to drink it. [Pulls a face.]

Top five things to do when you've got a hangover:

1. Lie in bed, moaning. [Cut to: shot of Anna lying on her bed with a pillow over her face. From under the pillow is coming a low moan.]

2. Eat a big cooked breakfast. [Cut to: still photo of a cooked breakfast and large mug of tea. Then to a photo of Anna looking slightly less ill.]

3. Watch *Bridget Jones's Diary*. [Cut to: Anna turning in aside to the camera. 'Doesn't have to be *Bridget Jones's Diary*. I've heard that some people don't like that film. Those people couldn't be my friends, but still. What I mean is, you need to watch a film that you love, one that you know almost off by heart and so you don't need to concentrate or use your brain. You don't want to use your brain on the film because you need to use your brain to keep yourself from throwing up again.] [Cut to: film of Anna sitting on her bed, rocking, holding a pillow and singing 'All By Myself' quietly.]

4. Have a shower or a bath. [Cut to: Anna in aside saying 'A shower might not feel too good on your head, in which case a bath would be better. But take your trusty bucket with you because you do not want to throw up *in* the bath. Trust me on this.] [Cut to: a photo of some sparrows frolicking in a bird bath with Anna in voiceover saying, 'Did you

really think I was going to show you a photo of me in the bath?!']

5. Drink lots and lots of water. [Cut to: shot of Anna guzzling from a litre water bottle and then looking queasy.] If you can't stomach cold water, try warm water – boiled from the kettle, not from the hot tap. Something like fruit or herbal tea will work too. Or, of course, a giant latte. [Cut to: shot of Anna drinking what looks like coffee from a mixing bowl.]

Top five things not to do when you're hungover:

1. Talk to your mother. [Cut to: film of Anna pretending to sob with her mobile next to her ear.]

2. Go shopping. [Cut to: a selfie of Anna standing in a shop queue, pretending to sob.]

3. Go for a run. [Cut to: a film of Anna running, slowly and heavily, pretending to sob.]

4. Have another drink. [Cut to: a photo of Anna holding a glass of wine in one hand, her hand over her mouth, pretending to sob.]

5. Housework. [Cut to: Anna kneeling in front of the toilet, pretending to sob.]

COMMENTS:

Daisy Locke: I'm glad someone's looking after you but you should be careful if your drinking.

Maria Rushton: This is SO FUNNY! I'm CRYING HAHAHA

Butterflyaway: Look at my channel :)

Chapter 9

Anna put on the new dress she'd bought for work – or rather, her mum had bought for her. She loved it, but she worried it looked a bit too much like something of Lola's. It was red with elbow-length sleeves and a dropped waist. She added black tights and black ballet pumps with a red heart on the toe, and clipped her hair up. Lola, she knew, would wear a dress like this with skyscraper heels, a wide belt and statement jewellery, but the dress was enough for Anna. She liked it. She looked different. She felt different.

Lola had phoned on Friday when Anna had been just past the worst of her hangover, but nowhere near back to normal. She'd asked Anna to come into the office on Monday morning for a 'chat'. Anna had mentioned it to her dad when he'd brought her stuff over on Saturday and he said it was probably to do some HR stuff and sign her contract.

He'd had a look around the house, but no one else had been in so he hadn't met any of the other housemates. He'd seemed to approve though, Anna thought, and had squeezed her and kissed her on the forehead when he left. Anna had spent the rest of the weekend recovering from Thursday night and working on her first Liverpool vlog. She hadn't decided whether to tell the others about her channel yet, but they were all out most of the time. In fact she hadn't seen them all in the house at once since Friday morning.

Alfie was in the kitchen when Anna went downstairs on Monday morning. He was sitting at the breakfast bar, reading something on his iPad and drinking a coffee.

'Want one?' he asked Anna, looking up. Then he said, 'You look really nice.'

Anna ran a hand back across her hair. 'Thanks. It's not too much?'

Alfie shook his head. 'No. You look great.'

Anna poured herself a coffee while simultaneously kicking herself for being so self-conscious. Why couldn't she have just smiled and accepted the compliment gracefully instead of coming across as so needy? Lola would have said something like, 'Nice? I look fabulous!' Anna smiled to herself. She was really looking forward to seeing Lola again. To being back in the office.

Once she'd drunk her coffee and collected her bag from her bedroom, she set off down Bold Street towards the theatre. Bold Street was already busy – a huge lorry was trying to turn into a side street and had got wedged halfway across, and a small crowd had gathered, giving advice on the best way to proceed. The pavement was wet where the street sweeper had been and the shops were just starting to open up. Anna tried to ignore the butterflies swooping in her belly and focus on the blue sky and the sounds and smells of the city.

She was really there. And she was on her way to work.

* * *

Anna pressed the buzzer and when someone answered hello, said, 'Hi! It's Anna!' and pushed the door as soon as it buzzed. On her first day of the internship, she'd pushed the door too late and had needed to buzz again, and felt like an idiot.

Inside, it still smelled the same – hot dust and paper and sawdust. She stood at the bottom of the stairs and breathed it in. Her stomach was flipping wildly. Maybe she shouldn't have had that coffee.

Upstairs, Gemma was sitting at the front desk and she smiled at Anna, but then answered the ringing phone so didn't have time to speak to her. As she talked on the phone, she gestured to Anna to go straight through to Lola's office, so Anna pushed open the double swing doors to the main, open plan, office.

It was quiet. Only a couple of people were in and they weren't people Anna had got to know particularly well, but they looked up and smiled and waved as Anna headed to the far corner and Lola's office.

Lola's door was open and Anna had only hesitated in the doorway for a second before Lola waved her in. She was typing on her laptop and said, 'Just a sec . . . Sit down . . .'

Anna sat down on the other side of Lola's desk and looked out of the window at the view of the square, the red-tiled ceilings and chimneys. Along the edge of one of the rooftops, someone had put a row of brightly painted plastic pigeons.

Lola closed her laptop and smiled at Anna and Anna felt her back straighten slightly. She smiled back, shyly. She'd spent so much time thinking about Lola lately – about how lovely she'd been to her, about how great it was to work with her – that it was almost like seeing someone you'd had a dream about. She felt like Lola could see into her head.

'You made it!' Lola said. 'Alfie said you moved in last week?'

Anna nodded. 'It's been really great. I can't wait to start work. Did you want me to start today, or—'

'That's actually why I asked you to come in,' Lola said. She stood up, walked around her desk and closed her office door before sitting back down. She leaned forward and smiled at Anna, before taking her glasses off and rubbing carefully at her eye.

'Last thing on Friday, I had a meeting with our chief exec.' She put her glasses back on. 'And one of the things that came out of that meeting was that we're not in a position to hire anyone else at the moment.'

Anna frowned. She hadn't known they were planning to hire anyone else. Was Lola talking about another assistant? Not an assistant to Anna, surely?

'I know I told you there was a job for you,' Lola said. 'And there was – it wasn't something I said lightly. But I'm afraid we're not in a position to offer you that job currently.'

Anna felt a chill creeping up her back. The back of her neck felt weird and cold. She shook her head.

'*My* job?'

Lola was looking at her with concern. 'I'm so sorry, Anna,' Lola said. 'There is no job.'

'But . . .' Anna said. Her mind felt blank. She could actually see a white screen. She waited for words to appear on it, but nothing came. 'But . . .' she said again.

'I'm so sorry,' Lola said. 'I promise you I argued for you. And if things change then we would love to have you. The work you did was so evident when I was getting information together for the meeting. It made it much easier for me. You know that I would have you start today if I could.'

Anna nodded. She still couldn't think properly.

'Do you want a cup of tea?' Lola asked.

Anna nodded and Lola went out into the main office, but was back in a few seconds – she'd obviously just asked someone to make one. Anna felt embarrassed that everyone else must have known exactly what was happening.

'Is there any chance you could still go to university?' Lola asked, sitting back down behind her desk. 'And then in three years, maybe—'

'Is that why?' Anna interrupted. 'Is it because I'm too young? And I haven't got a degree?'

Lola shook her head. 'It's nothing to do with that, I promise. It's not about you. There's a hiring freeze across the company. In a recession, people don't go to the theatre so much.'

Anna nodded. She knew that. And Lola knew she knew it. They'd talked about it when she was on work experience. They'd talked about things they could do, ways to make theatre more affordable and accessible. Lola had been impressed with Anna's ideas. Or so she'd said, anyway.

'You said you can't offer me the job,' Anna said.

Lola frowned. 'No. I'm sorry.'

'But you already offered me the job,' Anna said. 'And I accepted.'

Lola nodded. 'But you hadn't signed the contract.'

'Oh,' Anna said. 'Yeah.' She'd thought for a second that maybe it was too late – that because they'd offered her the job they had to give it to her. But she should have known it wouldn't be that simple.

'Of course I'm happy to give you a reference,' Lola said. 'And if I hear of anything anywhere else . . .'

Nodding, Anna stared past Lola, out at the roof opposite. At the multi-coloured pigeons.

'If anything changes . . .' Anna said.

'I'll be in touch,' Lola said. 'Of course I will. I really am so sorry, Anna. And I wish I'd known in time to stop you moving. What do you think you'll do?'

'I don't know,' Anna said. 'But I don't want to go home.'

Chapter 10

With a flick of her wrists, Nina flung the sheet across the double bed. She found it strangely satisfying, particularly when she remembered how hard it had been when she'd first taken the job. Back then, she'd ended up having to kick off her functional uniform shoes and crawl across the bed to get everything tucked in. Now she had a system and she barely thought about it. And the beds always looked a hell of a lot neater too. She changed the pillowcases, smoothed out the replacements and threw the soiled ones in her cart. One had mascara marks on it. She couldn't understand women who didn't take their make-up off at night – weren't they worried about what they were doing to their skin?

She got down on her hands and knees and checked under the bed for any abandoned condoms, lost shoes, phone chargers and any other of the sundry things guests tended to leave behind in hotel rooms. Some of them truly disgusting. But today there was nothing at all. She finished making the bed, then plugged in the Hoover.

And then she started singing. It was really the only time she allowed herself to sing, because no one could hear her over the sound of the vacuum cleaner. And she didn't want anyone to hear her. Because whenever anyone heard her singing they told her she should do it professionally, or they asked her if she ever did do it professionally, or, if they knew her, they asked her why she'd dropped out of college, and she really didn't want to talk about that. But she could sing while she Hoovered and make believe she was on stage doing some big production number – the hotel chambermaid who was discovered for her voice and became a big star. And maybe she sometimes let herself glance up at the red light of the smoke alarm and pretend it was a camera.

Whoever had cleaned this room previously hadn't done much of a job of it, Nina thought. There were actual cobwebs stretching between the arms of the ceiling pendant and for every one she Hoovered up, she saw more elsewhere. She needed rodent helpers like in *Enchanted*. She was holding the attachment up above her head and belting out the final notes of 'Bad Romance' when she felt someone grab her around the waist.

She screamed and brought the Hoover attachment down against the leg of whoever was standing behind her.

'Jesus Christ, Nina!' Jack yelled into her ear before letting go of her waist and grabbing her wrist.

'What the fuck did you think you were doing?' Nina yelled back, before realising she was yelling because the Hoover was still on. She turned it off. Their shouts seemed to still be bouncing around the room. There was no way they wouldn't have been heard. Someone would probably complain. Damn.

Jack was still holding Nina's wrist, a bit too hard. She twisted her hand away.

'I just came to say hello,' Jack said, rubbing his leg. 'Shit. That really hurt.'

'Good,' Nina said. 'What did you expect, sneaking up on me like that? You scared the shit out of me.'

'I think you can handle yourself,' Jack said. He pulled his jeans up, still trying to look at his leg, but his boot was covering the bit Nina had hit.

'God, you're fine,' she said, looking away from his bare skin. 'Stop being such a baby.'

'You could at least offer to kiss it better,' he said, looking up at her from under his fringe.

She knew it was a cheesy line. He'd been – was still being – a dick. But she really wanted to kiss it better.

'Kiss it yourself,' she said, flicking the vacuum cord at him.

Jack caught the cord and started winding it onto the back of the Hoover. 'Are you done now? What time are you finishing?'

'I'm done with this room, yeah,' she said. 'But I've still got four more. And then I'm done.'

'I'll come and help.' He started scooting the Hoover out of the room.

'No, thanks,' Nina said, pushing the cart behind him. 'I've had your help before.'

Jack grabbed the cart and looked at her over the top of the piles of clean towels. She knew that look.

'I haven't got time,' she said.

'You will if I help with the next room,' Jack said, pushing Nina back into the room.

'And what about your work?' Nina asked. 'Who's going to do that?'

'That's *my* problem,' Jack said. He wiggled the cart on its wheels and wiggled his eyebrows at Nina.

'Fuck,' she said, but she was already smiling.

She locked the door and pushed the cart up against it for good measure. Another staff member could still get in – they all had key cards to access the rooms – but at least if someone did come in, the door hitting the cart would give them some warning.

'Have you done the windows?' Jack asked, crossing the room.

Nina frowned. 'No. I don't do them every time.'

Jack pushed up the metal bar on the old window and swung it open. 'I think they need doing.'

'Even when I do them I only do the inside. There's a window cleaner . . .'

Jack held out a cloth and then, when Nina didn't take it straight away, folded her hand over it. 'They need doing though,' he said, his voice low. 'They're really . . . dirty.'

'Oh, God.' Nina laughed. 'Seriously?'

Jack grinned at her. 'Filthy.'

She leaned out over the window sill and started to wipe the window with the cloth. She felt Jack move his hips against her arse and immediately became aware of his erection. She braced one hand on the window ledge and pressed back.

'Wait, stop,' Nina told Jack. 'Alicija's down there. In the courtyard.'

'Call down to her,' Jack said. 'Say hello.'

'What?' Nina tried to look back at him over her shoulder, but she couldn't see his face.

'Call down to her,' he said as he pushed the skirt of her uniform up. Nina gasped and shifted her feet to keep her balance.

Nina leaned out a bit further – Jack's hands on her hips – and shouted. 'Alicija! Hi!'

Alicija looked up and grinned, waving a cigarette to show Nina what she was doing in the courtyard.

'Have you got much more to do?' Alicija called.

'Not on this floor,' Nina said. 'Just these windows.'

Her stomach clenched and she dug her nails into the wood of the window ledge as she felt Jack slide inside her. She heard the rustle of foil as he dropped the condom wrapper on the floor.

'Keep talking,' he said, his mouth against her neck.

'What about you?' she called. 'Almost finished?'

Her voice sounded falsely bright to her own ears, but Jack was obviously enjoying it – he groaned and moved his hands from Nina's hips up under her top, grabbing her breasts. Nina's knees actually went weak and she buckled against Jack then reached further out of the window for support.

Jack slid one hand down between Nina's legs and she shifted position again, leaning her shoulder against the wall to give him a better angle.

'No. I'd better get back in!' Alicija shouted, then she waved and, to Nina's relief, disappeared back inside the hotel. Nina didn't think she'd be able to carry on a full conversation now that Jack's hips and fingers were moving faster. She ducked back under the window and pressed her forehead against the glass.

'That was so . . . fucking . . . sexy,' Jack groaned directly into her ear.

Nina tipped her head back so he could kiss her shoulder at the base of her neck. 'I love that she had no idea you were fucking me,' she murmured.

Jack groaned again.

Nina felt her orgasm building. She took one hand off the window ledge and pressed it on top of Jack's, helping him get the angle exactly right. Her thighs were tingling and her stomach felt liquid and then it was spreading and taking over her whole body. She tried to keep her eyes open, to look out across the courtyard, into the other rooms containing people who had no idea what she was doing, no idea that Jack was deep inside her, but she couldn't do it. She closed her eyes tight, dropped her head back and let herself go.

Chapter 11

Sean hadn't planned to follow Charlie, he really hadn't. But Charlie and the Viking had left college just ahead of him and for a couple of streets they were going the same way and then, when it got to the street where Sean should have turned off if he'd been heading for home, he just . . . didn't. When they got to Berry Street, the Viking left – without a hug or a kiss, Sean was relieved to notice. And then he just carried on walking behind Charlie.

Not just because Charlie was very nice to look at from behind – he was wearing jeans that made his arse look amazing and a white T-shirt, through which Sean could see his shoulder blades – but because Sean kept telling himself at some point Charlie would stop and Sean would say, 'Oh . . . hey!' And Charlie would say what a coincidence it was that they were both . . . wherever they were. And then maybe Sean could suggest they go for a coffee and then, you know, get married.

Charlie crossed over Duke Street and Sean realised he was heading for Liverpool One. That was good. It was perfectly reasonable that Sean might also be going there; everyone likes shopping. It was better when you actually had money to spend, but whatever.

As he followed him, Sean thought of things they could talk about . . . They'd both done the Musical Theatre foundation course, so he could mention that. Or he could ask him what he'd chosen for his long-form essay. Sean thought about the class they'd had in which they had to pretend to be squirrels at Formby Point – Charlie had started slowly, but before long seemed to genuinely become a squirrel, all twitchy and shifty and sort of playfully mischievous. If someone had told Sean he'd fancy someone he'd seen embody the spirit of a squirrel, he would've laughed, but it really had just made him fancy Charlie even more. He was so bright-eyed and bushy-tailed.

Charlie didn't do what Sean usually did at Liverpool One – get a coffee and mooch about, gaze in the window of the Apple Store, go and read a few chapters of something, sitting on one of the sofas in Waterstones – he went straight to Lawler's, the toy shop.

Sean wandered up and down the row of shops nearby, but when Charlie hadn't emerged after ten minutes, Sean figured he could go in, have a look around. Nothing dodgy about that. Just a person, looking around a toy shop for something for his . . . niece's birthday. Yes.

Just inside the door, a member of staff was flinging a little toy plane that circled through the air and returned to him like a boomerang. He threw it straight at Sean and Sean ducked before realising the plane would circle back before coming anywhere near him. He felt stupid and almost turned around to go back out, but then the plane guy smiled at him – he had dimples, so cute – and Sean carried on inside the shop.

He couldn't see Charlie, so he wandered around, grinning at toys he'd had as a kid and wincing at the price of some of the Lego.

'Is there anything I can help you with today?' a woman asked him. Actually, Sean realised, turning to smile at her, she probably was about the same age as him. Could he work there? Did they need staff? What did it pay?

'Is there anything in particular you're looking for?' the girl said and Sean realised he'd just been staring at her.

'Yes, sorry!' he said, his voice coming out too loud. 'Niece! I need a present for my niece.'

The girl smiled. 'Aw. How old is she?'

'Um,' Sean said and looked around as if his imaginary niece was somewhere nearby, ready to give him her date of birth. 'Three?'

'Cute! And do you know what kind of things she likes? Are you looking for a game? Or Lego? Or a cuddly toy?'

'Cuddly toy sounds good,' Sean said. Surely even imaginary children liked cuddly toys.

'OK, great!' the girl said and Sean followed her across the store to a wall of cuddly toys.

'Shall I just leave you to have a look or do you need more assistance?'

'I think I'll be OK from here, thanks,' Sean said, even though he wasn't entirely sure he would. There was so much choice.

The girl left to serve someone else and Sean started picking up toys and looking at the prices. He couldn't afford any of them. There was a really super-cute seal pup that felt so soft Sean almost wanted to rub it against his cheek, but it was thirty-five pounds. Thirty-five quid! And that was one of the cheaper ones. Then again, he didn't know why he was worrying – it wasn't as if he really had to buy one.

Particularly since Charlie had probably bought whatever he'd come in to buy and had left while Sean was chatting to the assistant. He set off towards the door, but the assistant was suddenly in front of him again.

'You didn't find anything?' she said.

'No, I . . .' Sean said.

And then he saw Charlie. He hadn't left. He hadn't even been shopping. He was wearing the store's uniform of a bright yellow T-shirt with a black smiley face, but unlike the other assistants he was also wearing a black top hat (decorated with a yellow smiley face). And he was standing behind a table. And doing magic.

'Can I help at all?' the assistant said.

'No,' Sean said, dragging his eyes back to her smiling face. 'Thanks. I'm going to get this.' He reached out and grabbed something off the nearest table.

'Oh, lovely!' the assistant said. 'She'll love that.'

'Thanks, I'm sure she will.' Sean walked straight over to the checkout and put the box down on the counter, then turned to look back at Charlie. He had cups on the table in front of him and a wand – an actual magic wand – in his hand. In front of him, two small children were staring up at him in awe and Charlie was grinning right back at them.

'That'll be sixty-four ninety-nine.'

'What?' Sean said.

'Sixty-four ninety-nine,' the assistant on the desk said.

Sean looked at his imaginary niece's birthday gift. It was a Furby. And apparently they cost almost a hundred quid.

'Sixty-four ninety-nine?' he said.

The assistant smiled. 'Yes, sir.'

Sean took out his wallet. And then he took out his emergency credit card.

Chapter 12

'So how's the course going?' Alfie's father asked without looking up from his phone.

'Good, yeah,' Alfie said.

He looked out of the window at the building opposite. It was black and glossy and Alfie could see the reflection of the restaurant he and his dad were sitting in. Alfie lifted his hand to see if he could spot himself, but he couldn't.

'What have you been studying lately?' His dad glanced up over the top of his glasses, but then looked straight back down at his phone again.

'Corporate social responsibility,' Alfie parroted. 'Finance law. And Entrepreneurship.'

His dad's head snapped up and his fingers stopped moving over the keyboard. 'Why are you taking that?'

'I thought it would be interesting,' Alfie said. He picked up his glass and drank some of the iced water.

His dad curled his lip. 'It's not as if you'll need it.'

'Well, part of the module is about how businesses can learn from methods used by entrepreneurs,' Alfie lied. 'So it could actually be useful, I think. Even if I'm working with you.'

Alfie expected his dad to comment on the 'if' but he didn't. He probably wasn't really listening. Instead, he nodded. 'Right. How did you get on with Finance in the end? I know you were struggling.'

He was looking back at his phone again.

'I wasn't struggling,' Alfie said. 'There was just one paper I wasn't keen on.'

'But you passed?'

Alfie looked around the room. As usual he caught the eye of someone who was staring at him and his dad, presumably wondering what their relationship was. There was always one.

'Yeah, I passed.'

'That's the main thing,' his dad said.

I'm not sure it is, Alfie wanted to say. I'm not sure the main thing is working for the sake of it, or just to make money, or to make the most money. I'm not sure actually enjoying what you do isn't more important. Even if you're not the best at it. But he'd mentioned that to his dad before. When they'd talked about university. When he'd chosen his A levels. When he'd chosen his GCSEs, in fact. Alfie looked out at the building opposite again. Actually, even when they'd chosen the high school he attended. He'd long since learned it was easier to go along with what they wanted and find a way to make it into something he wanted too. Of course, he hadn't quite meant to take it as far as he had done this time, but it was his life: shouldn't he be able to live it his own way?

Yeah, he should, he told himself. But then he shouldn't expect his parents to pay for it. And he did. He drank the last of the water in his glass and watched his dad shoot his cuffs and then look around for a member of the wait staff.

'What are you up to this afternoon?' his dad asked without looking at him.

'I've got a shift at Bean.'

His dad glanced at him. 'How's that going?'

'It's great,' Alfie said. 'We've been really busy and I've got a fair bit of responsibility, so—'

'As long as it doesn't affect your studying.' His dad caught the eye of a waiter and gestured for the bill. Alfie hated when he did that.

'No,' Alfie said. 'It's useful, actually. I'm learning a lot about how businesses actually work.'

His dad laughed. 'That's not the kind of business I'm sending you to university for.'

Alfie rolled his eyes internally. That was the problem exactly. 'It's great,' he said. 'Malc – the owner – built it up from nothing. When he bought the shop it had been empty for years. He—'

His dad's phone rang and he answered it, holding one finger up to Alfie. Alfie knew it was probably for the best; he'd been wasting his breath anyway. But he was impressed with what Malc had done with Bean. He'd seen the photos of the state it had been in when he'd taken it over. He'd got it cheap because no one else had wanted to deal with the filth and the mess, or seen the potential. Alfie felt that recognising the potential in something like that was an excellent business lesson, but he knew his dad wouldn't agree. He was about taking over already-successful businesses and reaping the rewards of someone else's hard work, not doing the hard work himself.

His dad ended his call brusquely, and turned to Alfie. 'What were you saying?'

'It doesn't matter,' Alfie said.

Alfie's dad paid the bill and Alfie followed him out of the restaurant onto Strand Street.

'Back to work?' Alfie asked.

'Yes.' His dad took his car keys out of his pocket and looked up and down the road, as if trying to remember where he'd parked.

'What have you got on?' Alfie asked.

'Meetings,' his dad said. 'There's a development near Sefton Park we've been looking at.'

'Right,' Alfie said.

'So you'll be home . . . ?'

'In a couple of weeks,' Alfie said, as he always did. He wasn't sure when he'd last been home, but it was definitely longer ago than a couple of weeks. He hadn't even made it home during the summer holidays, when he was sure he would.

'Keep up the good work,' his dad said.

'Cheers,' Alfie said. 'You too.'

His dad smiled then, but still didn't actually meet Alfie's eyes.

As Alfie waited at the traffic lights, he watched his father walk towards the Liver Buildings and wondered why he still bothered with these lunches. When his dad had first suggested they meet for lunch once a month, Alfie had been sort of thrilled – it wasn't the kind of thing they'd ever done before and he liked the idea of sitting in a fancy restaurant with his successful dad, talking about their lives. But it had never been like that. His father acted as if he was checking on an investment. Alfie supposed he was.

He'd done the same with Lola when she was at university and she claimed she'd loved it, but then she'd always been able to ignore their dad's comments and barbs, whereas Alfie worried about every little thing.

The lights changed to red and then back to green, and Alfie was still standing there. He turned and headed back in the same direction as his father. Alfie saw him turn into Brunswick Street, and crossed over. If his dad saw him, there was nothing he could say. There was no reason for him to be down here, nowhere he could believably say he was going.

He heard the *blip blip* of his father's car – the BMW – unlocking and felt the tension leave his belly. It was fine. Good. And then he saw the woman emerge from the car next to his father's – one of those little mint-green retro Nissans he knew his dad hated. She walked around the car – she was tall and thin, of course, with long, shining, blonde hair and enormous sunglasses obscuring most of her face. But Alfie had known what she'd look like: all the others.

As his dad walked around the BMW and pressed up against the woman, dropping his head down on her shoulder, Alfie turned and left.

Chapter 13

Sean had just rounded the corner by John Lewis when he spotted Alfie and shouted his name.

'Hey!' Sean said, grinning, once Alfie was closer.

'Hey,' Alfie said. He looked miserable.

'What's wrong?' Sean said. 'You look . . .' He frowned.

'Pale?' Alfie said and smiled.

Sean smiled back. 'No. But I was thinking maybe "wan". Is wan a thing?'

'I look bad, is what you're saying.'

'No,' Sean said. 'You always look gorgeous. It's sickening. But you look . . . sad.'

'Yeah,' Alfie said. 'I just had lunch with my dad.'

'Ah,' Sean said, as they rounded the fountains opposite the Hilton. 'Weren't you going somewhere fancy?'

Alfie nodded. 'Brixton's.'

'How was it? The food, I mean?'

Alfie frowned. 'I don't even know. I ate it, but I didn't even notice, you know?'

'Your dad's pretty intimidating,' Sean said.

Sean had met Alfie's father when he'd first moved into the

houseshare and Alfie's parents were still taking an interest in who was living there. He was hot as hell – even better looking than Alfie, which wasn't easy – but terrifying. He had the confidence of someone with loads of money and who was used to getting exactly what he wanted, whenever he wanted it.

'Yeah,' Alfie said. 'And then when he left I sort of . . . followed him. And saw him with a woman.'

'Oh, shit,' Sean said.

'I don't know why I'm surprised . . .' Alfie said. And then he shook his head. 'I'm not surprised.'

They dodged a bunch of teenage girls in cropped tops and ripped jeans.

'He's done it before?' Sean asked.

'I first saw him when I was about five, I think,' Alfie said, shrugging. 'My parents had thrown a party and this woman was leaving – I called her Aunty. Aunty Jasmine. Mum was in the kitchen tidying up and Dad was at the front door, kissing Aunty Jasmine. Even then I knew not to say anything.'

'I'm sorry,' Sean said. 'That sucks.'

Alfie laughed. 'It does suck. My mum must know, right? If I've known since I was five, she can't not know. And that really pisses me off.'

They turned towards Liverpool One.

'You just never know with people's marriages,' Sean said. 'My parents always seemed completely sexless. I never even saw them touch each other. They hardly even looked at each other. But then they'd have a couple of drinks and get all gormless and soppy and tell me how happy they were and all that. And then Mum died and Dad went to pieces.'

'Oh, God,' Alfie said. 'How is he now?'

'I'm not sure,' Sean said. 'I had a really weird conversation with him last week. He was saying he was back at work.'

'And he's not?' Alfie frowned.

Sean shook his head. 'I don't think so. I don't think he can be. He's been retired for years now.'

'Your parents were—'

'Old,' Sean said, grinning. 'Yeah. Mum was forty-four when she had me, and Dad was fifty. They'd apparently been trying for years, which is why I always assumed they didn't have sex. I thought it had put them off.'

Alfie laughed. 'Parents, man.'

'So I don't know. He could be working. He seemed pretty confident about it. And then he didn't. God, I don't even know. And then he rang this morning and just wanted to talk about mice. In his lounge.'

'Mice?'

'Mice.'

They lapsed into silence. Sean tried to remember when they'd last hung out, just the two of them, but he couldn't. Lately Sean was usually at college or out with Molly, and Alfie was always working.

'So where've you been?' Alfie asked.

'Oh, God,' Sean said. 'I was hoping you wouldn't ask me that.'

Alfie grinned at him. 'Up to no good?'

'I did something incredibly embarrassing.'

Alfie raised an eyebrow.

'OK. So there's this boy I kind of like. At college.'

'Right,' Alfie said.

'Do you want to get a donut?' Sean asked, as they passed the Krispy Kreme shop.

'No,' Alfie said. 'Stop stalling.'

Sean grinned. 'I've never done anything like this before, honest. Well . . . that's not strictly true. I've never done anything like this . . . for a while? Is that better?'

Alfie laughed.

'So. I like him. I don't know if he really even knows I'm alive.'

'I bet he does,' Alfie said.

'Well, if he does he never shows it. So we were leaving college at the same time. He was talking to this guy I saw him having breakfast with the other day. They were leaving together. And I just wanted to know if, you know, if they were together. Because if they were I would, you know . . .'

'What?' Alfie said.

They walked up the steps and skirted past Waterstones.

'I don't know,' Sean said. 'I could maybe stop obsessing over him so much? If I knew he was taken?'

'Really?' Alfie said. In his, admittedly limited, experience it didn't always work like that.

'Well, you know, I thought it was worth a try,' Sean said. 'I should probably go in there and get a book I'm meant to get for college.' He stopped and looked at the shop, then shrugged and started walking again.

'So?' Alfie said.

'So they walked together for a few minutes and then the Viking – the boy he was with looks like a Viking, all hair and red cheeks – went off and Charlie was on his own.'

'At which point you realised you were being creepy and stopped following him,' Alfie said.

'Yes!' Sean said. 'Except no. I mean, I thought about it. It's not like I didn't know I was being creepy, I get points for that, right?'

'Oh, of course,' Alfie said.

'I just . . . I tried to make myself stop following, but my legs just wouldn't have it.'

'Damn your legs.'

'Right? Bastards. So I kept following him and he went into the toy shop and it turns out he works there. And I followed him in and accidentally bought a Furby for nearly a hundred quid.'

'Bloody hell,' Alfie said. 'And so what did you learn from this Introduction to Stalking?'

'That Furbys are really fucking expensive?'

'Useful,' Alfie said. 'Maybe next time you should just, you know, ask him out for a drink or something.'

'Ugh. You're as bad as Molly.'

'Why, what did she say?'

'Same. Ask him out. That's not happening.'

'Why not? I thought gay men were much more—'

Sean fake-screamed. 'That is such a cliché! It's not all glory holes and—'

'Oh, my God!' Alfie said. 'I wasn't thinking of glory holes! I just meant I thought it was meant to be easier for men to ask out other, you know, men.'

'But why should it be?' Sean said. 'I don't even know if he's gay.'

'Is he on the same course as you?' Alfie said, smiling.

Sean laughed. 'Oh, you are all about the stereotypes today! And no. As far as I know he has no interest in musical theatre. Anymore.'

Alfie grinned. 'You're right. I'm sorry. Maybe ask him for help with something college-related? Just to at least start a conversation. You've had a conversation with him, right?'

'Not exactly,' Sean said.

'I think that's probably your first step then. No, actually, your first step is to stop stalking him.'

'I'm not stalking him,' Sean said, pretending to be offended. 'I'm just, you know, casually following him around to see what his interests are.'

Chapter 14

Molly hadn't been able to believe it when she'd heard who the guest lecturer was going to be. She'd seen his films; she'd even travelled to Leeds to see him live on stage. Twice. She had a picture of him on her bedroom wall and pasted a printed-out screenshot of one of his many full-frontal scenes into the back of her diary. She felt a bit bad about that – out of the context of the performance the photo was objectifying, but Molly loved the way it made her feel and whenever she'd tried to tear it out and chuck it away she just hadn't been able to make herself do it.

So when her friend Clare had told her that he was coming here – that Roman Lucas was actually going to be taking classes and seminars and that Molly would be able to look at him and talk to him and learn from him . . . Molly had been speechless. It had worried Clare a bit, actually; she'd never seen Molly anything like speechless before.

'What's your problem?' Clare had grinned.

'I . . . love him,' Molly had managed to squeak out.

Clare had laughed. 'Do you? I think he's a right wanker.'

Clare wasn't the only one. Molly had overheard quite a few of the other students on her course saying the same thing. Molly was studying Acting and Dance and she heard more than one person joke that they didn't know Roman could dance and he had to be coming for that because he sure as hell couldn't act.

But Molly thought they were wrong. Yes, he'd been in a bunch of blockbusters and hadn't really impressed, but Molly had seen him in a couple of smaller, indie films and thought he was wonderful. And she'd seen him on a chat show a couple of years earlier and thought he seemed like a really nice guy, as well as being sexy as hell. She couldn't wait to meet him.

As she and Clare got themselves tea from the vending machine outside the canteen, Clare had grinned at her. 'I can't believe you've gone all moony over Roman Lucas.'

'I've not,' Molly said. 'I just think we're really lucky that he's coming here—'

'Yeah, I know,' Clare said, shaking her sugar sachet and then pouring it into her tea. 'You really get him. More than anyone else. If you could just get to talk to him . . .' Clare rolled her eyes.

'Shut up,' Molly said, smiling.

'Everyone thinks that, Mol,' Clare said. 'You're like one of those teenagers who's obsessed with some boy-band dork: "If I could just meet him!"'

Molly shook her head and fastened the plastic lid on her tea.

'Seriously though,' Clare said. 'He's coming as a teacher. He's not going to hang out with us. He's not coming to be our friend.'

'The lecturers hang out with us sometimes!' Molly said. They'd all been for an Indian with Danny Cotterill when he'd come to teach them stagecraft. It was one of Molly's favourite things ever. Snapping a poppadom and looking at this guy and thinking, You've been nominated for an Oscar . . .

'You never know,' Molly said.

'I do know,' Clare said. 'And you haven't got a hope.'

Molly drank some of her tea and smiled at her friend. 'We'll see.'

As Molly walked home from college, her mum rang.

'I can't stay on long,' she said. 'I'm back out to work in a minute. How's things?'

'Which work?' Molly asked, looking back up the road before crossing over.

'Cleaning,' her mum said. 'At Boots.'

'Oh, I didn't know you were still doing that!' Molly said.

'Different branch. They let me go from the last one and then someone rang from a new one. Have to get the bus there, but it's not too bad.'

Molly hated the thought of her mum getting a bus to a minimum wage-paying evening job after she'd worked all day as well, but she knew better than to say that since her mum would tell her she had no choice. And Molly knew she was right. Sort of.

'You been at work today?' Molly asked.

'Yeah,' her mum said. 'Not in the kitchen though. I've been on yard duty.'

'How come?' Molly stopped to look in the window of the cupcake shop and wondered if they delivered. She'd love to send her mum a box of cupcakes. Not that she could really afford to.

'My hands have been a bit . . . They're fine, they're getting better, but they weren't doing so good in the kitchen. The hot water, you know?'

'Mum!' Molly said. 'I thought you said you were going to wear gloves!'

'I do, most of the time. But I can't do everything with rubbery hands. Anyway, don't worry, they're not too bad now.'

'Make sure you wear gloves when you're cleaning though,' Molly said.

'I will, of course,' her mum said and then she laughed. 'I'm your mum, you know!'

'I know,' Molly said. 'Sorry.' She pictured her mum's hands, chapped and peeling with eczema and wondered if she should buy her some hand cream instead. Even though people were always buying her hand cream.

'How's college?' her mum said, as Molly gave up staring into the cake shop window and resumed walking down Bold Street.

'Great,' Molly said. 'You'll never believe who's coming as guest lecturer.'

'Ooh! Who?' her mum asked and even in just those two words her voice sounded brighter.

'Roman Lucas,' Molly said, smiling into the phone.

'Oh!' her mum said. 'Is he the one in that film we watched? The one with the huge penis?'

Molly snorted with laughter. Yes. He was.

Nina lay face-down on her bed and scrolled through her phone in case she'd missed a text from Jack. She was pretty sure he hadn't texted, but sometimes her texts didn't show up as unread and she missed them. There was definitely nothing from Jack though.

Clambering off her bed, she plugged in her record player and slid her *West Side Story* original cast recording out of her bookcase, wiped it with a non-static cloth and put it on, before flopping back onto the bed, forgetting that it made the needle jump across the record.

'Shit.' She sat up and returned the needle to the start, before deciding she'd skip the prologuey parts and go straight to the bits that made her cry. She always listened to *West Side Story* when she was feeling a bit sorry for herself. It either made her cry or made her feel lucky to be alive and listening to such gorgeous music. Sometimes both. She'd sung 'I Have a Love' at her first audition for the Academy so she didn't listen to that one any more.

She was sitting up against her headboard, singing along with 'Tonight' and imagining herself on a New York fire escape – or a New York fire escape on a stage set anyway – when her phone rang. She answered at the same moment she saw it wasn't Jack, but her mum.

'Oh, I am honoured!' her mum said, instead of hello.

'Hi, Mum,' Nina said.

'Is that *West Side Story*?'

'Yeah. Hang on, I'll turn it off.'

Leaving her phone on her pillow, she scooted down the bed and lifted the needle off the record, before lying back down and picking up her phone.

'Was that a CD?' her mum asked.

'No. Vinyl,' Nina said, without thinking.

'My vinyl? I wondered what had happened to that!'

'Sorry,' Nina said.

'Never mind. You can bring it back next time you come home. Remember home?'

Nina rolled onto her back. 'Yeah.'

'I assume you've been busy?'

'Yeah. College has been crazy. Second year is pretty full-on.'

And right there she'd missed her chance again. Every single time she spoke to either of her parents she planned to tell them she'd dropped out of college and every single time she failed.

'You'll let us know when you're doing a show, right? Isn't there a Christmas show this year?'

Nina sat up, pulling her knees against her chest. 'There is, yeah, but I haven't got all the details yet.'

She'd have to ask Molly about it. And then find a way of putting her parents off coming. Molly said they'd understand, but Molly didn't know Nina's parents. They wouldn't have understood her dropping out in the first place – not after all the time and effort they'd spent to get her there – and they absolutely wouldn't understand her lying to them all this time.

'Your dad would really like you to come home next half-term,' her mum said. 'Do you think there's any chance?'

'Yeah,' Nina said, her stomach flipping with guilt. 'Maybe. Can I let you know?'

'How did it go today?' Alfie asked Anna.

She was curled up in the corner of the sofa in her pyjamas, clicking mindlessly through dozens of TV channels, a cup of tea gone cold on the side table next to her.

'Not well,' Anna said. 'There's no job.'

'What?' Alfie said. He got up from the dining table where he'd been sitting with his laptop and came over to the end of the sofa.

Anna looked up at him, pulling a cushion into her lap and wrapping her arms around it. 'Lola had a meeting with the chief exec and there's a hiring freeze.'

'But she offered you the job, didn't she?' Alfie said, frowning. 'Shit. I bet that's why she rang me today. I missed a call when I was at work.'

Anna shook her head. 'She offered it, yeah, but I hadn't signed a contract or anything. And now there's no job.'

'Can they do that?' Molly said from the doorway. Anna hadn't even heard her come in. 'That's awful.'

'I think . . . I don't know,' Anna said. 'But I didn't sign anything so . . .'

'So what are you going to do?' Molly asked. She walked around the sofa, passing Alfie, and sat down next to Anna.

'I don't know,' Anna said.

Her voice cracked and she felt tears starting to come. She thought she'd done all the crying she was going to do. After she'd left the Phoenix she'd walked down to the Mersey and sat on a bench looking out at the river and cried until she felt sick. A couple of people had actually come over to ask if she was OK, so after a while she went to get a coffee in a cafe, but burst into tears there too so eventually gave up and walked back home and went back to bed for a couple of hours. She only went into the lounge because she knew Alfie was home and she was sick of her own moping company.

Alfie passed her a square of kitchen roll and she held it against her eyes.

'I'm really sorry,' Alfie said. 'You must be so disappointed.'

Anna looked at the kitchen roll and its two black curled-mascara imprints. Like a bit of her face, looking back up at her. How she still had any mascara left, she had no idea.

'It's . . . I mean, I am.' She picked up her mug and drank some of the cold tea. 'I know it's not so bad. I know much worse things happen. I just . . . I was really looking forward to it.'

'What are you going to do?' Molly said. 'Are you going to go home?'

'I don't want to,' Anna said. 'Maybe I have to, I don't know.'

'Oh, stay,' Molly said. 'I'm sure between us we could find something for you to do. Can she do some shifts at Bean, Alfie?'

Alfie sat down on the chair in the corner and leaned forward, his elbows on his knees. 'I should think so.' He smiled at Molly. 'She can do your shifts. Maybe she'll be on time.'

Anna looked over at Alfie and then at Molly. Maybe she *could* stay. Just because she didn't have the job she thought she had didn't mean she had nothing, did it? She had the first month's rent paid, so that gave her a month to find something and start paying her own way. She could do that. Couldn't she?

'Lola said she was going to talk to some people at other theatres. She said she'll do her best to find me something.'

'She will, I'm sure,' Alfie said. 'I know she likes you a lot and she said you were brilliant at the job.'

Anna's mouth twitched. Brilliant, but not brilliant enough, apparently.

'Seriously though,' Molly said. 'You should stay and try to find something else. We'll all help you.'

'Thank you,' Anna said.

'You're welcome,' Alfie said. 'You just need a plan and you'll feel a lot better.'

Anna looked at her new friends in her new home and realised she felt better already.

SPARKSLIFE: Dumped

by AnnaSparks 9,696 views
Published on 12 September

[Transcript of Anna's vlog]

No. Not like that. Today I want to talk about something I've been putting off. Because it's bad news. For me, I mean. Actually, it was terrible news for me. I did try to make a video about it before now, but I kept crying so I had to stop. You really don't want a video that's just five minutes of me [cuts to video of Anna sobbing noisily. This video moves up to the right hand corner of the screen and carries on playing – without sound – while Anna keeps talking in the main screen.].

So I moved here for a job. It was at the theatre where I did an internship in the summer holidays. I absolutely loved it there. You know – I talked about it a lot. So when they offered me a proper job, a full-time job with money and everything, I jumped at it. Even though it meant not going to university.

And I know some of you didn't agree with that decision. My parents didn't really agree with that decision. And knowing that has actually made it much harder to do this. To talk about this, I mean. To tell you what happened. Because what happened is this: I moved to Liverpool, and then I found out that there wasn't a job any more.

[The main picture is briefly replaced with the smaller shot of Anna sobbing. This time with sound. And then it scoots out to the side again.]

Yeah. I know. I have a little bit of money – enough to stay here for a couple of months – but no job. And no prospect of a job. It's not like I'd been job-hunting or interviewing or anything; I'd literally been offered this one job. This one job that I thought was kind of my dream job. And now it's been taken away from me.

So I did a lot of [Anna points to the smaller picture of her sobbing] and then I realised I just have to get on with things. I need to get another job. I haven't yet, but I'm working on it. OK, I'm not even really working on it. But I am thinking about it.

So that's my news. It was very bad. But I'm OK. And everything's going to be fine. Probably.

COMMENTS:

> Daisy Locke: I'm so sorry to hear this, hun. I'm sure you'll find something soon. (((hugs)))

Amber Books: I think you should go to university. You can do your dream job once you've got your degree, but it's important to get an education.

SophSimps: What was the dream job? Can you find something similar somewhere else? Have you even looked?

Daisy Locke:
+ SophSimps: She already said she hasn't looked yet, but she's going to.

Butterflyaway: Good luck with whatever you try to do, Anna. You're so talented. Can you look at my channel?

Chapter 15

Anna hadn't thought it would be easy to find a job, but she hadn't realised it would be so hard either. She'd been to the Job Centre, but it had completely freaked her out and she'd left without speaking to anyone. She'd popped into a few local shops to ask if they were looking for staff, but no one was. A guy in a bar a couple of streets away took her mobile number and said he'd call if anything came up, but she suspected he'd just actually wanted her number for himself.

She'd spent the last few days recording for her vlog and working on edits of videos she'd been meaning to get around to for a while. She tried to post three times a week since she first started vlogging, but she didn't always manage it. And she'd mentioned to her viewers that she might not be able to do that after the move. She had promised at least one video a week though, so she had to stick to that. Also, she wanted to. She didn't quite feel like herself when she wasn't vlogging. And she'd noticed that when she was doing things, she was already rewriting them in her head in the way she was going to present them in a vlog. It was a bit weird, but it was also fun for her.

Back from another fruitless job search, she made herself a tea and took it upstairs to the lounge. She sat down at the dining table with the local paper and a pen and then folded her arms on the table and dropped her head down onto them.

'Hey!'

Anna jumped in her seat and let out a shriek.

'Sorry!' Nina said, from the sofa. 'Didn't you know I was here?'

Anna shook her head. 'Are you OK?'

'Knackered,' Nina said, shuffling up on the seat and resting her chin on the back of the sofa. 'No joy today then?'

Anna shook her head. 'Nothing. How long did it take you to find your job?'

Nina frowned. 'Oh, well, I wasn't really looking. My parents had come to visit me and they were staying at the hotel. It was sort of a spontaneous decision.'

'I see,' Anna said, although she didn't really. 'So what were you doing before that?'

'I was at the Academy with Sean and Molly.'

'Oh, yeah?' Anna said. 'I think Sean said something about that. So why did you leave?'

Nina shook her head. 'I don't really want to talk about that, if it's OK?'

'Of course,' Anna said. 'Sorry.'

'Sorry, I don't want to be rude, it's just that Sean and Molly go on about it a lot. It's no big mystery – I just . . . before I went there I was a big fish in a small pond, you know? And then when I wasn't, I found I wasn't good enough. That's all.'

Anna nodded. 'That sounds hard.'

Nina smiled at her. 'What are you going to do?'

Anna sighed, heavily. 'I don't know. I just need to keep looking, I think. And take anything that comes up and keep looking for something better. And I need to ring Lola.'

She couldn't face Lola yet. She felt stupid about what had happened. Yes, Lola had offered her the job, but Anna was the one who dropped everything. She felt like she'd been ridiculously naive.

'You don't think you'd be better off going home?' Nina said. 'It's going to be hard. I've got a shitty job and it's not much fun.'

'You're still here though,' Anna said. 'You didn't go home.'

'No,' Nina said. 'I didn't. But I think my situation's a bit different.'

Anna wanted to ask how, but Nina had already said she didn't want to talk about it.

'I definitely want to stay,' Anna said, opening the paper again and picking up her pen.

'OK,' Nina said, lying back down. 'Good luck.'

'What's the matter with you?' Molly said, sitting down next to Sean in the canteen. He was slumped with his head resting on the table. 'Did you do it? Did you talk to him?'

'Yes,' Sean said, turning his head to one side and looking up at her. 'This is me, celebrating.'

'Oh, Sean. What's the problem?' Molly picked up his polystyrene cup and sniffed it. 'Do you want me to ask him for you?'

Sean sat up and stared at her. 'Yes, that's exactly the image I'm going for. Can you do it now? Can you? Can you?'

'Is this tea?' she asked. 'It doesn't smell like tea.'

'It's coffee,' Sean said.

'It doesn't smell like coffee either.' She put it back on the table. 'If you don't do it, I will.'

'Hells no,' Sean said. 'I'll do it. I just need to, you know, psych myself up. And I need money. If I ask him out and he says yes, I'd have to say, "You're cool to pay, right?"'

'I thought your dad was sending you some money.'

'Yeah, he keeps saying he will and then he doesn't.' Sean shrugged. 'I don't know that he's even got any.'

'You could take him somewhere free,' Molly said, picking up a bag of crisps. 'Like the park. That's romantic.'

Sean rolled his eyes. 'Yeah, that's not happening."

'I'm going to see Adam's mate's band tonight in a pub near the park. Not exactly romantic, but if you wanted more of a cazh invite . . .'

'Nope,' Sean said. 'And those crisps were here when I arrived.'

Molly dropped the crisps back on the table. 'Harry really fucked you up, didn't he?'

'By making me fall in love with him and then fucking off? Nah, that was fine.'

'He didn't make you fall in love with him. You forget that I was there. You had heart-eyes the minute he walked in the door.'

'That's because he was beautiful. A beautiful bastard. Could it have been worse? Or better?'

'Everyone needs to get their heart broken at least once,' Molly said. 'It's character-building.'

'And now he's building his character in London's Glittering West End,' Sean said.

'He's very talented,' Molly said, seriously. And then grinned. 'Wanker.'

'Do you really believe that?' Sean said. 'About getting your heart broken? Because what about childhood sweethearts who stay together for ever? That's better, isn't it?'

'Maybe,' Molly said. 'I don't know. How do they know what they're missing?'

'Maybe they don't feel like they're missing anything. I don't think my parents ever did.'

'My parents didn't,' Molly said. 'Because they just shagged everyone anyway.'

Sean groaned. 'I don't know how we're meant to know what we're doing with them as role models.'

'You can be my role model,' Molly told him. 'And I'll be yours.'

'I'm not taking relationship advice from you,' Sean said. 'You'll just tell me to shag everyone, just in case.'

'Don't knock it til you've tried it,' Molly said. 'You're young. You should be sowing oats.'

'I haven't got the energy,' Sean said. 'And I've blunted my needle.'

'You should see a doctor about that.'

'Ha,' Sean said. 'Anyway, I'm done for the day. Are you not?'

Molly shook her head. 'I'll see you at home later. And if you see Charlie, just say, "Do you want to get a coffee?" Tell you what, wait till we see him in here and I'll go over with you. You can say, "Me and my sexy friend Molly are going to get a coffee – wanna join us?" That way if he's *not* gay . . . KERCHING!'

'He's so gay,' Sean said.

'You're so gay,' Molly said.

'Your mum's so gay.'

Sean's phone rang and he answered it, grinning at Molly.

'This isn't over,' Molly said, picking up the coffee again.

Chapter 16

After she'd finished work, Nina waited for Jack on the steps in front of the hotel. She watched him come through the main door – which he wasn't meant to do – then he stopped, frowning, looked up and down the main road, and lit a cigarette. He was halfway down the steps before he saw her and she thought she saw annoyance flicker across his face, but then he smiled.

'You're not supposed—' she started to say, gesturing at the cigarette, but Jack grabbed her and kissed her hard.

'From now on, I'm going to do that every time you nag,' he said, against her neck.

'I don't nag,' she said, licking her top lip where Jack had caught it against her front teeth. 'And if Janice sees us here she'll—'

'You said that on purpose, didn't you?' Jack said when he'd stopped kissing her again.

Nina smiled. 'What are you doing?'

'What? Now? I was going to go and get a drink. You coming?'

Nina grabbed Jack's hand and she let herself forget about the day she'd had cleaning up other people's crap and just be with Jack, who was clearly in a surprisingly good mood.

They walked towards Lime Street and Jack turned into one of his favourite pubs, dropping his cigarette on the floor outside. Nina didn't really like it – she preferred the bars on and around Bold Street – but Jack had apparently been coming to this place since he was a kid (they weren't bothered about underage serving, he said).

'How was your day?' Nina asked Jack, as he sat down opposite her, putting the bottle of lager he'd bought her on the table. Nina had actually wanted wine, but he hadn't asked.

'The usual,' he said, shrugging.

'Mine was so boring,' Nina said, pulling the bottle towards her. 'It's the same every day. Like, exactly the same.'

She'd been thinking about it since she'd listened to *West Side Story*. When she was little, her plan had been to run away to London at the first opportunity – or even New York if she managed to save enough for the fare. She imagined herself in a tiny flat, even just one room really, but somewhere exciting, the centre of things. She used to go through her mum's Next Directory choosing the furniture she'd have. She didn't think she'd need much because she imagined she'd be out all the time, working and socialising. She'd pictured herself auditioning and getting a perfect role almost immediately – something small but pivotal. And then her career would just grow from there. That had been her plan. It hadn't quite worked out.

She scuffed her shoes on the sticky floor. 'I want an adventure.'

Jack raised one eyebrow at her and grinned.

'Not like that!' Nina said, smiling back at him. 'I was thinking about it today. You know what I've always wanted to do? Go to the airport and pick a flight randomly. Just take my passport and money and sort everything else out when I get there.'

'But you haven't got any money,' Jack said.

'I haven't even got a passport,' Nina said. She swigged her lager. 'I need to do something though. I feel restless.' She held the heel of her hand against her chest. 'Here. I can feel it. Something wants to burst out. Is there a fountain we can go and jump in?'

'That's your idea of an adventure?' Jack said, looking at her chest.

'I meant naked,' Nina giggled. 'Is that any good to you?'

'Better,' Jack said. 'Definitely better.'

'So is there one?' Nina said.

Jack frowned. 'I can't think of one, no. But if I find one I'll let you know.'

'Oh,' Nina said, slumping back in her seat. 'Where would you go? If you could go anywhere in the world.'

Jack frowned. 'California, maybe? Definitely America though.'

'I'd love to go to New York,' Nina said, sighing. She pictured herself on Broadway, looking up at her name in lights and then forced her brain to wipe the image away.

Jack pulled a face. 'I'm thinking Santa Monica. Or Venice Beach. I could see you in a bikini in the surf.'

He grinned and Nina felt her stomach flip.

'Oh, yeah? Can't see you on a surfboard though.'

'No? I think I'd be great.'

'Only cos you think you're great at everything.'

Jack grinned again. 'What's wrong with that?'

Nina swigged her lager, shaking her head. 'Nothing at all.'

Jack drained his beer, checked his phone and then said, 'How about Whitby?'

'What about Whitby?' Nina asked.

'I'm going there. Next week. To see my mum.'

'Whoa!' Nina said, staring at him.

Jack snorted. 'I know, right?'

'What's she doing there?' The last time Jack had mentioned his mum, she'd been living in the south of France, renovating a cottage and managing some gites.

'She's got a gallery, apparently. And she runs retreats.' He pulled a face.

'Wow,' Nina said.

Jack laughed. 'I know. So. Do you want to come? I mean, it's not much of an adventure, but it's better than jumping in a fountain.'

'Seriously?' Nina said. Her stomach was already fluttering at the idea.

'Yeah. I think so. I mean . . . why not?'

Nina would have preferred 'I don't want to go without you' but just the fact that he wanted her to go was good enough.

'I just . . . I didn't think you really wanted to see her.'

'I didn't,' Jack said. 'I mean, I don't know if I do. But she sent the money and I might as well have a few days away and see . . .'

'See what?'

'See how things are. She's on her own. The boyfriend's gone, apparently.'

Nina nodded. She'd suspected that it had been Jack's mum's boyfriend that had really been the problem, even though Jack had never said so.

'It sounds good,' Nina said. 'It'll be nice.'

'It'll probably be a fucking disaster,' Jack said. 'But at least I'll know, eh?'

Nina nodded.

'So? You gonna come?'

'Definitely,' Nina said.

Nina had lost count of how many drinks they'd had, but last orders had been called – a while ago, it felt like – and they'd finally been chucked out of the pub.

'You know people touch that for luck?' Jack said, pointing up at the bronze of a naked boy, high above the ornate doorway of what used to be Lewis's department store. The front of the building was covered with scaffolding so Nina could only just see the statue, but she'd seen it every time she'd walked past for as long as she'd lived in Liverpool.

Nina laughed. 'No, they don't.'

'They do!' Jack said. 'People have been doing it for years. Lucky Penis.'

'How could people get up there without the scaffolding?' Nina asked, looking at the flat slabs of the walls.

'There's footholds from where people have done it before—'

'That's probably what they're repairing,' Nina said.

Jack ignored her. 'That scaffolding'd make it a piece of piss though . . .'

'No way,' Nina said. 'You'd fall and break your neck.'

'Wanna bet?' Jack said, grinning at her.

'Not particularly. It's stupid anyway. How could touching the dick of a statue bring you luck?'

'Say "dick" again,' Jack said. 'That'll bring me luck.'

'You are not doing it!' Nina shouted, as Jack grinned, turned, and ran across the road.

Nina waited at the crossing, even though there weren't any cars. He couldn't seriously be planning to climb that thing, she thought.

'You're not doing it!' she said again, once she'd crossed.

'You said you wanted an adventure!'

He was practically hopping on the spot, he was so excited.

'Yeah, *me*,' Nina said. 'Not you.'

'I'll show you, then you can do it.'

Nina laughed. 'No. Way.'

'It's easy,' Jack said. 'Watch me.'

Nina looked around. The corner they were standing on was quiet, but there were people on the steps in front of Lime Street station and a few people were still smoking and talking outside the pub they'd just left.

'You keep a look out,' Jack said. 'And then when I've got it in my hand I'll shout and you can take a photo.' He handed her his phone.

'Don't,' Nina said. 'Seriously, Jack. You'll fall.'

'I've never fallen when I've done it before,' Jack said. 'And there wasn't even scaffolding then.'

He was already starting to clamber up the scaffolding, as if he was on a kids' climbing frame.

'I can't look,' Nina said. 'Call me when you're up there.'

But she couldn't help sneaking glances every now and then; Jack did look like he knew what he was doing. His hands and feet would only grope or reach for a couple of seconds before he found the next bar to hold on to and Nina couldn't help admiring the way his bum and thighs looked in his torn jeans as he climbed.

He was halfway to the statue when a man shouted, 'Hey!' from the pub opposite.

'Bit busy,' Jack called without turning round.

'You can't nick it!' the man yelled.

'He's not trying to nick anything,' Nina couldn't help but shout back.

Jack was almost at the statue's plinth when a bus stopped at the traffic lights on the corner and someone shouted, 'Wanker!' out of an upstairs window.

Jack held up one finger, again without turning round, and Nina started to actually hope he would get there, hope he could do it without anyone stopping him. It was ridiculous – pointless, dangerous and irresponsible – but Nina couldn't help admire his fearlessness.

The lights changed, the bus moved on and Nina carried on watching Jack, her phone in her hand ready to take the photo as soon as he reached the statue. Jack had now made it to the top of the frame the statue was standing on, and was just a metre or so away. Nina held up her phone and Jack grinned down at her as he reached out and grabbed the statue's penis. Nina took a photo and Jack shouted, 'You get it?'

'Yes!' Nina yelled. 'Now come down.'

'Hang on,' Jack called. He crouched down in front of the statue and Nina worried he was going to do something hugely inappropriate, but instead he turned and sat down on the plinth, his legs hanging down over the frame.

'Take another one!'

Nina took another photo and shouted, '*Now* come down!'

'OK, OK,' Jack called, grinning.

As he turned, his left leg slipped and swung under the scaffolding.

'Stop it!' Nina yelled, assuming he was messing around for her benefit. But then his right leg swung too and he was hanging on the edge of the scaffolding by his hands, his legs swinging, trying to find the next pole.

'Oh, my God,' Nina said, half under her breath.

She heard someone shout something and cars honking, but then Jack found the scaffolding and carried on climbing down. He'd almost made it to the bottom when his foot slipped again and he dropped heavily onto the pavement.

Nina stared for a second, thinking she might be sick, but then she heard Jack say, 'Fuck!' and she gasped out a breath.

'Are you OK?' she asked, falling to her knees next to him.

'I've never done that before,' he said.

'Are you all right?!'

'I'm fine,' he said.

'Bloody *hell*, Jack!'

He grinned. 'Don't suppose you got a photo as I fell, did you?'

Chapter 17

The pub was even dingier than Molly had expected. Her shoes were sticking to the floor and when Adam guided her to a table, Molly had to shuffle her chair back because so much beer was pooled around the cardboard coasters.

'Drink?' Adam said.

Molly looked over at the bar and thought about wine, but decided on a beer instead. While Adam was at the bar – Molly saw him chatting to a bunch of other boys who looked just like him: messy hair and band T-shirts and hipster glasses – Molly fiddled with her phone and looked around at the other customers. They almost all looked the same. There was only one other girl there and she was just staring down at her phone.

Molly wondered if maybe she could just leave. Adam probably wouldn't be that bothered; he had so many mates here anyway. She'd met him at college. He was a music student. She wouldn't usually be interested in a music student – they worked all night and slept all day, and usually she wanted to be out at night. But not tonight. Tonight she'd rather be at home. Maybe sitting on the terrace with a beer, listening to Sean talk about Charlie. She could have an early night. She was pretty tired . . .

That was a slippery slope though, she knew. She was young and free and out with a hot man. And the band might be good. She decided to stay.

The band was not good. The singer was terrible and at one point the drummer knocked one of his drums over and everyone just watched as it rolled across the low stage and dropped onto the pub floor. Molly suspected Adam had actually come along just to take the piss; there was no way he could think this lot were any good.

And Molly felt like she was getting a migraine. Actually she felt like the band *was* a migraine. She could feel the beat of the bass in her teeth.

'I'm just going outside!' she yelled at Adam.

He gestured at her with his beer bottle, grinning.

'Need some air!' she yelled.

He kept nodding and smiling.

So she left.

Leaning against the wall of the pub, she could still hear the band. She felt like she could still feel them through the brick. Maybe she would be better off at home – she could get chips on the way. But then she'd have to ring a taxi and she didn't know exactly where they were, and Adam was nice and she didn't want to worry him. Surely they couldn't play for much longer?

She went back inside and bought herself another drink, but couldn't even stay inside long enough to drink it. The band had moved on to U2 cover versions and Molly couldn't take the mullering they were giving 'All I Want Is You'. And she didn't even like the original version.

Back outside, she sat down on a bench seat in the beer garden and scrolled through Twitter on her phone. This was not one of her best ever dates.

'Hey,' someone – a man – said. 'Are you all right?'

Molly was all ready to tell him to fuck off, when she looked up. He was older. Quite a lot older. And utterly gorgeous.

'Yeah, thanks. I'm fine. Just . . . getting some fresh air.'

'Right,' he said.

He was looking at her with a slight frown. Like he recognised her. Or thought maybe he should recognise her. Molly frowned back. She didn't know him, did she? She didn't think so. She was pretty sure she'd remember someone who looked like him. He was properly gorgeous. Not like Adam; gorgeous like a grown up. Cropped hair, dark eyes, clean-shaven. He was wearing a tie, FFS.

'Can I get you a drink?' he said.

Molly looked at her bottle. It was empty. She hadn't realised.

'That would be nice,' she said. 'Thanks.'

She watched him walk inside. He was wearing a suit without the jacket because it was still warm, even though it was late. He looked expensive. Professional. Molly had never been with anyone like him before. She wondered what it would be like. A man, not a boy. Or a girl. Interesting.

He came out of the bar with a bottle of lager for her and a Guinness for himself.

She wrinkled her nose.

'You don't like Guinness?' he said.

'Tastes like cold coffee to me.'

He smiled tightly. 'It's an acquired taste.'

'I don't understand that,' Molly said. 'Why would you acquire it?'

He sipped his drink and then grinned at her. 'That's a very good point. But somehow I did and now I like it.'

He licked the foam off his top lip and Molly crossed her legs. He wouldn't be interested in her, she knew. Even if he had bought her a drink. He'd be waiting for someone and just passing the time. But she wondered what it would be like to be with someone like him. It was ridiculous even to think about it – she'd just been scrolling through Roman Lucas's Instagram and thinking about what it would be like to be with *him*. Maybe she thought about sex too much . . .

'What are you thinking about?' the man asked.

Molly laughed. 'I was wondering if I think about sex too much.'

'Not possible, surely,' he said, smiling.

'Do you think?' She looked at him from under her lashes. If he was interested, now was the time to let her know. Now was the time she would know.

He stared at her. 'People don't think about sex enough. They settle for OK when they could have . . .'

'Mindblowing,' Molly said.

'Yes.'

'Oh, my God,' Molly said. The car door handle was stuck so deeply between her shoulder blades she worried she'd have to have it surgically removed. But when she looked down at Michael's – his name was Michael – face between her legs, she figured it was worth it. She'd never come like that before. All the times she thought she'd come, she'd been wrong. She'd actually seen stars. Or maybe she'd burst a blood vessel in her eye.

She wriggled her bum along the leather seat and her skirt back down her hips.

'I need to get back,' she said.

'Boyfriend?' Michael asked, shifting in the seat until he was sitting up with her feet in his lap.

'Not a boyfriend, no,' she said. 'But I was on a date.'

'Not much of one.'

'No, not much of one.'

Molly swung her own legs round so she was sitting alongside Michael.

'Why don't you tell him you're leaving and I'll take you home,' Michael said.

Molly looked at him. She wanted to do that. Actually, she wanted to go home with him – see where he lived, learn more about him, ask him about grown-up life stuff. But she knew that wasn't going to happen.

'Or we could go to a hotel,' Michael said. He said it completely casually, like he did that kind of thing all the time. Maybe he did, Molly thought.

'I don't know about that,' she said. 'We've only just met.'

'But we got to know each other pretty quickly,' Michael said and smiled.

Molly grinned at him. 'Only a small part.'

'Less of the small,' he said.

Molly swung one leg across the seat so that her thigh knocked against his. 'You know what I mean. I don't know anything about you. You could be a mad axe murderer. Or a Tory.'

Michael laughed and Molly felt it deep in her stomach. She needed to get out of the car right now or she would go home with him. And he probably was a Tory. He was clearly rich and rich people generally were, weren't they? She pulled her leg back and opened the door.

'I'm serious,' he said. 'Let's go somewhere. I promise I'm not an axe murderer.'

'That's what all the axe murderers say,' Molly said. She clambered out of the car, knowing she was giving him an excellent view of her arse.

'Give me your number,' Michael said.

Molly turned. 'What?'

'Your mobile number. Give it to me.'

He had his own phone in his hand ready to put her number in.

'You've got terrible manners for a rich bloke,' Molly said.

He smiled. 'Please may I have your phone number?'

Molly took the phone out of his hand and typed her number in then slammed the door and headed back inside the pub.

Chapter 18

On the terrace, Anna carefully carried one of the iron chairs over to the railing and moved another one so she could put her feet up. Bold Street was dark and mostly quiet. Anna could hear some shouting coming from somewhere near Central Station and cars swishing along Berry Street at the opposite end, but Bold Street itself was peaceful. She turned the fairy lights on and then tipped her head back to look up at the few visible stars.

A few years earlier she and her parents had gone on holiday to Northumberland. They rented a cottage in the middle of nowhere: they had to drive through a farm to get to it and more than once they were stuck behind a crowd of sheep or pheasants or cows, Anna's mum getting more and more frustrated while her dad tried to placate her with, 'Relax! We're on holiday!' which only seemed to annoy her more.

One night, Anna had been closing her curtains to go to bed when she'd looked out of the window and seen the sky filled with stars. Her parents had already gone to sleep – they always went to bed really early on holiday and then got up early so they could get out and 'make the most of the day'.

Anna tiptoed downstairs, stepped into her wellies, unlocked the front door, and crunched out over the gravel driveway to the walled garden opposite, where she sat down at the picnic table much like the one on the terrace. Only then did she allow herself to look up and it was as if her brain couldn't quite take in what she was seeing.

The sky was full of stars. Not even just full – *crammed* with stars. So many that she couldn't get her eyes to focus on them properly. It was as if her eyes were trying to take in more than they could handle and so were skittering about in a panic. Anna found it frustrating; she wanted to really see, but her eyes wouldn't let her.

Instead she shuffled up so she was sitting on the table and then lay back and stared straight up, letting her eyes relax. It was completely overwhelming. She felt like a bug on a leaf. She felt tiny and pointless, but also enormous and important and vital. She wanted to jump up and get on with her life – eighty years or whatever she might get suddenly seemed like nowhere near enough time to do all the things she wanted to do and go all the places she wanted to go. But at the same time she felt like there was no need. She was just a tiny speck in an unimaginably big universe. It didn't really matter what she did; the pressure was off.

She didn't feel that way now. There were nowhere near as many stars in Liverpool as there had been in Northumberland. There were, of course; she just couldn't see them as clearly. They were still there. She squinted. She could see the Big Dipper – the only constellation she ever confidently recognised – and she could also see what she thought was probably the North Star. Was that always the brightest star in the sky? Or maybe that meant it was a planet. Someone had told her that at school. Maybe Venus? Or Jupiter.

She had that feeling again. The tiny and also huge feeling. She needed to stop feeling sorry for herself and get on with things. Time was running out.

She opened her laptop and switched on the camera. She didn't have her make-up on, but she figured she could edit it in some way that it didn't matter – maybe turn up the contrast or use still photos intercut with film of the terrace and the view. She pulled her hair out of its ponytail and fluffed it around her face, before pressing record.

'I can't sleep,' she whispered. 'So I've come out onto the terrace to talk to you guys.'

Alfie lay on his bed and stared up at the ceiling. There was a crack running from corner to corner. Had it always been there? There'd been a crack, he thought, but not that long. Maybe the ceiling would collapse and bury him in rubble in his bed. It probably wasn't ideal that his first thought was relief that at least he wouldn't need to do his Economics essay. He frowned. There was an enormous cobweb in one corner too. He closed his eyes. He felt more wired than tired, but he had college in the morning so he knew had to get some sleep.

But every time he tried to sleep, he pictured his dad with that woman. And then he thought about college and work and how much he actually had to do and he felt completely overwhelmed. And then he thought about lunch with his dad, which led to the woman again, and he was going round and round in circles driving himself mad.

And he was worried about Anna. When he'd talked to Lola she'd been sure she'd be able to find Anna a job somewhere, even if it wasn't the kind of job she was expecting, but Alfie couldn't help feeling bad for her, though it was nothing to do with him. It was his sister who'd let Anna down and Anna was sharing his house . . . He wanted to do something to help. But he really had enough on his plate. Which was why he couldn't sleep.

He sat up and shook himself. He'd have to get rid of that cobweb if he wanted to sleep. The mop must still be on the terrace from when Anna had been sick her first night. Great. It'd be disgusting by now.

He headed up the stairs and into the lounge, but stopped when he saw Molly's hoodie hanging over the back of one of the dining chairs. She'd told him once that she'd had it for years – the cuffs were frayed and the elastic around the hem had gone baggy – but she obviously loved it. He loved it on her. It made her look softer and more vulnerable than the usual stuff she wore. He loved the way she dressed; she always looked completely herself in her dungarees and seventies charity shop coats, but whenever she was wearing the hoodie, he wanted to curl up next to her and smell it.

He picked it up, thinking he'd fold it and leave it on the sofa where she could find it in the morning. But instead of folding it, he lifted it to his face and inhaled. It smelled exactly like her. Like vanilla and amber and that strange lipstick smell. He pictured himself pressing up against Molly and smelling her neck. The feel of her skin under his lips, her hair in his hands. It was only when he felt an erection starting to stir that he dropped the hoodie back on the chair. What the hell was he doing?

He turned to go out onto the terrace and saw Anna standing just inside the patio doors, staring at him.

'I—' he started, even though he really had no idea what he was going to say. Even from the other side of the room, he could tell Anna was blushing.

'Sorry,' she said. 'I was out on the terrace. I couldn't sleep.'

'Me neither,' Alfie said. 'That's why I . . . I came to get the mop. There's a cobweb . . . and . . . God, I'm really sorry, this is embarrassing.'

Anna smiled. 'You like Molly.'

Alfie nodded. His stomach clenched with nerves. He hadn't told anyone before. 'Yeah.'

'She doesn't know?' Anna asked.

Alfie shook his head. 'And I've never done anything like –' he gestured at the hoodie – 'that before. Honestly. I don't want you to think I go round the flat, like, fondling her stuff or anything.'

Anna laughed. 'No. I know.'

'I would prefer it if you didn't . . . say anything. To any of the others.'

'God, no!' Anna was horrified. 'God. No. I wouldn't say anything.'

'I just . . . Thank you. I know I need to say something to her. I've tried. But you've seen Molly. She's always rushing about. She's always seeing people, different people. And it's hard because she lives here. I wouldn't want her to feel uncomfortable, you know. If she wasn't interested.'

Anna nodded. He was so nice. She couldn't quite get her head around how nice he was. How could Molly not like him? She wanted to say so. She wanted to say something encouraging, but she couldn't seem to manage it.

'So what were you doing?' Alfie asked, gesturing at the terrace.

'Oh!' Anna glanced back over her shoulder and then put her hands up to her hair, which was down. Alfie hadn't seen it down before; she usually had it in a ponytail. But it suited her loose. 'I was just recording a message. For my friend.' She pulled a band off her wrist and fastened her hair back up. 'But I've finished now. I'll just . . .'

She went back out onto the terrace and closed her laptop. Alfie followed her out.

'Do you mind some company?' he said. 'Or are you going back in now?'

Anna shook her head. 'No, that would be great. It's really lovely out here.'

She sat back down at the picnic table and Alfie sat opposite.

'So why can't you sleep?' she asked him. 'It can't just be the cobweb. Unless you've got a phobia of spiders?'

Alfie smiled. 'No, I don't mind spiders. I've more got a phobia of . . . not getting things done.'

'You do a lot,' Anna said, smiling. 'I don't know how you fit it all in.'

'I don't really,' Alfie said. 'I'm behind on my college work. I should really do more shifts at Bean because it's busy and I need the money. I just . . .' He shook his head.

'There's only so much you can do though,' Anna said. 'You don't want to make yourself ill.'

Alfie smiled. 'You're right. I just need to, I don't know, take a time out every now and then. Stop letting it all get on top of me.' He tipped his head back and looked up at the stars. 'This helps.'

'I was just thinking that,' Anna said. 'Do you think that one's a star or a planet?' She pointed at the brightest star overhead.

Alfie frowned. 'A planet, I think. Aren't the brightest stars planets?'

Anna looked at him. 'That's what I thought, but I wasn't sure if I'd made it up.'

He smiled. 'I mean, they're all planets anyway, aren't they? Just not in our orbit? Or something?'

'I don't know. It makes my brain hurt.' Anna looked up again. 'Is that a . . . shooting star? No. It can't be. It must be a plane.'

'Where?' Alfie asked her.

The white light was moving, but it didn't have a flashing light or a red light. It was moving in a sort of smooth curve.

'Ah, I know that one,' Alfie said. 'That's the International Space Station.'

Anna shielded her eyes with her hands so she could see it better. 'Seriously?'

'Yeah. Incredible, isn't it?'

'So there's people in there?'

'Yep. They're probably looking down, thinking, What are those two doing up at this hour?'

Anna laughed. 'That's amazing though. We're looking up at something in space.'

'I know,' Alfie said. 'Puts things into perspective.'

'I was just thinking about that,' Anna said.

'I'd better get back to—'

'Your cobweb?' Anna said.

'I was going to say bed,' Alfie said, standing up. 'But, yeah, I'd better deal with the cobweb too.'

'Night then,' Anna said, smiling up at him. 'I'm going to stay out here for a bit.'

SPARKSLIFE: Crushed

by AnnaSparks 10,324 views
Published on 17 September

[Transcript of Anna's vlog]

So. Something kind of weird and kind of funny happened last night. I saw one of my housemates doing something . . . a bit odd. It wasn't anything bad or anything, it was just . . . it was a bit embarrassing for both of us. It turns out that he's got this mega crush on another of my housemates. He's known her for a while and he's just, you know, completely mad about her.

And it made me think about crushes. Because I love having a crush. I really do. I love it when you think about this person all the time and you talk about them as much as you can without giving away that you like them (but your friends know anyway and every time you say their name it's like there's flashing lights and a big arrow with 'CRUSH' on it – so embarrassing). And . . . maybe I shouldn't say this because it's probably just me and you're all going to think I'm a freak, but when I've got a crush on someone I kind of feel like they're watching me all the time. So whatever I'm doing, I do it with them in mind, like I want to impress them and make them see that they should be going out with me? That's not just me, is it? Is it? Oh, God. [Anna puts her head in her hands.]

Anyway, I thought I'd do a Top Five Greatest Crushes. Of mine. So far. Ready?

1. Fred from *Scooby Doo*. Shut up.

2. The teaching assistant at primary school. He always did the reading and he was really good at it. And then he took a job teaching English as a Second Language in Japan. And I was so upset. I did make him a lovely leaving card though.

3. Robert Pattinson. I mean, obviously.

4. Mr [quacking sound over the name] who was my Geography teacher. I know, it's such a cliché to have a crush on a teacher, but I went to an all-girls school so whaddaya gonna do? Mr [quack] had blue eyes and a beard and he wore really tight trousers. Some would say too tight. I would not.

5. Emmet in *The Lego Movie*. Don't pretend you wouldn't.

Chapter 19

Because she had nothing else to do, Anna had offered to do the shopping. She'd been to Morrison's on Church Street and was walking back up Bold Street when she noticed a 'help wanted' sign in the window of a fish restaurant. She put her bags down on the pavement and peered in through the windows. She must have walked past it every time she'd been up and down the street, but she hadn't actually noticed it before. It looked nice: bright and clean with candles on the tables and fairy lights around the mirrors. She could see the staff in their white shirts and little black skirts. They were chatting and laughing and she made herself push the door open before she could change her mind.

'I was wondering if the job was still available?' Anna said to the first person who approached – a woman who didn't look much older than Anna, with long blonde hair tied back in a low ponytail.

'Er . . .' She wrinkled her nose. 'I'm not sure. I'll have to ask Tony. Hang on a sec.'

She had a strong Scouse accent and it made Anna feel a bit more relaxed – this wasn't a snobby place. She could work here.

The girl disappeared through a door at the side of the restaurant and Anna stood and waited, feeling self-conscious. The other girls she'd seen through the window were at the back of the restaurant now, setting tables and chatting. Anna looked at the bar on the right-hand side and wondered if she'd be expected to mix drinks or anything. She didn't know how to do anything like that. But then she'd never worked as a waitress either . . . They wouldn't need someone with experience, would they? She was a quick learner.

She was wondering whether to lie and say she'd had a Saturday job at a restaurant back home or whether that was something they were likely to actually check up on, when the girl came back through the door followed by a very short older man.

'I'm Tony,' he said, holding his hand out to her. 'Good to meet ya.'

Anna shook his hand and said, 'Anna.'

'So you're interested in the job?' he said. 'Have you got any experience?'

'Yeah, I . . .' Anna started and then changed her mind. 'No, but—'

'Hang on,' Tony said. 'Why don't you come through to the office and we can have a chat. The girls are trying to set up and don't want to be tripping over us. Just leave your bags here,' he said, gesturing at Anna's Morrison's carrier bags. And then he shouted to one of the girls, 'Can you put these behind the bar, Zosia, love?'

Anna felt a twinge of nerves as she followed him through the door – yes, they were in a public place, but she was still going somewhere private with a complete stranger – but there was something about Tony she'd liked instantly, so she wasn't overly worried. She still took her phone out of her pocket though.

The office was tiny and messy with a computer on a desk in one corner and piles of boxes and bags in the other.

'We'll get organised one of these days, eh?' Tony said, sitting down behind the desk and smiling at her.

Anna sat down on the slightly wobbly chair on the other side of the desk and tried to look enthusiastic, trustworthy and capable. Which wasn't that easy when she was just sitting there.

'So do you have any restaurant experience?' Tony asked, before turning to the computer and tapping on the keyboard. 'Sorry, just going to make a couple of notes. I type faster than I write, now. How bad is that?'

'Oh, I do too,' Anna said. 'Um . . . I don't actually have any restaurant experience, no. But I am a very fast learner and . . .'

'Hmmm?' Tony said, turning back from the computer to look at her, his eyebrows raised and a small smile on his face.

Anna had stopped because she'd half expected him to say he couldn't help if she didn't have restaurant experience. 'Sorry,' she said. 'Um, I'm a very fast learner and I'm responsible and . . . conscientious.' That's what her school reports had said. Always conscientious.

'That's good,' Tony said, tapping on the keyboard. 'I mean, experience isn't strictly necessary. It's better, but, you know, it's not rocket science.' He smiled brightly. 'You know the job's not here though?'

'I . . .' Anna started and then stopped. Obviously she'd thought the job was there; the sign was in the window. So where was it?

'Sorry,' Tony said. 'We didn't get much interest when we advertised it there, so we thought we'd try here.'

'So, um, where is it then?' Anna asked.

'It's in the chip shop. Up on Berry Street. Do you know it?'

Anna thought maybe she did. Across the road from the bombed-out church. She'd never been in there, but she'd been vaguely aware of the smell of vinegar and batter when she'd walked past.

'It's not glamorous, I know,' Tony said. 'But if you're just looking for a job . . .'

'I am,' Anna said.

'And if any jobs came up here, you'd be first in line to move over. If that's what you wanted.'

'Sounds good,' Anna said.

'So what do you think?'

Anna nodded. 'Um. What does it pay? And when could I start?'

Tony tapped at the keyboard again and a printer that Anna hadn't noticed started whirring to life.

'I'll give you all the details now,' Tony said. 'You go home and have a read and talk it over with your parents or whatever and then give me a call.'

'I will,' Anna said. 'Thank you.' She stood up.

'Sorry it's not what you were expecting, love,' Tony said.

'No,' Anna said. 'Thanks. That's OK.'

She followed Tony back through to the cafe.

'Don't forget your bags,' Tony said.

'Thanks,' Anna said. She took them from him, stood back while he opened the door for her, and crossed the road towards home.

* * *

'I'm going over,' Molly said, staring at Roman Lucas across the canteen. He was sitting with two girls Molly knew by sight but had never spoken to, and Alex from wardrobe, who Molly knew well enough to go and sit down with. Not that she'd ever done that before.

'Why would you do that?' Sean said, glancing up at Roman Lucas and then back at his essay notes. 'I've written total bollocks so far. Have you done yours already?'

'God, no,' Molly said. 'You could ask him for advice on your essay.'

'Yeah, no,' Sean said. 'I won't be doing that.'

'You haven't had a class with him yet, have you?'

Sean shook his head. 'Not yet, no. Does he sing? Does he dance?'

'Not that I know of,' Molly said. 'But that's not what he's here for, is it? He's here to teach us about The Profession.'

'Right,' Sean said, rolling his eyes. 'I can't wait to learn how to project when rolling out of the way of a burning car.'

'You're a snob,' Molly said.

'Yep,' Sean agreed. 'And so are you, usually. You're just suspending it now cos you've got lady wood.'

Molly laughed. 'I have. I really have.'

'Which reminds me,' Sean said. 'Have you heard from the mystery car shagger?'

Molly shook her head. 'I didn't really expect to, to be fair. We were like ships passing in the night . . .' She curved an arc through the air.

'Yeah, that sounds much nicer than an anonymous bunk up in the back of a car.'

'Shut up,' Molly said. She pouted as she looked over at Roman Lucas again. 'You don't think he's hot?' she asked Sean.

Sean sighed and put his pen down on top of his notebook. 'Objectively, yes, of course he is. But he's not my type.'

'Hot is not your type?'

'I don't fancy all men, Molly.'

Molly snorted. 'No. Just most.'

Still staring at Roman Lucas, Sean tipped his head on one side. 'He's got a nice smile . . .'

Molly looked over. Roman Lucas was laughing at something, his head thrown back. He had the most perfect jawline. And throat. She wanted to run across the canteen and lick it.

'But his eyes are too close together,' Sean said.

'For what?' Molly said.

'Binoculars.'

'Right. You've lost it. Finally.'

'It's good that we don't have the same taste in men, Molls. Means we'll never fight over one.' He bumped Molly with his shoulder. 'Now, can you stop drooling over Planet Hollywood there and help me with this fucking essay?'

'Meh,' Molly said. 'I still think I'm going to go over.'

'You are not going to leave me here floundering with actual work while you go over there to flirt. No. I forbid it. No.'

Molly snorted. 'Forbid it. OK. I'll help. Just this once. But next time we see him in here – or anywhere else – you're going to come over to talk to him. Be my wingman.'

'I'm nobody's wingman,' Sean said, fake-hautily.

'Just be a friend then. A friend who helps a friend flirt with a guest lecturer.'

'Right,' Sean said. 'Yeah, I can be that.' He pushed his notebook over to Molly. 'Now read this and see if it makes any sense at all. It's gibberish to me now.'

While Molly read Sean's essay notes, Sean drank his coffee and watched Roman Lucas. The two dancers were clearly in full flirt mode, flicking their hair, touching him on his arm, laughing uproariously at everything he said. Alex from Wardrobe was much more low-key, but Sean thought maybe he was interested too – he was certainly listening intently to everything Roman Lucas was saying.

'What does this say?' Molly asked, pointing at a line of Sean's notes.

Sean leaned over and squinted at the book. 'Something about . . . influence on other artists? God, my writing is bloody awful.'

'You think?' Molly said. 'I'm getting a headache in my eye.'

Pushing his now-cold coffee across the table, Sean pulled a bottle of water out of his bag and gulped some down; it was always way too hot in the cafeteria. As he put the bottle on the table, he glanced over at Roman Lucas, only to see him looking straight back at him.

Sean's mouth was wet from the water and he licked his bottom lip. And Roman Lucas didn't break eye contact. Interesting.

'Shit, Sean!' Molly said, hitting him in the arm.

'What?' Sean said, turning to look at her.

'This is really good!' She held the notebook up and shook it.

Sean shook his head and looked back at Roman Lucas. He wasn't looking any more. He was looking at Alex, who seemed to be telling him something serious, judging by the look on his face. And Roman Lucas looked interested and sympathetic, leaning slightly towards him and nodding.

Sean realised he wanted him to look back up again. To look at him.

'What are you doing?' Molly asked.

'Just wondering what they're talking about,' Sean said.

'What's it to you?' She put the notebook down on the table and pointed at the left-hand page. 'This is mostly bollocks. But this stuff . . .' She twirled her finger over the right-hand page. 'But this is really good. You should scrap all that and focus on this.'

'Is there enough there for the full essay though?'

'I think so,' Molly said. 'And you've got room to branch out from that and expand on the original idea.'

'Great,' Sean said. 'That's really helpful. Thanks.'

'Why have you gone weird?' Molly asked. 'Is Charlie here?' She craned around the room.

Sean shook his head. 'Just tired, I think.'

Alex stood up and seemed to be thanking Roman Lucas. The two dancers looked completely unimpressed. Roman Lucas stood up too, and he and Alex crossed the room towards Sean and Molly.

'Fuck,' Sean heard Molly say under her breath.

'Be cool,' Sean said.

'You did not just tell me to be cool,' Molly said, without moving her mouth.

Sean watched Roman Lucas put his hand on the small of Alex's back as he steered him around a table. He watched him tug his phone out of his jeans pocket with his other hand and Sean felt a twitch in the front of his own jeans.

He was still looking when Roman Lucas glanced over at him, did that chin-up thing, and say, 'Hey.'

Roman Lucas had already left the cafeteria before Sean had focussed his mind enough to say anything back.

Nina knocked and then opened the door with her staff card.

'Oh, sorry!'

The man was sitting on the end of the bed putting his socks on. He glanced up and looked startled, but Nina had pulled the door closed before he had a chance to say anything.

'Housekeeping!' she called brightly through the door. 'Should I come back?'

The door opened and the man was standing in front of her. She could smell last night's alcohol coming off him in waves.

'No, I'm just checking out,' he said. He swung a small suitcase up beside him.

'I hope you've enjoyed your stay,' she said, as she'd been told to, the smile plastered on her face.

'I have, thanks,' he said.

He brushed against her as he passed and she had to stifle a shudder. Was it porn that made so many men think a woman knocking on their door had to be interested? Even if she'd knocked for a clearly stated reason? It was so tedious.

Nina pulled the trolley over to the door and took out the pile of fresh towels, bedding and toiletries, leaving them next to the door where she could reach them easily. Pulling on disposable gloves, she headed into the bathroom. She always made herself get the worst bits out of the way first otherwise she didn't quite trust herself not to run away, and she really needed this job.

The smell in the bathroom was horrible and the sink was ringed with beard shavings, and globules of shaving cream wobbled on the countertop.

Holding her breath, Nina lifted the loo seat and flushed before squirting the bowl with heavy-duty bleach and putting the lid back down.

The bedroom wasn't as bad. An empty beer bottle stood on the bedside table, alongside a rolled up copy of *The Sun*, and a few more bottles lay on the carpet underneath the bedside table.

Nina pulled off the bedspread, pulled back the quilt and sheets and had to stifle a scream.

Right in the middle of the bed was a turd.

She'd heard about this from other girls, but she'd never come across it before. Apparently it was a thing. Some people liked to leave a turd in the bed for the maid to find. A power thing, presumably, rather than a bowel control problem.

He'd gone now. And there'd be a note on the file to say he wasn't welcome back.

Nina was having a last look around the room when she saw the wallet. It had dropped down the back of one of the old chests of drawers. Modern hotels had them fitted to the wall for exactly that reason, but The Campbell prided itself on its olde worlde charm and traditional furnishings, so they were forever retrieving things from down the backs of the cupboards and beds.

The wallet was an expensive-looking one: brown, leather, folded over but bulging. Probably receipts and crap rather than cash, Nina thought. But then she opened it. She sat down on the floor and looked around the room. She knew she was alone – she'd locked the door behind her – but she shouldn't have even opened the wallet, let alone do what she was about to do.

She pulled the thick wedge of cash free and counted it. Two hundred and forty pounds. In twenties. New-looking twenties. This guy had at least six credit cards as well, along with all sorts of membership and loyalty cards. Receipts and various bits of paper. But no photos. No ID apart from his cards. Nothing that looked sentimental.

The train to Whitby cost nearly a hundred pounds and Nina didn't have it. She'd waited to see if Jack was planning to buy her ticket, but he hadn't mentioned it again. If she wanted to go with him – and she really did – she'd need to pay for herself.

Nina stood up and put the wallet on the bed then lifted her skirt, tucked the money into the top of her tights, and smoothed the skirt back down. She opened the wardrobe door and looked at her reflection in the mirror. She couldn't tell the money was there, but she took it out and repositioned it inside her knickers, just in case.

She tucked the wallet inside the dirty sheets that she'd left piled behind the door. In the corridor she dropped the sheets into the laundry bin on the side of the trolley. She'd have to remember to get the wallet out later.

As she waited to be sure the next room was empty, she told herself that if the customer had been nice, if he hadn't left a turd in the bed, if he'd been a regular customer, she would have handed the wallet in. But he deserved to lose it after what he'd done. Maybe it'd teach him a lesson. Maybe next time he stayed in a hotel, he'd think about karma.

Chapter 20

Anna had spent the morning in her room, editing a vlog. She'd set up a tiny desk under the window, pulled up the blinds and opened the small window at the top so she could listen to the sounds of the street and not feel quite so isolated from the world.

The job in the chip shop was only part-time – a couple of afternoons a week – and the pay was awful, so she knew she'd need something else as well, but she felt like she'd made some progress, at least. And she'd also shown some initiative, so she thought she could go home to her parents, tell them that while the theatre job had fallen through, she'd found herself something else (maybe say it was in the restaurant rather than the chip shop) and ask if they could lend her a bit of money until she found something full time or with better pay.

She had no idea whether they would go for it or not, but it was worth a try.

She still hadn't told any of the other people in the house about her vlog channel. She'd thought about it when Alfie had almost caught her filming, but she knew they'd probably want to watch some of the videos and she just didn't feel ready for that yet. She almost felt like AnnaSparks was a different person and even though AnnaSparks was a lot more confident than Anna Parkes, Anna Parkes almost felt protective of her. What if the others thought having an online alter-ego was stupid? What if they laughed? What if they thought it was a waste of time? These were the kind of things AnnaSparks wouldn't worry about. But Anna Parkes absolutely did.

She hadn't intended to create this other identity when she'd started vlogging a couple of years ago, along with her friend Eleanor. They'd been watching various YouTubers for a while and decided to give it a go for a laugh. Eleanor had lost interest almost immediately – particularly since she'd been hoping for hundreds of thousands of views, leading to money and fame, and instead their first few videos had been lucky to get views into double figures – but Anna became addicted almost as quickly and worked extra shifts at the bakery to save up for a camera and tripod. She just felt different when she was filming: more confident, more mature, less worried about what people thought of her. So when she'd created her own channel, she decided to give herself a different look, sort of a mask to hide behind. She'd toyed with wearing an actual mask, maybe some sort of superhero one – but after watching a few tutorials, decided to go with make-up and her hair down. She certainly didn't look unrecognisable, but she looked different enough that she didn't think it would be obvious to any but her closest friends (so, really, just Eleanor) if they saw the thumbnail of one of her videos on YouTube.

At first she'd watched the views and subscriber numbers as obsessively as Eleanor had, but when they weren't moving much, she'd stopped worrying about it and focused more on actually making the videos and, funnily enough, that's when she started getting more views and more comments and more messages.

Now she wasn't sure who she'd be if she wasn't also AnnaSparks.

'Alfie?'

Alfie was almost running down the corridor when he heard his name being called. His trainers squeaked on the floor as he stopped and turned to see his seminar tutor leaning out through the door of her office.

'Have you got a minute?'

Alfie didn't. He was already going to be late to Bean because his last lecture had overrun, but since he knew why Ms Nguyen wanted to speak to him, he thought he'd better get it over with.

'I wanted to talk to you about your essay,' she said, as soon as Alfie sat down in her office.

Alfie nodded. 'I know. It wasn't good enough, I just—'

Ms Nguyen held her hands up. 'No, no, that's not it at all. It was excellent. Well-researched, thoughtfully argued, and actually about five thousand words too long.'

'Oh! Oh, right,' Alfie said. 'I'm sorry about that, I—'

Ms Nguyen frowned. 'You don't need to apologise. Granted, we set a word count for a reason, so it would be preferable for you to stick within the limits, but it wasn't waffle. It was relevant to the topic.'

'OK,' Alfie said. 'Good. Thank you.'

Ms Nguyen flicked through Alfie's file on her desk and glanced up at him over the top of her wire-rimmed glasses.

'The thing is, that your work is brilliant. Everything you've handed in has been excellent. And I was wondering if you've chosen a project yet.' She smiled.

'The outline's due at the end of next week,' Alfie said. He hadn't thought about it yet; he hadn't had time. It was one of the things on his to-do list. The fourth thing, if he remembered rightly.

'You know what you want to do it on?' Ms Nguyen asked.

'I do, yes,' Alfie said. 'I mean, I don't have all the details yet, but . . .' He couldn't think of a way to finish the sentence. There was no way to finish that sentence.

'Good,' Ms Nguyen said. 'I was wondering if you might consider expanding on the topic of your last essay. This essay.' She tapped the papers on her desk. 'Ethical economics seems to be something you're passionate about.'

Alfie glanced up at the clock on her office wall and felt his stomach cramp. 'I am. I mean, it is.'

'Good, good,' Ms Nguyen said. 'So you'll give it some thought?'

'I absolutely will. Thank you.'

Ms Nguyen frowned again. 'You're an excellent student, Alfie.'

'No,' Alfie said. 'Thank you. I really appreciate it. And I'll get the outline to you as soon as I can.'

'The end of next week is fine,' Ms Nguyen said.

Alfie started to get up, but Ms Nguyen spoke again and he dropped back into his seat, trying not to sigh with frustration.

'I do have one concern . . .'

Alfie's stomach sank. 'OK.'

'Like I said, you're an excellent student. But university isn't just about studying.'

'No,' Alfie said.

'Are you having fun?'

'Now?' Alfie wanted to ask. Instead he said, 'Fun?'

'Yes.' She took her glasses off again. 'Do you relax? Do you go out? Do you have friends? A couple of staff members have mentioned that you don't seem to hang out like the others do. You're always rushing out of seminars and lectures.'

'I have a job,' Alfie said.

'I know you do,' Ms Nguyen said. 'But do you also have a life?'

'I . . .' Alfie looked down at his hands, which were balled into fists against his thighs. He forced himself to relax them. 'I do. Yes. I've got good friends. My housemates. And the people I work with.'

'That's good to hear,' Ms Nguyen said. She leaned forward, concern evident in her expression. 'I don't want you to get overwhelmed.'

'I'm not,' Alfie said. 'I won't.'

'Good,' Ms Nguyen said and then smiled. 'You're free to go.'

Alfie left.

'Look at this,' Sean said over his shoulder to Molly as they pushed through the swinging doors to the lecture room. 'When has it ever been this busy this early?'

'Last time we had a guest lecturer,' Molly said. 'The only difference is that last time it was a Pussycat Doll and the first few rows were boys like this . . .' She put her chin on her clasped hands and fake-beamed.

'Still,' Sean said, heading along the front row of seats. 'This is ridic. He's not even that famous.'

'Why are we sitting down here?' Molly asked. Sean pretty much always wanted to sit right up at the back, where he could check his texts or generally tit about without anyone noticing.

'I'm going home straight from here. I want to make a quick getaway.' He pulled his bag up on the seat next to him and got out his notebook and pen.

'Is your dad OK?' Molly asked.

Sean nodded. 'I think so. Bit weird, but . . .' He shrugged. 'I just thought it was time I went back. See how he is. And I'm going out with Louis and Connor tomorrow night.'

'Oh, God,' Molly said. 'Ladz on the town.'

'Yep, that's us. Lock up your women.'

'So you're going to be taking notes,' Molly said, gesturing at Sean's notebook. 'Even though you don't think he's got anything worthwhile to say?'

'I can work on my essay,' Sean said. 'Anyway, it's best to be prepared. Who knows, appearances may be deceptive. Maybe he'll be inspiring and brilliant.'

'The Pussycat Doll was great,' Molly said. 'And you thought she'd be shit too.'

Sean miaowed and pretended to clean his face with his hand.

'Litter box,' Molly said.

The seats started to fill up and Charlie passed them, heading up towards the back.

'Fuck,' Sean said under his breath.

'Bad kitty!' Molly said.

'Why is he here?'

'Because this is open to everyone,' Molly said. 'Did you really not expect him to come? Everyone always comes to these things.'

The door opened and Roman Lucas walked in and a frisson of excitement ran around the room. He was wearing jeans and a black jumper and black-rimmed glasses and he perched on the edge of the desk at the front of the room and grinned up at them all.

'Hey,' he said.

There were a few giggles, but the main feeling in the room was that everyone was holding their breath.

'Mr Byrne was going to come and introduce me,' Roman Lucas said about the Head of Department, whom they all actually called Tom. 'But I said I just wanted to come and say hello and get on with it.'

He fiddled with the cuff of his jumper. 'But I wore my special teacher specs to give me an air of authority.'

He glanced over at Sean and Molly; Molly sat a little straighter in her seat.

'Did it work?' Roman Lucas said.

An hour later everyone seemed completely relaxed, including Roman Lucas. He'd told them they could call him Roman after one girl put her hand up and asked a question to 'Mr Lucas' but Molly only seemed to be able to think of him as Roman Lucas. He'd told them how he'd got started in acting, talked about his favourite films to work on, some of the worst experiences he'd had, best and worst directors he'd worked with, what it was like to attend the Oscars ('boring as fuck' apparently) and then he'd started asking them questions, about the college, about their courses, about what they wanted to do with their lives and careers.

The time had flown by and at the end Sean had almost – *almost* – forgotten he was a Hollywood star who had appeared in some of the crappiest films Sean had ever seen. He had, however, come to share Molly's opinion that he was hot as hell. At the end of the class everyone started to leave, but quite a few students gathered around Roman at the front, asking more questions, and Sean thought he saw someone take a sneaky selfie with him in the background. He wanted to do the same. He wanted a picture of Roman Lucas on his phone.

Chapter 21

'Hello, sweetheart,' Anna's dad said as she dropped into the passenger seat.

Anna's stomach fluttered. She hadn't realised how much she'd missed her dad, but the car smelled just like him: his lemony-woody aftershave and the cigarettes he sneaked when her mum wasn't around. She leaned over and hugged him, kissing him awkwardly on the side of his jaw.

'Are you doing OK?' he asked, rubbing his face with embarrassment.

'I am, yeah,' Anna said. 'Thanks.' She opened the glove compartment and rummaged until she found the packet of Tic Tacs her dad always left in there. She never really wanted one, it was just part of her getting-into-the-car routine; it would be really weird not to have one.

'Making friends?' her dad asked, pulling out from the waiting bay.

'Yes!' Anna said. 'Really lovely friends. Everyone in the house is so nice, it's fantastic.'

'And your mum said you haven't started at work yet?'

Anna shook her head, even though her dad wasn't looking

at her, but at the road.

'No. Not yet.'

She hoped he didn't ask any more questions. She planned to tell them both together, at home, probably after dinner when they'd had a glass of wine or two. They might be more receptive to supporting her for another couple of months then.

Anna stared out of the window at the shops and the streets she'd seen over and over in the sixteen years she'd lived in Meadowvale. Even though the shops had changed – what used to be a Netto was now a Wetherspoons, the toy shop she'd loved visiting when she was little had become a Tesco Express – it all seemed the same. Boring. Suburban. She couldn't quite work out why the charity shops and newsagents on Bold Street seemed so much more vibrant than the charity shops and newsagents on the high street here, but they did.

As they pulled into the driveway, Anna felt her stomach starting to clench. It was awful how she almost dreaded seeing her mum. It was just that she knew she'd have so much to say about what Anna was doing wrong. And that was before she knew about the job. Or lack of job. Anna told herself it was just one evening and then she could go back to Liverpool again in the morning. Get her mascara and her toy rabbit, tell her parents about the job, maybe ask them for another couple of months' money, and get out. How hard could it be?

'Anna,' her dad said, and she turned to look at him. 'Your mum . . .' he started. 'Your mum misses you,' he said.

Anna was about to say something like 'As if' but the look on her dad's face made the words die in her throat.

'OK,' she said instead.

'It's hard for her,' he said. 'You leaving like this.'

'But you thought I was going to uni anyway,' Anna said. 'What's the difference?'

Her dad turned the steering wheel until Anna heard the lock click on. 'Your mum likes things to go a certain way,' he said. 'And when they don't go the way she expected, she finds it hard to adjust.'

'It's my life though,' Anna said. 'Shouldn't she be happy for me to do what makes me happy?'

Her dad shifted in his seat and gave her a sad smile. 'She is happy for you. Really. It's just hard for her to show it. OK?'

Anna nodded. 'OK.'

The house felt different as soon as Anna walked in and she stopped in the hallway to see if she could work out what it was. She couldn't see anything that had changed – a plant used to be on the table in the corner, maybe? – so she figured it was just because she'd been away. How weird that she lived there for so long, been away for such a short time and it already felt different.

She walked right through to the kitchen where she knew her mum would be dishing food out, having prepared it to time perfectly with Anna's arrival. She couldn't see her mum at first because she was getting something out of the microwave, but then she shut the microwave door with her elbow and smiled tightly at Anna. Her face looked flushed and some tendrils of hair had escaped from her hairband, making her look a bit more relaxed, but the kitchen was hot and Anna figured she was probably stressed. As usual.

'Hey, Mum,' Anna said.

Her mum reached up and tidied a strand of hair away. 'Your train was on time?' she said.

Usually Anna would bristle at the idea that her mum was more interested in train timetables than in her, but instead she said, 'It was, yeah,' and smiled.

Her mum smiled back. 'It's nice to have you home.'

Anna blinked at her. 'It's nice to be home,' she said.

As Anna headed to the stairs, intending to take her bag up to her room, her dad called her from the lounge.

'Can you come in here a sec?'

'I'm just going to take my bag up,' Anna said.

'Just come and have a word first, love,' her dad said.

Dropping her bag, Anna joined her dad in the living room. She'd expected him to be in his usual chair in front of the TV, but he wasn't; he was sitting at the dining table.

Anna sat opposite him, smiling. 'Very formal.'

He flexed his hands and for a second Anna felt like she was at a job interview.

'Is everything OK?'

Her dad puffed out his cheeks and Anna's stomach clenched again. Bad news. There was definitely bad news.

'Your mum and I are fine,' he said. 'Let me say that first.'

'You're scaring me,' Anna said.

He shook his head. 'Oh, no, no. No need for you to be scared. We just . . . It's the business. We've had to close the business.'

Anna couldn't think for a few seconds. She wasn't even sure what business he meant. And then her eyes widened. 'Your business?'

He nodded. 'We've been struggling for a while and it got to a point where we just . . . couldn't continue.'

'Right,' Anna said. 'OK. So what are you going to do? For work?'

'We have . . . a few plans,' he said. 'But that's a bit further down the line. The most immediate thing – and this is what we wanted to talk about . . .'

Anna noted the 'we' even though her mum was still in the kitchen – she could hear her crashing dishes and opening and closing the oven doors.

'. . . is that we're selling the house,' her dad finished.

'This house?' Anna said, stupidly, as if there was any other house they could be selling.

Her dad nodded. He was biting his lip. Anna wasn't sure she'd ever seen him look quite so nervous.

'If there was any other way . . .' he said. 'It's too big for us now really anyway. Now that you've moved out. And it really doesn't make sense for us to have so much money tied up in the house while there are debts in the business . . .'

'Debts?' Anna said.

'Oh, for God's sake,' her mum said, coming into the room carrying a casserole dish with oven gloves. 'Anna doesn't need to know about all that. All she needs to know is that the house is up for sale.'

'It's up for sale?' Anna said. 'Already? I didn't see a sign.'

'We're selling it privately,' her mum said.

'So it's not up for sale?' Anna said. 'It's already sold?'

'A sale's been agreed,' her dad said. 'Nothing's definite yet.'

As her mum headed back to the kitchen, Anna heard her

tut to herself, which suggested things were more definite than her dad was letting on.

'So when will you be moving, do you think?' Anna said. 'I mean . . . is it going to be soon?'

'Probably before Christmas,' he admitted, standing up and getting a bottle of wine out of the cabinet.

'Can I have some?' Anna said.

Her dad looked at her, his eyebrows knotting together. 'A small glass, maybe.'

He took three glasses out of the cabinet and set them on the table. Anna's mum came back in with another dish and sat down.

Anna's dad poured about half a glass for Anna, but filled his own and her mum's almost to the top. But it didn't matter how much they drank, Anna thought; there wasn't any point in asking them for money now. So what was she going to do?

Once dinner was over, Anna headed upstairs to her room. As soon as she opened the door, she saw why her dad hadn't wanted her to go up there before he'd spoken to her. Her chest of drawers was gone and in its place was a stack of cardboard boxes.

Anna stood and stared. She knew it wasn't her room any more, she knew she'd moved out, but she just hadn't expected her parents to move on without her so quickly. The house had been the same for as long as she could remember; she couldn't really get her head around the idea that they wouldn't be living there any more.

She heard her mum coming up the stairs and hoped she was going to the bathroom rather than coming to talk to her. She was out of luck.

'While you're here,' her mum said from behind her, 'it would be helpful if you could sort out some of your stuff. Take some back with you, and if there's anything to go to the charity shop . . .'

Anna didn't even turn round. 'I'll have a look, yeah.'

'Good,' her mum said.

Anna shut the door, not even checking to see if her mum was still standing there. She knew that her mum's way of dealing with difficult emotions was to pretend she didn't have emotions, but didn't she even think about how hard it might be for Anna? She'd literally just had the concept sprung on her and now she was supposed to just pack up her stuff. And the fact that the business had failed she would have to think about later. Go through the bedroom she'd slept in for her entire life and decide what she wanted to keep for ever and what she never needed to see again.

And she knew that her mum's 'suggestion' was more than that. She knew that anything she left could well end up in a skip, her mum justifying it with, 'Well, you left it in your room, I assumed you didn't want it . . .'

Even though Anna was tired and fed up, she opened her wardrobe and started sorting through her clothes. She'd ask to borrow suitcases in the morning.

She'd divided her clothes into keep, charity shop, and bin piles when there was a knock on her door and her friend Eleanor put her head round. She was, as always, smiling and looking worried at the same time.

'Hey!' Anna said, clambering up off the floor where she'd been reading one of her old diaries. 'How did you know I was home?'

'Your mum told my mum at Slimming World. Can I come in?'

'Course,' Anna said.

'I meant to text you,' Eleanor said.

Anna nodded. 'No, me too. It's just been a bit . . . mad.'

'For me too,' Eleanor said.

She sat down on the end of Anna's bed, her back against the wall, and Anna thought of all the times they'd been in this room together, doing homework, avoiding doing homework, watching TV, talking about the boys they had crushes on. Eleanor was as rubbish with boys as Anna was.

'So I leave for uni tomorrow,' Eleanor said, pulling her sleeves down over her hands.

'Wow,' Anna said. 'Tomorrow?'

Eleanor nodded. 'I'm really scared.'

'You'll be fine,' Anna said. 'It'll be amazing.'

'If it's so amazing, why didn't you want to go?' Eleanor asked. She picked up one of Anna's sweatshirts off the bed. Anna had had it for years and it was much too small now; she didn't know why she hadn't got rid of it sooner.

Anna shook her head. 'It just didn't feel right.'

'And Liverpool feels right?'

Anna nodded. 'It really does. I love it.'

'How's the job?'

Anna stood up and put the diary she'd been reading into the bag she was taking back with her. 'You haven't seen the vlog? There is no job.' She watched Eleanor's eyebrows shoot up. 'Don't tell anyone, OK?'

Eleanor nodded. 'What happened?'

Anna sat up on the other end of the bed, leaning back against her pillows and told Eleanor what had happened with Lola and the Phoenix.

'So what are you going to do?' Eleanor asked.

'I'm going to keep looking for a job,' Anna said. She didn't want to mention the chip shop. 'It's all I can do really. I can't come home. Not now. Do you know about the business?'

Eleanor nodded. 'Are they going to be OK? Your parents?'

'Dad says so,' Anna said. 'I don't know. They've never really talked about it to me, you know? But they both seem positive about it. You know, for them.' She smiled.

'Mum said she was surprised they were taking it so well,' Eleanor said. 'She said she thinks they've been stressed with it for a while and it's probably a relief.'

'Maybe,' Anna said. 'They've always worked really hard on it. They probably need a break.'

'Would you not go to uni?' Eleanor said. 'I mean, you only didn't go because of the Phoenix, right?'

Anna shook her head and pulled her knees up to her chest. 'Not only because of the Phoenix. I didn't want to go anyway.'

'You never said.'

'No, I know. I felt like I should want to go. And you were so excited about it . . .'

'We were supposed to both go!' Eleanor said. 'Together. To the same place. And be in halls together!'

Anna laughed. 'That was never going to happen.' Eleanor was going to Exeter, which was much further away than Anna had even considered.

'It would've been cool though, wouldn't it?' Eleanor said.

Anna grinned. 'Yeah. You'll have to come and visit me in the holidays. My room's tiny, but I can fit a mattress on the floor. Just about.'

'I'll definitely do that,' Eleanor said. She flicked through an old copy of *Heat* magazine that Anna had found in a drawer. 'Aren't you scared?'

Anna frowned. 'Sort of. But it's a kind of good-scared. You know, it means that something's happening. I was never really scared here because I was always bored.'

'We weren't always bored!' Eleanor said.

Anna shook her head. 'Not with you. With this place. Are you scared?'

Eleanor nodded and then laughed. 'I think you're mad.'

Anna smiled. 'I might be.'

They sat in silence for a little while and then Eleanor held up one of Anna's hoodies and said, 'Are you getting rid of this?'

Chapter 22

'Hello?' Sean shouted as he stepped into the hall of the house he'd grown up in.

The house smelled a bit dodgy, but it always did since his mum had died – his dad just wasn't as hot on cleaning as his mum had been. It didn't smell any worse than usual, at least.

'Dad?' Sean shouted. He took a breath, wondering what he'd do if he walked in and found his dad dead.

'Seany?'

Sean blew out his breath. 'Where are you?'

'Garden!'

Sean headed through the house into the lounge. His dad was crouched on the small patio outside. His jeans were baggy at the arse and Sean could see his crack. He rolled his eyes.

'What are you doing?'

'Come out here, I don't want to shout.'

Sean stepped through the patio doors and went to sit on the three small steps up to the garden. His mum had bought a stone lion for each side of the steps and she'd been really proud of them. One of them was missing its snout, Sean noticed now. Was it called a snout on a lion?

His dad had his toolbox next to him and was doing something to the bricks under the patio door.

'What are you doing?' Sean said again.

'I've got mice,' his dad said. 'I'm blocking up the hole.'

'You've got mice where?' Sean leaned to one side, but he couldn't see the hole.

'All over the show. They started out here. Tiny things, running about. Then they started coming up to the window and tapping to come in. And then they started coming in.'

'They were tapping to come in?' Sean said, grinning. He was picturing mice knocking and waiting impatiently.

'Dead right,' his dad said. 'I couldn't hear the telly for all the knocking.'

'How loud could it be?' Sean said.

'Not bad when there was just the one. But when the rest of them turned up it was a right racket.'

'So, hang on. Did you get traps or anything?'

'Course I did. Didn't do anything. And they're coming through here.' His dad sat back on his haunches and pointed at the brick. It was one of those air bricks with the holes.

'I think they're important,' Sean said. 'I don't think you're meant to block them up. You told me that, actually.'

His dad shrugged. 'No big deal. Better to block it up than to have mice running round the house.'

'All over the house?' Sean said. 'Or just in the lounge?'

'All over. I can hear them in the walls at night.' He knelt back down and carried on poking at the brick.

'I think you need an exterminator,' Sean said.

'Nah, this'll get rid.'

Sean watched for a bit longer, trying to ignore the feeling of worry in his belly. 'Can I make you a tea?' he said, eventually.

'That'd be great, yeah. Thanks, lad.'

In the kitchen, Sean wiped the countertops that were scattered liberally with crumbs. He changed the bin, which was definitely contributing to the house's off-smell and then he threw away all the out-of-date food in the fridge. Once he'd taken a tea out to his dad, he took his own cup of tea up to his old bedroom.

It was exactly the same as when he'd last been home. A while ago. It didn't even feel like anyone had been there, as if his dad had shut the door behind Sean and forgotten about it.

In fact, the whole house was a bit like that – his dad hadn't got rid of any of Sean's mum's stuff either. For a while, one of her cardigans had hung over the back of the chair in the dining room, but eventually Sean had taken it to the charity shop, along with a bag of her clothes from the wardrobe she shared with Sean's dad. Sean had been slightly nervous that his dad was intentionally saving everything and that he'd hit the roof at Sean's interference, but he hadn't even mentioned it. Sean wasn't sure he'd even noticed.

Sean lay down on his bed and wondered about the mice in the walls. Could that really even happen? He'd heard of people having mice, but usually they talked about getting a couple of traps and that was it. And he needed to Google that air brick thing in case blocking it up was going to fill the house with carbon monoxide or something.

Sean stared up at the ceiling and thought about all the years he'd laid on this bed, wishing to be away. And now he was away. But he had to keep coming back. He didn't want to come back. But admitting that was like admitting he didn't want to see his dad, and he did. He just wished his mum was still here. Then it would have felt like coming home. Now it just felt like coming to a house. A sad and depressing house.

Sean pushed open the double doors of what had been his local pub, but now seemed to have been completely transformed into a gastropub-stroke-wine bar. Everything had changed; the layout was completely different and disorientating.

'Hey!' said a boy who looked about fifteen, approaching from behind the bar. 'Do you need a table?'

'No . . .' Sean said, craning his head to see if any of his friends were there already. 'I don't think so. Not yet anyway.'

'Meeting people?' the boy said.

'Yeah,' Sean said. He really couldn't be more than sixteen. 'But I don't think they're here yet.'

'No problem. If you just want to get a drink in the bar area, when you're ready for a table, call me over.'

'Right,' Sean said. 'Great.'

'Or if you need anything else,' the boy said.

'Yeah, great,' Sean said. Was that flirting? Had he been flirting with him? Sean glanced back over his shoulder as he walked through to the bar, but the boy was already greeting an older couple who must have come in just behind Sean.

The bar area was much more open and bright than it had been when Sean had last been in. He squinted and tried to superimpose his memory of the old layout over the new one. There'd been a sort of snug in the far right corner, he remembered – wooden dividers and bench seats. Now that corner was decorated with Penguin Books wallpaper and one of those green glass-shaded brass lamps stood on a small wooden table next to a leather wing-backed armchair. Sean ordered a drink at the bar and then sat in the leather chair. He felt ridiculous, but also thought it would be a laugh for his friends to come in and find him sitting there like a prince.

His phone vibrated in the front pocket of his jeans and he pulled it out to find a text from his best mate, Louis, telling him he was going to be late. He knew that. Louis was always late. Sean drank his lager and watched a group of women in the far corner of the bar. They'd pushed a bunch of the smaller tables together and were all talking intently across their glasses of wine. Sean couldn't decide if they were on a night out or having some sort of meeting. Maybe a book group. His mum used to come to a book group here, he remembered. She always worried because she hadn't finished the book, but then come home pissed and happy.

Sean shook his head and looked back towards the main door. Even the door was in a different place, he realised. Why had they even renovated? It probably would have been cheaper and easier to knock it down and start again.

He was still staring at the door, his eyes slightly unfocused, when Connor came in, looked straight over at Sean and burst out laughing.

'Look at the fucking state of you!' he said, while he was still halfway across the bar. A couple of the women in the corner turned round and tutted.

'I won't stand . . .' Sean said, imperiously waving his hand.

'Should I kneel?' Connor asked, grinning.

'Bit early for that,' Sean said. 'You haven't even bought me a drink yet.'

Connor threw his head back, laughing, said, 'Same again?' and turned back towards the bar before waiting for Sean's answer.

Connor put his and Sean's lagers on the table and pulled over another chair.

'We should move,' Sean said, starting to stand.

'No, no,' Connor said. 'We're fine here. And Louis needs to see you on your throne.'

'I do feel very regal . . .' Sean said. 'So how's things?'

'Pretty much the same.' He swigged his lager. 'You?'

'Good, yeah. College is great. Dad seems a bit . . . I dunno.'

Connor frowned. 'Yeah. I didn't know whether to say something about that.'

Sean felt a shiver run down between his shoulder blades. 'What do you mean?'

'My mum said he gave her a lift home one day – I think they bumped into each other at the Co-op or something? Anyway, she said he seemed fine – was chatting away and everything – but didn't stop at any red lights. By the time they got home, she was shitting herself.'

'Fuck,' Sean breathed. 'I don't know what . . .' His head seemed to be full of a rushing sound. 'Tell your mum I'm really sorry.'

'I will. But it's not your fault. I just thought I should say something.'

'Yeah. No, it's better to know. Thanks.'

He drank some lager, staring down at the carpet. The new carpet that seemed to have a pattern of feathers and roses. The old carpet was mostly beer and trodden-in cigarette ends.

'Fuck, that was a conversation killer, eh?' Connor said. 'I'm going for a piss and when I get back you can tell me who you've been shagging in the 'pool, OK?'

Sean huffed out a laugh and downed the rest of his lager.

'Oh, here he is!' Connor said, as Louis walked in and looked in the wrong direction, towards the restaurant area.

'Are we getting food?' Sean asked.

'Better had,' Connor said. 'Or we'll be wankered.'

The boy who'd greeted Sean was now talking to Louis.

'I think that lad was flirting with me when I arrived,' Sean said.

'That one?' Connor said, leaning forward to have a look. 'Christ, he looks about fifteen.'

'That's what I thought! Glad it's not just me.'

'I think he's flirting with Louis too,' Connor said. 'Look at him; he's gone all fluttery.'

He was right: Louis was in full flirt mode. But then he almost always was. He had one hand on the boy's arm and was patting his own chest with his other hand.

'This is like a nature documentary,' Connor said. 'The ho-mo-sex-ual in his natural habitat.'

Louis got his phone out and Sean half lifted out of his seat to get a better look.

'Is he getting his number?!' Connor said, incredulous. 'He's only just in the door!'

'Look at it this way,' Sean said. 'He may actually stick with us tonight, since he's already pulled.'

'Yeah, or head off early to meet that kid after his shift.' Sean shook his head. '"That kid", listen to me.'

Connor laughed. 'Yeah, you old git. Why so jaded? You should be sowing your oats.'

'That's what Molly keeps telling me.'

'Oh, yeah?' Connor said, sitting a bit straighter and picking up his lager. 'How is Molly?'

Sean was prevented from answering by Louis spotting them and practically running across the bar.

'All right, Prince Charming?' he said, before dropping down on Sean's lap and kissing him loudly on the forehead.

'You're a bit over-familiar for a commoner,' Sean said, hugging Louis with one arm.

'Nothing common about me,' Louis said. 'Did you see I just got that boy's number?'

'We saw,' Connor said. 'And boy is right.'

'He's not as young as he looks,' Louis said. 'He worked here before it was done up.'

'Did he?' Sean said. 'I don't remember him.'

'You wouldn't,' Louis said. 'You were all loved up.' He wiggled on Sean's knee and kissed him on the temple. 'Sorry. Banned topic.' He pretended to zip his lips and then got up and headed over to the bar. 'Same again?'

Sean smiled. He'd worried that things might be a bit awkward being back home, out with his mates again. Particularly since he hadn't seen them for a while and he hadn't even spoken to Connor for a couple of months, but nothing had changed, apart from the pub.

'Are we eating here?' Sean said an hour or so later. He was at the point where if he didn't eat soon, he'd be past it and he'd just get drunker and drunker and . . . he didn't really want to do that.

'Bit wanky?' Connor said. 'Why don't we go to O'Connell's?'

'Is it open?' Sean asked. 'What time is it?'

'They open late on Saturdays now,' Louis said. 'Yeah, let's go there – it'll be like old times.'

They left the pub – Sean and Connor having to wait a couple of minutes outside while Louis had another chat with the greeter boy – and then they were walking up the pedestrianised street towards their old hangout.

'Isn't this nice?' Louis said, linking arms with Sean. 'It's good to have you home.'

Sean laughed. 'It's good to be home.'

'How's that sexy housemate of yours?' Louis said, as they waited at the traffic lights.

'Alfie?' Sean said, smiling.

'You didn't tell me about Molly either,' Connor said.

'God,' Sean said. 'I will give you a full update on my housemates as soon as I've got some cheesy chips inside me.'

'Dirty bastard,' Louis said, as he pulled open the door to O'Connell's.

They all trooped up the stairs, walked straight through the main space and opened the door to the outside terrace. There were a couple of teenagers standing at the far end, blowing their cigarette smoke out over the canal, but apart from that it was empty.

'Score,' Louis said, pulling a couple of chairs over to one of the small metal tables. 'You go and get the food, Con.'

Connor saluted sarcastically – Sean grinning at how Connor

was capable of saluting sarcastically – and then went back inside.

'So how's things really?' Louis asked, as soon as they were both sitting down.

'Great,' Sean said. 'Honestly. Nothing to report really. My dad's not doing so good, but . . .'

'God, yeah, Connor mentioned that. Fucking hell. That's a bit rough.'

Sean nodded. It really was.

'And no men? Seriously?'

Sean shook his head. 'Nah. Not really. There's a boy at college I like, but I haven't even spoken to him.'

'Why the fuck not?' Louis asked, pulling a packet of cigarettes out of his jacket pocket and offering Sean one.

Sean shook his head. 'Lost my bottle, mostly. Also, how awkward would it be if something happened and then it went wrong and I had to see him every day? Oh, wait . . . I know exactly how awkward because that's already happened.'

'So – what? You're never going to go out with anyone ever again because it didn't work out with Haz?'

Sean winced at the nickname and Louis waved his hand. 'Sorry.'

'Not . . . never again,' Sean said, glancing down at the dark water in the canal, reflecting the lights from the restaurant. 'Just . . . not yet. I dunno. He poked a finger at a droplet of water on the edge of the metal table. 'It still hurts.'

Louis dropped his cigarette under the table and scuffed it with his foot. 'Of course it does. He was your first love.' He grinned. 'Even though it should have been me.'

Connor joined them at the table, carrying a tray with three bowls of cheesy chips, three bottles of lager and a pile of ketchup sachets.

Sean smiled at Louis. 'You were my first kiss, if that helps.'

'You told me it was me!' Connor said, fake-affronted.

'You were mine,' Louis said. 'But you were asleep, so you never knew.'

'Oh, I knew . . .' Connor joked.

Sean smiled at his friends and picked up a cheesy chip. It was good to be home.

Sean's first thought when he woke up was 'mice' but once he'd come round a bit he realised whatever he could hear was much too loud for mice, whatever his dad said. It sounded like dishes smashing. Or crashing, at least.

Sean got out of bed and wondered what you were supposed to do if you thought someone had broken into your house. Presumably you weren't meant to just let them help themselves to everything. But going downstairs to challenge them didn't seem like a sensible idea either. He got his mobile out and looked at it. He didn't want to phone the police and then have them come round and it be mice. Or a fox. Or whatever made noise in houses in the middle of the night.

He dialled nine and nine on his phone and then crept down the stairs with the phone out in front of him as a torch. By the time he got to the bottom of the stairs, he could hear his blood rushing in his ears and he was close to just pressing the third nine and running back up the stairs, slamming the door behind him.

But then he heard singing. He stopped in the hall and cocked his head as a weird sensation came over him. He could remember tiptoeing down the stairs as a child, hearing his dad singing this exact song. It was something old. Whenever his parents had friends round when Sean was little, his dad would get out his guitar and sing it, one foot on the sofa (Sean's mum turned a blind eye to shoes on cushions on these occasions).

Sean pushed open the dining room door. His dad was standing in the kitchen washing dishes. Sean could see his reflection in the black window behind the sink. He looked fine. He looked happy. But Sean had washed the dishes before he'd gone to bed.

'Dad?' he said.

His dad jumped and turned, clutching his chest. 'Seany! You scared the crap out of me!'

'Bloody hell, Dad!' Sean said. 'You scared the crap out of *me*! I thought you were being burgled!'

'I'm just doing the dishes,' his dad said, pointing at the sink.

'Yeah, I can see that. But why? It's three in the morning!'

His dad looked confused. 'Is it?'

Sean looked down at his phone and then up at the clock on the dining room wall, which was in the same place it had been for his whole life.

'Yes! Ten past three now.'

'In the morning?'

'Yes! That's why it's dark.'

His dad shook his head and laughed. 'I didn't realise.'

'You didn't notice it was dark?'

His dad frowned and looked puzzled. 'I did. I thought that when I first came downstairs, but then I just . . .' He shook his head again.

'Dad,' Sean said. 'Is everything OK?'

His dad crossed the kitchen and sat down at the dining table. 'I didn't want to say anything cos I didn't want to worry you.'

Sean sat down at the end of the table. In the seat his mum always used to sit in. 'Well, I'm worried now, so you might as well tell me.'

'It's these pills the doctor gave me. They sometimes make me a bit . . . confused.'

'What are the pills for?' Sean asked.

His dad tipped his head forward and rubbed the back of his neck. 'They're for Parkinson's.'

Sean felt his stomach lurch. 'Shit, Dad!'

'Don't swear, Sean. I know. I should've told you, but it's not that big a deal.'

'You did tell me,' Sean said. 'You told me Doctor Magennis said it wasn't Parkinson's.'

'Yeah, that's what he said at first. And then I went back in with my dead foot—'

'Your what?'

His dad's eyebrows shot up. 'Did I not tell you about that? Yeah, my foot kept going heavy and then it'd be all right again, but Magennis sent me to see this specialist. A woman.'

'Yeah, they have them now,' Sean said, smiling.

'I know, smart arse. I'm just saying. She was a lot better than Magennis – asked more questions. Got me to walk up and down. Did loads of tests. And she said it's Parkinson's. But

Magennis didn't seem convinced when I went back to him, so I don't know.' He shrugged. 'But he's given me all these pills just in case and they make me feel a bit fuzzy sometimes.'

'It's the pills making you feel fuzzy?' Sean asked. 'Not the Parkinson's? And are you sure you're taking them properly?'

His dad shook his head. 'I don't know. I think so. I've got one of those little plastic boxes with the days of the week on. Makes me feel like a right old fucker.'

Sean smiled. 'Don't swear, Dad.'

His dad smiled back and he looked just like his old self. 'I'm OK, Sean. Honestly. I'd tell you if I wasn't.'

'OK,' Sean said. 'But you have to. Because you're here on your own and I'm in Liverpool and—'

'I'll tell you.'

'Good.'

'Now, do you need some money?'

'Dad, I always need money.'

His dad nodded. 'I'll give you a cheque to take back with you.'

Sean smiled. 'That would be great. Thanks.'

SPARKSLIFE: Crashed

by AnnaSparks 8,196 views
Published on 21 September

[Transcript of Anna's vlog]

I've just been home for the night for the first time since moving to Liverpool. I had a plan to ask my parents for a bit more money – I haven't told them that the theatre job fell through and I thought it was because I didn't want them to make me go back home again. But I learned while I was at home that that wasn't the reason at all.

The real reason is that I don't think I want their help. Or maybe that's just what I'm telling myself because they're not going to help me; they can't help me. I learned while I was at home that everything is changing. Everything I've had my whole life is basically going away, being taken away. And I'm sort of OK with it. It's sad, of course, but also I kind of feel like change is good. Or will be good at some point, anyway.

So, no, my parents can't help me. But I was thinking that I want to do this on my own. Maybe that's stupid, I don't know. But I made this decision and lots of people thought it was the wrong decision – my best friend came round to see me – she's doing the thing everyone expected me to do, she's going to university, and she thought maybe I should do that too. But it was so clear to me that it's not what I want. That it wouldn't have been the right decision for me.

But also I'm not on my own. My housemates are great. I haven't got to know all of them that well yet – they're all busy – but I already know that at least a couple of them are going to be really good friends.

So that makes me think that moving to Liverpool – even without the job I thought I was moving there for – was the right decision for me. IS the right decision for me. And now I just have to make it work. Wish me luck!

And while I'm asking you for luck – more luck – I just want to thank you all for your support. I've talked before about how vlogging has really helped me become more confident and your (mostly!) sweet and supportive comments always really help me too. It's always good to know that I can come here and talk things through and you guys will listen and tell me to go for it. I really appreciate it. Thank you.

COMMENTS:

Anna Benford: Good luck!

Melly Mel: You know what the right decision for you is. I wish I had your confidence.

Butterflyaway: I think you can do anything you choose to do. Go for it ;) ;) ;)

Daisy Locke: Change IS good! You'll be fine. You inspire me to be braver.

Chapter 23

It had been a surprisingly hot day, so it was still warm even as the sun was going down, and the huge beer garden was busy and buzzing. Sean flopped down at the nearest empty table under a red umbrella and handed some cash to Molly.

'I know, chivalry's dead, but can you go please? I'm shagged.'

Molly pointed at him. 'I'll need to hear about that. What are you drinking?'

Sean and Anna both asked for beers and Molly skipped around the tables to the bar. Anna watched her spot someone she knew and wave and shout.

'She knows everyone,' Sean said. 'I couldn't work it out when I first met her. But it's because she'll talk to anyone. You know when someone smiles at you in the street and you think, what do you want?'

Anna laughed.

'Molly talks to them. I got the train with her once and she actually started a conversation with the people sitting opposite us. I didn't know where to look. I think she grew up in a commune or something.'

'My mum basically told me to trust no one,' Anna said.

'She's right!' Sean said. 'People are freaks and you should avoid them wherever you can.'

Anna smiled and fiddled with a beer mat. She knew Sean was at least as friendly and kind as Molly. She bet he'd chat away on the train too.

'How was home?' Molly said when she got back with the drinks. 'Was it hideous?'

Anna smiled. 'My parents have lost their business and sold our house.'

'Shit!' Molly said.

'My dad's got Parkinson's,' Sean said. 'So it sounds like we both had a brilliant time!' He smiled at Anna.

'God,' Anna said. 'That's awful. Now I feel bad for feeling sorry for myself.'

'Nah,' Sean said. 'Your thing is shit too. Are they going to be all right?'

'I think so,' Anna said. 'They seem OK about it – almost relieved – but they're pretty good at denial. What about your dad?'

'Same really. Says it's not a big deal, but I don't think he's dealing with it very well.' Sean leaned back in his chair, spreading his arms out and turning his face up to the sun. 'And I don't feel like I *can* deal with it. What is this shit? Where are the adults?!'

'We're the adults now,' Molly said, in a horror-movie voice.

'Jesus.' Sean leaned forward on the table. 'I spoke to my Aunty Jean and she said she's going to keep an eye on him, but, you know . . . she's got her own life and a job and everything. I sort of feel like I should be doing more.'

'But you've got a life too,' Molly said. 'I think this with my mum. I worry that she's doing too much and getting stressed and struggling for money, but there's only so much *I* can do.'

'This is a cheery fucking conversation,' Sean said. 'No more talk about parents, knackered or otherwise, OK?'

'I'll drink to that,' Anna said, holding her bottle up.

They were on their second drinks when Alfie arrived, looking exhausted.

'You look like a man who needs a drink,' Sean said, standing.

'Oh, you get up now,' Molly said. 'But you made me get yours!'

'I'm refreshed now,' Sean said. 'And I can always get up for Alfie.'

Anna laughed and pulled out the chair next to her for Alfie to sit down. Alfie smiled at her and sat.

'Long day,' Alfie said, rubbing his face. 'College and work stuff. Doesn't matter.'

'You need to get drunk,' Molly said.

Alfie laughed. 'That's your answer to everything.'

Molly grinned at him. 'No, not to everything. But to a lot of things. You never relax. You need to let yourself go.'

'That seems to be a popular opinion lately.' He tipped his head forward and rubbed the back of his neck. 'You could be right.'

'Shit,' Molly said. 'I don't think you've ever agreed with me about this before now.' She turned to Anna. 'I've never seen Alfie drunk. Too much of a control freak.'

'Usually I have to look after you lot!' he said. Sean was still at the bar, so Alfie picked up Sean's lager and swigged it.

'Balls,' Molly said. 'We can look after ourselves. Ish. Live a little.'

'Right,' Alfie said, clinking his bottle against Anna's. 'To living. A little.'

Anna wasn't sure how many drinks she'd had by the time they moved inside the bar. They'd got hot dogs and chips from the stall outside and Alfie had bought them all soft drinks, despite everyone taking the piss out of him for not being able to let go of looking after them.

Inside, the music was louder and bright lights flashed along with the beat. They crammed into a booth around a table with Anna pressed up against the wall, Alfie next to her and Molly on the end. Alfie's thigh was pressed up against Anna's and she wriggled in her seat, but there was nothing she could do. She didn't really want to do anything; she liked sitting pressed up against him. As she reached for her drink, her arm brushed against Alfie's and he turned and smiled at her.

'You all right?'

She nodded and swigged some of her drink.

'Come on, Anna!' Molly said, slipping off the end of the bench. 'Come and dance.'

'God, no!' Anna said, laughing.

There wasn't a dance floor and no one else was dancing, but Molly didn't care – she was already moving, swinging her hips from side to side and shimmying her shoulders.

'Come on!' she said to Anna. 'Don't make me dance on my own!'

'Maybe after this drink,' Anna said. She thought about the comments on her last vlog. Her followers telling her she was brave and inspiring. They wouldn't think so if they could see her now, she knew.

'I'll dance with you,' Sean said, shuffling along the seat and joining Molly.

Anna wasn't surprised to see that Molly was a brilliant dancer. She was completely unselfconscious, adding little moves and singing along. Sean was brilliant too, but spent more time joking and messing around. Anna wondered what it would be like to be so confident and comfortable in your own skin. Maybe she should pretend to be AnnaSparks. But she wasn't sure she could convince herself without the hair and make-up.

'Want to join them?' Alfie said when the song changed. 'I love this song.'

'I don't know it,' Anna said.

'No way!' Alfie said. 'It's a classic.'

Alfie stood up and reached for Anna's hand to help her off the seat. As soon as his skin touched hers, she felt a shiver run up her arm. What would AnnaSparks do, she thought to herself and, grinning, stepped away from the table and started to dance.

Alfie was a much more self-conscious dancer than Sean, and Anna was relieved that she wasn't going to be the only one who didn't look like a professional dancer. Every now and then she could hear Alfie singing along with the song – it was called 'Rock With You' – and he had a nice voice. When the song changed to something faster, Molly pulled Anna towards her and spun her around. Anna had the sensation of light and colour and music and she laughed out loud.

When she'd stopped spinning she saw that Nina and Jack had arrived and were sitting in the booth the rest of them had abandoned.

'Come and dance!' Anna yelled at Nina.

Nina glanced at Jack, as if she was asking for permission, and then shook her head. Anna was about to go over and convince her, but she felt hands on her waist and turned round to see Alfie smiling down at her, wiggling his shoulders in a way that made her laugh out loud.

On the way to the loo, which was down the stairs and along a corridor, Anna realised that she was a bit drunk. And also that her feet were killing her. But when she looked at herself in the mirror, she realised she looked happy. She looked more like AnnaSparks than Anna Parkes, even without the hair and make-up. She grinned at herself in the mirror and pulled her shoulders back. She wanted to dance more.

When she came out of the loo, Jack was leaning against the wall opposite. Anna looked back at the loo door, wondering if she'd been in the men's by mistake, but it was definitely the right one.

'Hey,' Jack said.

Anna smiled. He was so good-looking. Ridiculously good-looking. Nina was so lucky.

'Are you having a good night?' he asked.

Anna nodded. 'I really am. I need to dance more. You should come and dance.'

'I don't dance,' Jack said and smiled. 'I like watching you though.'

Anna felt her stomach plummet. It made her feel unsteady on her feet. She opened her mouth to respond, before knowing what she was really going to say, but he was already moving past her, heading into the loo. As he did, he brushed against her, his hand grazing her breast, and putting his mouth close to her ear, said, 'You are sexy as fuck.'

'Do it!' Sean was saying when Anna sat back down in the booth.

Nina was shaking her head, but she was laughing.

'Do what?' Anna asked, her stomach still twisting.

'Sing!' Alfie said, leaning over so his mouth was next to her ear. It made her shiver. 'They've got a karaoke machine.'

'Oh, go on!' Molly said. 'I want to hear you sing!'

'Come on!' Sean said. 'Jack's gone so you don't need to worry about making a show of yourself.'

'Thanks!' Nina said, still laughing. 'I love that you think I'll make a show of myself. That's really encouraging.'

'Jack's just gone to the loo, I think,' Anna said. His name felt strange in her mouth. She couldn't look at Nina.

'Yeah, then he's going,' Sean said. 'He's got to be up early in the morning.'

'I talked him into one drink,' Nina said. 'But we're going to Whitby tomorrow. I'm not staying long either.'

Anna felt almost dizzy with relief. She'd had no idea how she was going to be able to deal with Jack after what he'd said.

'Come on, Neens,' Sean said, grabbing Nina's arm and hugging it. 'You know you want to.'

Nina shook her head.

When the bar closed – flashing the lights on and off – Anna was disappointed. She wasn't ready for the night to end.

'Can we go somewhere else?' she said, as they stepped outside into the still-warm air.

Molly grinned. 'Get you! Party animal!'

'I'm going to get back,' Nina said. 'Have fun.'

'Are you sure?' Alfie asked her. 'I can walk you back, if you like.'

Nina laughed. 'It's literally there.' She pointed up the road.

'So are we going back or on somewhere else?' Alfie asked.

'How drunk are you?' Sean asked him.

'I'm fine, mate,' Alfie said.

'So we're staying out then!' Sean said. 'We need to stay out till Alfie's wankered.'

Chapter 24

They headed up the cobbled street, Sean and Molly walking ahead, bumping each other's shoulders and laughing. Anna looked up at Alfie and smiled. He grinned at her and her stomach gave another flip.

She liked him. She'd liked him as soon as she met him. He was sweet and kind and funny and, yes, sexy. She could still picture him with his towel wrapped around his waist on the day she'd arrived at the house. He actually had a six pack. She had no idea how – because when did he have time to go to the gym? – but he did. He could dance. A bit. And he even had nice feet.

She couldn't believe she was thinking about his feet.

'Here?' Sean said, stopping outside a door with music blaring from inside.

'Depends if we want to talk or dance,' Alfie said.

'I want to dance!' Molly said.

'Me too,' Anna admitted. She'd never done anything like this before – the only time she'd gone out with friends at home, it had been to a feeble under-eighteens night where everyone had been too self-conscious to dance and the whole purpose of the evening had been who could get off with who.

'It's nice downstairs,' Sean said. 'Honest.'

They followed him down the steps and where Anna had been imagining either a dingy bar with sticky floors or an intimidatingly cool space, it was actually really lovely: one side of the room was lined with overstuffed, multi-coloured booths, and white fairy lights looped from tree branches that criss-crossed the ceiling.

'I'll get the drinks,' Alfie shouted. 'You get seats.'

Being a week night, it wasn't too busy, so they easily slipped into another booth. Molly and Sean sat opposite Anna and she was aware that meant Alfie would be sitting next to her again. The thought of it made her stomach slosh with nerves.

Alfie put four bottles of lager on the table, then headed back to the bar and returned with glasses and an old Grolsch bottle filled with water .

'You are too grown-up!' Molly yelled at him.

He just grinned back.

Anna even liked that about him. She liked that he wanted to take care of them all, that he was responsible, that he was organised enough to be working and doing a degree and taking care of the house and their friends – even though he was clearly exhausted.

She felt herself lean slightly towards him without even meaning to. And she felt him lean slightly towards her too. Her stomach flipped. She glanced over at Molly who was grinning at her with one eyebrow raised. Anna shook her head. Nothing was going to happen.

* * *

'You and Alfie?' Molly said later, in the loos.

The bathroom was accessed through a door in the trunk of a tree in the corner of the room. Anna hadn't been able to find it and had gone back to their table to ask Sean where it was and Molly decided to go with her.

'Oh, no,' Anna said, looking at Molly in the mirror. 'No.'

'Why not?' Molly said, pulling a lipstick out of her bag and leaning forward to reapply.

'I . . . I wouldn't want to make it awkward in the house,' Anna said. She'd been about to say that she thought he liked someone else, but knowing Molly she'd be determined to get it out of her.

Molly shook her head. 'You're too nice.'

She pouted at herself in the mirror then stuck her finger in her mouth and pulled it out.

'It's to stop the lipstick getting on your teeth,' she told Anna when she saw her staring. 'The bits that would go on your teeth go on your finger.' She washed her hands. 'And actually Alfie's too nice too, so you'd be perfect together. Or is that what you don't want? Do you like bad boys?' She tipped her head on one side.

'God, no,' Anna said. 'I mean . . . I don't really know what I like.' Although that wasn't strictly true. She looked at herself in the mirror – her eyes were wide and worried. 'What's the deal with Jack?'

'What do you mean?' Molly asked.

'I mean . . . is it serious? Him and Nina?'

Molly was looking for something in her tiny black box of a bag. 'I don't know. I think maybe it's more serious for Nina than it is for him. But he's still around, so maybe that's just the vibe he wants to give off, you know?'

Anna nodded. She didn't know really. But maybe him saying what he said earlier was just his way of messing with her. He hadn't meant it. Anna stared at herself in the mirror – he can't have meant it anyway. It wasn't anything close to true.

Molly pulled a pencil out of her bag and started filling in her eyebrows.

'I could show you how to do this, you know?' Molly said. 'Make-up? I mean, you look lovely, but I could really make you look . . .' She pulled a pouting pose and then grinned.

'No. Thanks,' Anna said. 'I don't . . . like to wear a lot of make-up.'

Off-screen, at least, Anna thought. She wondered what Molly would think if she showed her what she looked like as AnnaSparks. Would she be impressed? Or annoyed that she'd kept it secret?

'That's cool,' Molly said. 'And maybe if you wore your hair down . . .'

Anna shook her head and Molly laughed. 'No worries. It's cool that you know your own style.'

Anna almost laughed. That wasn't it at all.

'If you change your mind, you know where to come,' Molly said, closing her bag with a snap. 'I'll make you look fabulous, honestly, even more gorgeous than you are now. It'll knock Alfie's socks off.'

'I don't—' Anna started, but Molly rolled her eyes. 'You do. I can tell. I think it's amazing. You'd be brilliant together.'

Anna washed her hands again, just for something to do. She held her wrists under the cold tap to cool her down then patted cold water on her cheeks.

'You should dance with him,' Molly said. 'And then I'll get Sean to leave you alone later.'

'Oh, don't,' Anna said, horrified. 'He'll know and it'll be really embarrassing.'

Molly shook her head. 'Don't worry. I'll be subtle.'

Anna didn't meant to pull a face, but she must have done because Molly said, 'I can be subtle! Sometimes! Trust me.' She put her arm around Anna and they headed back into the bar.

Anna allowed herself one more drink and then switched to water. Even so, she felt a bit unsteady on her feet and kept bumping against Alfie as they danced.

He didn't seem to mind though and she wasn't sure, but she thought maybe he was bumping into her too, on purpose. She had no idea what to do about it, so she just kept dancing and smiling at him every time she caught his eye, which did seem to be happening more and more. And then the bar was closing and they were back at their booth finishing their drinks and then they were walking up the stairs and out into the night.

'I miss the erection section,' Sean said, as they stopped on the street.

'The what?' Anna asked. She gulped at the fresh air and realised suddenly how tired she was.

'You know?' Sean said. 'When they used to play slow songs at the end of the night and everyone could slow dance together. Well, I mean, straight couples could slow dance – the gay boys had to go outside and feel each other up behind the bins.'

'We could slow dance here,' Molly said. 'You'd have to make do with me though,' she told Sean.

'That's OK,' Sean said. 'I've been out with boys with bigger boobs than you.'

'Shut it, you,' Molly said. She grabbed him and they started waltzing in the street. Everyone else who'd left the club had headed down towards Ranelagh Street or up to Berry Street and the four of them had the street to themselves.

Anna laughed as she watched Sean and Molly.

'Shall we?' Alfie said, holding his arms up as if he was suggesting a proper dance.

Anna couldn't think of anything to say, so she just took a breath and stepped into his arms. Alfie's chest pressed against hers and she felt the breath go out of her. She wanted him to kiss her. She glanced up at him and he was looking down at her. She wondered if he was thinking about kissing her too. She knew that in theory she could kiss him – she didn't have to wait for him to kiss her – but she couldn't. She wouldn't be able to make herself do it. He was moving slowly from side to side, not even stepping, more swaying and he was singing under his breath. She closed her eyes and moved along with him, trying not to think about the fact that they were on the street and there was no music apart from Alfie's vague humming. She wanted to just experience it, enjoy it without overthinking it. She could still hear Sean and Molly's feet on the cobbles, could hear them giggling, but knew that they would be laughing at themselves, not at Anna and Alfie.

'Are you OK?' she heard Alfie say, his mouth next to her ear.

She shivered. 'I'm fine,' she whispered.

'You feel like you're falling asleep,' he said. He stepped back, still holding her. 'We'd better get back.'

Anna opened her eyes and smiled at him. He was looking at her mouth and when he looked back up and met her eyes, she thought she saw something. She thought maybe he was thinking about kissing her. She tipped her face up towards his and he looked down at her mouth again and then said, 'I'm glad I came out tonight. It's been brilliant.'

Anna stepped back, so she and Alfie were no longer touching.

'It has,' she said. 'I've had fun.'

'We should do it again,' Alfie said.

Anna wasn't sure if he meant all of them or just the two of them so she just nodded and then turned to find Sean and Molly. They were still dancing – side by side now, not in hold – at the far end of the road, beyond their house. Sean was pretending to be serious, but Molly was laughing and it made Anna laugh just to look at them.

'They're nuts,' Alfie said.

Anna nodded. 'But they're great.'

'You're happy?' Alfie said. 'In the house?' He pulled his keys out of his pocket as they walked the few metres to their front door.

Anna looked up at her room. She'd left the fairy lights on around her window, which she knew she wasn't supposed to do, but it was just so welcoming when she came back.

'I am,' she said. 'I love it.'

'Good,' Alfie said. He opened the door and Anna followed him inside. She could hear Sean and Molly running to join them, but she suddenly felt overwhelmed with tiredness.

'I'm going straight up,' she told Alfie. 'Before I fall asleep right here.'

'OK,' he said. He stepped towards her and Anna got that feeling again. The feeling that he was going to say something or do something. Her stomach flipped over and she waited, but instead he just said, 'Sleep well.'

Chapter 25

Whitby was all bright blue sky and seagulls and tourists. Nina loved it instantly. She couldn't quite believe she was there with Jack or that he let her take his hand as they left the station and keep hold of it as they walked through town towards his mum's house.

'It's on the other side of the harbour,' Jack told her. 'In the old town.'

'You've been here before,' Nina said.

Jack nodded. 'We used to come here when I was a kid. She had a thing about Dracula.' He pointed at the ruined abbey on the top of the hill.

'That sounds healthy,' Nina said, smiling.

'She used to do re-creation things. It was weird. But she said she felt like a different person here. She always said she'd move here eventually.'

'I'm not surprised,' Nina said. 'It's gorgeous.'

'Yeah,' Jack said. 'It's pretty cool. Even better at Halloween. They have this gothic festival thing . . .'

They crossed the bridge and turned left into a narrow cobbled street full of tourists.

'It's in one of the yards,' Jack said, pointing at a tiny side-alley between a pub and a shop. 'Bit further down.'

They passed a market square on the left with stalls selling everything from massive wicker baskets to knitted *Despicable Me* minion hats and then Jack stopped so suddenly that Nina bumped into him.

'This is the one,' he said, looking up the alley.

Nina followed him in and past a dog lying down on a cushion and tied to a bench with a bit of rope. The dog raised its head and wagged its tail listlessly.

They climbed a few steps and then a few more and Jack stopped in front of a bright red door.

'This is it,' he said.

'OK,' Nina said.

Jack knocked and they both waited. Nina's belly was fluttering and she could hear her heartbeat in her ears so she couldn't imagine how Jack felt.

'She's probably out,' Jack said.

'No. You told her what time we were getting here, right?'

Jack nodded. His jaw looked tight and he was squeezing her hand.

And then the door opened.

'She's so nice!' Nina whispered, as Jack's mum went into the kitchen to get them all drinks.

'She is,' Jack said. 'Most of the time.'

Jack's mum had flung her arms around both of them, squeezing all the breath out of Nina. She kept saying how tall Jack was, how handsome, how 'grown-up'. And how beautiful

Nina was. She didn't look at all like Nina had expected her to – she had blunt-cut dyed orange hair, perfect forties style make-up and she was wearing dungarees over a Blondie T-shirt.

'I've only got one spare room,' she said, coming back in with cups and a teapot on a tray. 'You two are OK to share, right?'

'Mum!' Jack said and Nina looked at him, laughing.

His mum laughed too. 'Don't make me get the baby photos out.'

'I knew I shouldn't have brought you,' Jack said to Nina and she laughed. She felt like his girlfriend. For the first time. Not just some girl he liked to hang out with, have sex with, but his actual girlfriend. It was disorientating.

'I thought we could go out for dinner tonight,' said Jack's mum, who'd told Nina to call her Bella. 'There's a pub at the bottom of the road, right on the water. It's nice. Relaxed. The food's not amazing, but—'

'Sounds fine,' Jack said, glancing up from his phone.

Nina wondered for a second who he was texting or if he was on Facebook and then rolled her eyes at herself for feeling possessive. What did it matter what he was doing on his phone? She was here with him in Whitby. That made her his girlfriend, didn't it? Or certainly closer to being his girlfriend than someone who lived in his phone.

The pub was literally at the bottom of the road. Once they'd got to the bottom of Bella's steps, they just had to stagger down a short, steep cobbled street – luckily there was a handrail along the side – and then they almost fell into the pub. It was hot and dark and busy inside, but Bella pushed through to a reserved table on the waterside and they all sat down.

'Go and get the drinks, love,' she said to Jack, handing him a twenty-pound note.

He rolled his eyes, but he still went.

'You're good for him,' Bella said, once Jack had gone.

Nina smiled back. 'Do you think? I don't know. I hope I am, but . . .' She let the sentence drift.

'He had a hard time with his dad.' Bella fiddled with a beer mat on the table. 'And then his stepdad – my second husband – he was a right arsehole. So he's not always been easy, Jack. And he'd tell you the same about me, I'm sure. But he's a good boy at heart.'

'I know,' Nina said.

'He's working, yeah?' Bella asked.

Nina nodded. 'That's how we met. We both work in the same hotel.'

'Oh, yeah? That's good. I just want him to have some stability, you know?'

Nina nodded. She wasn't sure Jack was as interested in stability as his mum was, but then he was eighteen – what did she expect?

'And your parents, do they live nearby?'

Nina shook her head. 'No. They live in Derbyshire.'

'But you go and see them?'

Nina picked at her fingernails under the table. 'Not as often as I should.'

'Oh, you should, love,' Bella said. 'Really. You'll miss 'em when they're gone. Not that you need to worry about that for a while yet, I hope.'

Nina nodded. She did need to go home, she knew. Maybe she'd do that at half-term.

'Here he comes!' Bella said, grinning up at Jack.

'Some bloke at the bar said to say hello to you,' he said to Bella.

'Oh?' Bella said, sitting up straighter in her seat and trying to look over at the bar.

'Like that, is it?' Jack said.

Nina heard the edge in his voice and looked at him out of the corner of her eye. His jaw had gone tight.

'No!' Bella said, laughing. 'No! Just a mate. People are friendly round here. Everyone looks out for each other.'

'How's your work going?' Nina asked.

She could practically feel Jack bristling next to her – it didn't seem like what his mum had said had reassured him at all.

'Oh, it's great!' Bella said, beaming at Nina. 'This place is so inspiring. I've started weaving again. And I've been making these tiny bird sculptures with wire and feathers. I can just sit and look out over the roofs and the next thing I know I've got another idea. I can't remember when I was last so productive.'

'How did you get started?' Nina asked, when Jack hadn't offered anything.

'When I was pregnant with him!' Bella said. 'I'd never really done anything creative before then. Not since school. Not that it was that long after school when I fell with him.' She rolled her eyes. 'At school I'd been interested, but not very good, you know? I could do what they asked me, but I didn't have any ideas of my own. And then when I was pregnant I was just full of ideas, all the time! I started painting and knitting and felting! I hadn't even known what fucking felting was! 'Scuse my language, Nina love.'

Jack snorted at that and Nina leaned against him. He didn't resist and so she started to let herself relax a bit.

'One day I was in the bath – it was in the morning. That was the other thing when I was preggers, couldn't get enough baths. Thought I was having a mermaid for a while there. So my huge belly was looming out of the water and it was getting cold, so I started pouring water over it with a sponge. Like basting a chicken. And then suddenly the water droplets looked like the most beautiful things I'd ever seen. Honestly, I couldn't get over it. I was looking at them and thinking how had I never noticed how incredible they were before? The light was reflected and they changed colour and for every one that fell, there'd be another one. And I started thinking about life and birth and death and all that bollocks . . .' She waved her hand and took a sip of her drink. 'And that day I went off to this craft shop and bought all these crystal beads and started making jewellery. I'd never done it before. Hadn't even really thought of it as a thing you could do. And I sold some to my friends and they really took off and by the time Jack was a few months old, I had a little stall in the market.'

'Wow,' Nina said.

'Yeah,' Jack said. 'And then my dad left and she didn't make anything for years.'

'Well, that's how creativity works, love. It's a fragile thing and it doesn't take much to get the confidence knocked out of you.'

'That's what happened to me,' Nina said before she could change her mind. She drank some of her lager. 'I wanted to be a singer. But then I went to performing arts school and . . .' She shook her head.

Bella reached across the table and grabbed both of Nina's hands in hers. 'Listen to me. One thing I've learned over the years is that you can't let things affect you like that. Yes, you can get your confidence knocked. And sometimes – more often than sometimes – it's so much easier not to create. But you have to keep going. Because if you don't . . . it's not pretty.'

'Bloody hell,' Jack said. 'Who ordered the therapy session?'

Nina smiled, but her eyes had filled with tears. Bella was still holding her hands and she half-hoped that Jack would bugger off somewhere so she could talk to his mum more, without him taking the piss.

'My parents think I'm still at college,' Nina said.

'Oh, sweetie,' Bella said. 'We need to talk more about this. But first I think we should get some grub in us. You up for going back to the bar, Jack?'

'No,' Jack said, but when Nina looked at him, he was smiling.

'I'll go then,' Bella said. 'Fish and chips all right with you both?'

Nina nodded and wiped her eyes as Bella headed off to the bar.

'You daft cow,' Jack said.

Nina laughed. 'Your mum's lovely.'

He put his arm round her. 'Yeah, she can be. The thing is, if that bloke at the bar so much as winks at her, she'll fuck right off and leave us here. That's why I kept the change from the drinks.'

Nina rested her head on his shoulder and thought about college. Could she go back? The idea of it made her stomach clench with fear, but she didn't want to work at the hotel for ever, that was for sure.

She felt Jack's hand on her thigh, creeping higher and she wriggled in her seat as he kissed her neck.

'What if I went back to college?' she said.

He looked up, frowning. 'You want to do that?'

'I think so,' she said. 'Maybe. I don't know if I could get back in, but if I could . . .'

'What would you do for money?' Jack asked.

'I'd probably still have to work at the hotel. Part-time. Like I did in the first place.'

Jack nodded. 'I'd have to find myself another cleaner then. You know, for when you're not there.'

He grinned and Nina smiled, but she felt a twist of nerves in her stomach. Because she wasn't sure he was actually joking.

Back at the house, Bella made a big show of telling them she'd be in her bedroom, watching TV, and they were to treat the house as their own.

'Was your mum just telling us to go and have sex?' Nina asked, once they were back in their small room.

Jack laughed. 'Basically, yeah.'

'She's not like my mum,' Nina said.

'I bet your mum wouldn't let me in the house, would she?' Jack said.

Nina laughed as she knelt on the bed to close the curtains and looked out across the red-tile rooftops to the harbour beyond, lights from the arcades on the far side twinkling red, yellow and blue.

'Probably not, no.'

'We'd best make the most of it now then, eh?' Jack said.

Nina dropped back on the bed and looked up at Jack, who was already stripped down to his underwear.

'I've had a really good day,' she said.

'So have I,' Jack said, undoing the button on her jeans and pulling them down as Nina held her hips up off the bed.

'Glad you brought me?' Nina couldn't resist asking.

'Not sure yet,' Jack said, dropping her jeans on the floor and running his index finger up her inner thigh. 'You'll have to convince me.'

'I think I can do that,' Nina said. She pulled his head down for a kiss and was surprised to find him relax against her. Usually he held himself off. Usually he preferred her to be on top. Or for him to be behind. She slid one foot down the back of his thigh and gently bit his bottom lip, feeling rather than hearing him groan against her mouth.

'I'm definitely glad I brought you,' he said.

I love you, Nina thought, but wasn't stupid enough to say.

Chapter 26

'Sharda will show you how to work the coffee machine,' Alfie said, steering Anna behind the counter and pointing at Sharda. 'But that'll need to be later when it's a bit quieter.'

'What should I do till then?' Anna asked.

The cafe was already quite busy and Anna was worried she wouldn't be able to manage.

'Don't worry about it,' Alfie said. 'If you just watch what me and Sharda do and maybe you can take stuff over and clear the tables?'

'I can do that,' Anna said. 'And thanks again for—'

Alfie shook his head. 'Don't worry about it. We're short-staffed, you need a job. It's a no brainer.'

Anna stepped back so she was slightly out of the way of the flurry of activity behind the counter. Last night in the bar, Anna had told Alfie about her parents' business and how worried she was about money and Alfie had suggested she come in, do a shift and learn the ropes so that she could take shifts as and when in the future.

She did wish she didn't feel so much like a spare part though. Alfie and Sharda obviously worked well together and had a routine. It was all cupboard doors opening and closing and the coffee machine steaming and the sandwich press beeping, while Anna stood there feeling a bit useless.

An older man with a very red face came to the counter and said, 'All right, love?' to Anna.

'I . . . um . . .' Anna said, pathetically.

'The usual, Ted?' Alfie asked the man and Anna was flooded with relief to know she didn't have to deal with him at all. Alfie knew him. Alfie had it under control.

Anna watched Alfie making Ted's coffee and getting him a pastry from the cabinet.

'Could you pass me a knife?' he asked Anna, gesturing at a cutlery tray under the counter. Anna grabbed a knife and put it on the plate with the pastry and actually felt she'd achieved something. Putting a knife on a plate – yay, go Anna. She tried to study what Alfie was doing with the coffee machine, but it was all so fast, so practised, that she couldn't work it out.

Ted was chatting to Sharda about a restaurant he'd been to the night before so Anna took a moment to look around the cafe. It was long and narrow with tables on both sides at the front and down one side opposite the bar area. The walls were covered with paintings by local artists, most of which were for sale.

'I'm going to go and have a look at the paintings,' Anna said. 'So I know if anyone asks.'

'Good idea,' Alfie said, as he poured froth onto the top of Ted's latte.

Anna stepped out from behind the counter and walked around the cafe, avoiding tables where customers were sitting, but keeping a look-out in case anyone needed anything. She collected a couple of dirty plates and one customer stopped her to ask for another latte, which she asked Alfie for when she got back to the counter.

'What do you think?' Alfie asked.

'About . . . ?'

'The pictures?'

'Oh!' Anna said. 'I like them!' She hadn't liked them all, but there had been some paintings of the river as well as some bright abstract paintings that she really did like.

'People usually point to the ones they like,' Alfie said. 'Rather than asking for them by name. But it's good to familiarise yourself.'

'Is there anything I can do?' she asked. 'Or should I just watch?'

'Just watch for now,' Alfie said. 'Don't worry, we'll put you to work soon enough.'

Smiling, she leaned back on the cabinet behind the counter and watched Alfie. He was brilliant with the customers – smiling and chatting and remembering people's names – plus he was obviously very comfortable making the drinks and getting the food. He seemed to be able to sense what people wanted and more than once suggested something that turned out to be correct when the customer hadn't been able to remember or say what they wanted.

During a lull, he cleaned the counters, sorted out stuff in the cupboards and eventually handed Anna a box of sugar sachets so she could go and refill the bowls on the tables.

'Am I OK to take my break?' Sharda asked at about two-thirty.

'Oh, God, yeah, sorry,' Alfie said, looking up at the time. 'Sorry, I totally forgot.'

'You'll be OK?' she asked.

'Yeah, we'll be fine,' Alfie told her.

'It's usually pretty quiet mid-afternoon,' Alfie told Anna, once Sharda had gone. 'Are you hungry? Do you want a sandwich?'

'Please,' Anna said. She'd been too nervous to eat earlier and her stomach had been gnawing away for the past half hour.

Alfie made her a latte while talking her through the steps – she didn't think she'd remember, but at least he did it slowly – and then he gave her a chicken sandwich and told her to go and sit in the window for a bit.

Anna sat and looked out onto Bold Street, eating. In the side street opposite the cafe, someone had set up something that looked like a small, portable soup kitchen. They had a huge flask on a trolley and about twenty people were queuing.

'Alfie?' she said, picking up her mug and plate and taking them back to the counter. 'Have you seen there's like a soup kitchen over the road?'

Alfie frowned. 'No? I haven't seen anything like that before.' He headed through the cafe and looked out of the window.

'Will you be OK here for just one sec?' he said to Anna.

Anna nodded and then, as she watched him head out through the door, immediately started to panic about all the things that could go wrong while she was alone in charge of the cafe. She knew Alfie was only just over the road, but still.

None of the remaining customers even looked up from their phones or newspapers though and a couple of minutes later, Alfie was back.

'What is it?' Anna said.

'It's very cool actually,' Alfie said. 'It's a charity collective. I wanted to ask if there was anything we could do to help and they do actually need a space, particularly in the evenings. I'd have to ask Malc – he's the owner – but it's something to consider.'

'Have you got time to work here in the evenings too?' Anna said.

Alfie shrugged. 'Some evenings I have. I don't always have coursework.'

'Yeah, I know, but when do you ever get a break?'

Alfie smiled. 'Ah. Yeah, I don't do relaxing very well. I feel like . . . I've got all these things I want to do and I need to make the best possible start. You know? So I want to learn as much as I can at uni, but also learn as much as I can from working here and from the people I work with. Then when I finish uni I'll be in a good position to set up on my own.'

'Set up what?'

'Coffee shops.' He smiled. 'Ethical, fair trade, environmentally friendly coffee shops. I've been thinking about some sort of co-op aspect, so it's interesting what they're doing . . . Sorry, I can talk about this all day. Are you OK? Do you want another latte?'

Anna shook her head. 'I haven't finished this one yet. And Molly was right – you need to relax more.'

She'd guessed that Alfie worked hard from stuff the others had said, but she'd had no idea just how driven and ambitious he was. It made her feel a bit overwhelmed.

'I relaxed last night!' Alfie said, smiling, and Anna's stomach flipped at the memory of them dancing on the cobbles outside the house.

'Actually,' Alfie said. 'I'm going to see a film tonight. Do you want to come?'

Anna drank the last of her latte in the hope that the mug would hide the blush she knew was spreading across her face.

Chapter 27

Sean pushed out through the main doors and stood for a second at the top of the stone steps, rolling his shoulders back and stretching his neck. The sun was shining, it was actually properly warm and he thought about maybe walking down to the river, maybe even getting the ferry over to New Brighton for a walk on the beach. He could text Molly and see if she wanted to go too.

He turned to head down the steps and saw them, leaning against the railings. Well, Charlie was leaning back against the railings and the Viking was leaning against Charlie. Sean noticed that their hips were perfectly aligned – they were exactly the same height. He saw the Viking's hands holding the front of Charlie's jacket and then he saw their faces, eyes closed, mouths pressed together.

All of the sunshiney happiness he'd been feeling just seconds earlier drained right out of him and he suddenly felt so weary that it was all he could do not to sit right down on the step. There was no way he was walking down to the river now; he couldn't even face walking past Charlie and the Viking. Instead, he turned and walked back through the double doors into the foyer and headed down the corridor towards the canteen. He needed a coffee. And probably some cake.

It was ridiculous to feel like he'd lost something, he knew – he'd never even spoken to Charlie – but still . . . he'd been working up to it. And now he'd have to start from scratch with someone new.

'Shit!' He slammed into the side of someone who'd come out of one of the studios off the corridor. A phone skittered across the floor towards Sean and he bent down to pick it up.

'Sorry,' he said, holding it out. To Roman Lucas. He'd smacked into Roman Lucas and knocked his phone out of his hand. Sean smiled. He couldn't wait to tell Molly.

'My fault, I think,' Roman Lucas said. 'I was joining a main road from a side street. I should've indicated.'

Sean was still holding his phone. He laughed. 'I was basically driving with no headlights so I definitely have to share the blame.'

'You should never admit blame in the event of an accident,' Roman Lucas said.

He took his phone from Sean's hand and, as he did, brushed his thumb across the back of Sean's fingers. Sean remembered Roman's hand in the small of Alex's back in the canteen and felt something curl in his stomach. He looked at Roman Lucas's face to find he was looking right back at him. He definitely was objectively good-looking, Sean thought, Molly was right about that.

'I saw you in the canteen the other day, I think,' Roman said. 'You were with the girl with the bright red hair?'

'Molly, yeah,' Sean said. 'She's one of my housemates.'

'You were at my seminar too,' Roman said. 'What course are you on?'

'Musical Theatre,' Sean said. 'Your seminar was great. Really useful.'

'I'm glad,' Roman said. 'I've no fucking idea what I'm doing.'

Sean laughed. 'Well, it didn't show.'

Sean tried to think of something else to say, but the only things that came to mind sounded too fannish and he wasn't even a fan.

'So is your phone OK?' he asked, finally.

Roman glanced down at the phone in his hand. 'Seems fine. No harm done.'

'Good,' Sean said. 'Sorry again. I'd better . . .' He gestured vaguely towards the canteen.

'Yeah, me too,' Roman said. 'See you at the next seminar then.'

'See you then,' Sean said.

They both started walking in the same direction.

'Awkward,' Sean said after a few steps.

Roman laughed. 'You're not going to the canteen, are you?'

'I am, yeah,' Sean said.

The canteen was crowded and noisy. Some students seemed to be rehearsing something on one side of the room – they'd pushed tables together and a couple of people were sitting on them while others were sitting on the floor.

'Wow,' Roman said. 'I didn't realise people actually did that.'

'Yeah,' Sean said. 'It gets a bit Kids From Fame every now and then.'

Roman laughed again and Sean realised that every time he made Roman laugh, his heart did a lurchy thing in his chest.

'There's seats through there, I think,' he said, indicating the bar.

'Great,' Roman said and followed him through.

* * *

'Help!' Anna said, as soon as Molly opened her bedroom door.

'What's up?' Molly said. She was wearing Hogwarts pyjamas and had a piece of bread sticking out of her mouth.

'OK, don't freak out . . .' Anna started.

'Ooh!' Molly said, backing into her room and gesturing at Anna to follow her. 'This sounds promising!'

'I'm going out with Alfie tonight,' Anna said.

'He asked you out?!' Molly pulled the bread out of her mouth and dropped it on a plate on her bed. 'Go, Alfie!'

'No, I don't think so,' Anna said. 'He's going to see a film tonight and he asked if I wanted to go with him. It's not, like, a date.'

'It sounds like, "like, a date" to me,' Molly said. 'Where's the film though? If it's at FACT, it'll be some tedious documentary. He's always trying to get us to go and see them with him and no one will.'

'He didn't say,' Anna said. 'That'll be it though, I bet. Not a date.'

'Still a date,' Molly said. 'Definitely still a date. What's the problem? Need condoms?' She grinned.

'Oh, my God!' Anna said. 'No! I need something to wear. Do you think you've got anything I could borrow maybe?'

Molly looked Anna up and down. 'I don't think anything of mine would fit you. You're so tiny.'

Anna looked down at herself. She'd never thought of herself as tiny before, but she definitely didn't have Molly's boobs or bum.

'What time is it?' Molly said. 'Have you come straight from Bean?'

'Yeah,' Anna said. 'The shops'll be shut though, I think.'

'I know one,' Molly said. She stepped into a pair of ankle boots, grabbed a hoodie off the back of the chair in front of her dressing table and said, 'Come on.'

As they stepped out onto Wood Street, Nina was walking up towards them.

'Neen!' Molly said. 'Are you busy? We've hardly seen you since you got back from your hols.'

'Are you in pyjamas?' Nina asked, looking down at Molly's legs.

'Doesn't matter,' Molly said. She hooked her arm through Nina's. 'Come with us. Anna's got a hot date with Alfie and we need to get her an outfit.'

'You're going out with Alfie?' Nina asked Anna. 'Really?'

'It's not a hot date,' Anna said. 'We're just going to see a film.'

'Ugh, God, not one of his documentaries,' Nina said, allowing Molly to pull her along. 'Sorry. I mean, I'm sure it'll be a wonderful evening.' She grinned at Anna.

'Shut up, you,' Molly said. 'It will be a wonderful evening because Anna will fall asleep on his shoulder and he'll wake her with true love's kiss.'

'Yeah,' Nina said. 'That's definitely what'll happen.'

'Shit,' Molly said, as they turned the corner into a small cul-de-sac. 'We might be too late.' She let go of Nina's arm and ran a few steps to a low building with metal shutters halfway down the window. She ducked under and pushed the shutters back up. The sound of screaming metal made Anna wince.

'Anyone in?' Molly shouted through the letterbox.

The door opened and Anna heard someone say, 'Should've known it was you, gobshite.' Molly was pulled inside and Anna and Nina followed her in, ducking under the shutters.

Inside, the shop was like a grotto. Scarves and bags and hats hung from the ceiling and clothes rails took up almost all of the rest of the space. Molly was hugging the woman who then stepped back and introduced herself as Talia. She had shiny bobbed black hair, perfect winged eyeliner and one of those bull-ring nose piercings.

'What do you need?' she said.

'But . . . aren't you closed?' Anna asked.

'I will always open for Molly,' Talia said. 'I don't have a choice. She literally forces the door open.'

'You love me,' Molly said, bumping Talia with her hip.

'God knows I do,' Talia said, rolling her eyes.

'We need a dress,' Molly said. 'For Anna.'

Talia looked Anna up and down and said, 'Right. Stay there,' before disappearing into the clothes rails.

'I never really wear dresses,' Anna said.

'That's why you need a dress,' Molly said. 'It doesn't need to be fancy. Dresses can be casual. Don't worry, Talia knows what she's doing.'

'What do you think of this?' Nina said. She was holding up a black top that was almost sheer, but embroidered with multicoloured stars.

'Gorgeous,' Molly said. 'Try it on.'

'Is there a changing room?' Nina asked, holding the top out in front of her.

'There's only us here,' Molly said, reaching for Nina's jacket. 'Come on, get 'em off.'

'God, you're annoying,' Nina said, but she pulled off her jacket and handed it to Molly before pulling her work shirt off over her head and dropping it on the floor. Molly bent down and picked it up.

'Don't,' Nina said. 'It'll be sweaty.'

Molly draped it over the coat and Nina pushed one arm into the top. Anna noticed she had a bruise on her ribs and another on her shoulder.

'How did you do that?' Anna asked, pointing at the bruise on Nina's ribs. 'It looks sore.'

Nina pushed her other arm into the top. 'Ugh, work. Forever bumping into shit. I'm a right clumsy cow.' She pulled the shirt closed and said, 'What do you think?'

'Very Christopher Kane,' Talia said. 'It looks gorgeous on you. You have to have it.'

'How much is it?' Nina asked.

Talia waved her hand. 'Don't worry about that now. Go and find a mirror.'

While Nina was pushing through the clothes rails, Talia handed Anna three dresses.

'I wasn't sure how formal you wanted to go, so I grabbed a selection.'

Anna felt self-conscious getting undressed in front of Molly and Talia, but they immediately fell into conversation – Talia had been in her last year at the Academy when Molly had started – and so Anna pulled her T-shirt off and pulled the first dress on over her jeans. It was fitted and A-line and Anna liked it, but it was more of an evening dress – Anna thought, anyway. She took it off and Talia held her hand out for it without taking her eyes off Molly.

The next dress was a sort of loose shirt-dress, black and patterned with little red and yellow birds. Anna felt something leap in her stomach just looking at it and she couldn't get it on fast enough.

'That's the one,' Molly said.

'Definitely,' Talia agreed.

'Do you think so?' Anna asked, looking down at herself. She pulled at the neckline; it was a bit lower than she usually wore.

'If you don't buy it I'm buying it for you,' Molly said.

'Thank you,' Anna said, smiling. 'It's OK, I'll buy it.'

'Are you taking that too, darling?' Talia shouted to Nina.

Nina reappeared wearing a red *42nd Street* T-shirt. 'I kind of want this too . . .'

It turned out that one of the reasons Molly had taken them there was that Talia allowed her friends to pay for stuff in instalments and so Nina got both tops and Anna got the dress and they could both still afford to eat.

When they got back to the house, Alfie was in the kitchen, talking to Sean.

'Hey,' he said to Anna. 'You ready to go?'

'I was just going to get changed,' Anna said.

'You look fine like that,' Alfie said. 'And it starts soon.'

'Oh,' Anna said. She glanced at Molly who rolled her eyes and mouthed 'Boys!' at her.

'You still want to come?' Alfie said.

'Yes! Definitely!' Anna said.

'Great,' Alfie said. 'Let's go.'

Anna handed the bag with her dress in to Molly and followed Alfie out of the house.

The cinema didn't have normal cinema seating. Instead the small room had lines of two- and three-seater leather sofas.

Anna sat down at one end of a three-seater and Alfie dropped down at the other end. She tried to turn her body towards him without making it too obvious. She really didn't want to sit staring straight ahead, as if he wasn't there. Alfie turned almost totally towards her, his right foot propped on the knee of his left leg.

'You did really well today,' he said, smiling. 'At Bean.'

'I enjoyed it,' Anna said. 'Thanks again for—'

Alfie grinned. 'Honestly, you don't need to keep thanking me. It's good to know there's someone else I can call on when I need staff. Or when Molly doesn't turn up.'

Anna smiled. 'Well. OK. But I am grateful. You seem to really enjoy it.'

'I love it,' Alfie said. 'I've been thinking about suspended coffee and the co-op stuff. You know, after talking to that woman today?'

Anna nodded. The soup-kitchen woman.

'What's suspended coffee?' she asked.

'Oh, it's really cool,' Alfie said. 'A customer can pay for their own coffee and then for another that a homeless person can come in and ask for.'

'How would they know there was a coffee there for them?' Anna asked.

'We'd put a sign in the window explaining how it works. I talked to Malc, the owner, earlier. He's happy for us to do the suspended coffees, but he said we'd need investment if we wanted to open in the evenings. He suggested I should talk to some charities and maybe apply for a grant.' He shook his head. 'I don't know. I'd love to do it, but—'

'It sounds like a lot of work,' Anna said.

Alfie nodded. 'Yeah. But I'm supposed to be putting together a project for college and maybe it'll work for that. I don't know.'

The lights went down and the film started. It was indeed a documentary, a documentary about coffee and Ethiopian coffee farmers, and fair trade. When Anna had first seen what it was, she'd been worried that she might actually fall asleep, but it had turned out to be really interesting.

Even so, she'd been completely aware of Alfie throughout the entire film. They were sitting on a three-seater sofa, so they weren't close together, but once Anna crossed her legs and accidentally kicked Alfie's shoe and when she mouthed 'sorry' at him, he smiled back at her. But that was it. There was no tub of popcorn for their hands to touch in. There was no yawning as an excuse to put his arm around her. There was nothing even slightly romantic at all.

Anna hadn't really thought it was a date – she knew Alfie had dropped it into the conversation and he was probably just being nice, but she'd still half-wondered, half-hoped that he may have been interested in her. Even a bit. But no. Apparently not.

'Hot date?' Sean said, when Anna and Alfie got home and joined him on the terrace.

Anna blushed, but Alfie laughed and said, 'No, we've just been to see a film.'

'Oh, God,' Sean said to Anna. 'Not one of Alfie's fascinating documentaries. Are you OK?'

'It was good!' Anna said, smiling. 'How was your day?'

'Well, I'm glad you asked,' Sean said. 'I had coffee with Roman Lucas.'

'Wow!' Anna said. She would have much preferred to see one of Roman Lucas's films. There was a romantic thriller she'd read about that she kept meaning to get on DVD.

'I KNOW!' Sean grinned. 'I must admit, I wasn't that bothered when I heard he was coming to teach, but he's really nice. And I'm pretty damn sure he was flirting with me.'

Alfie laughed. 'You think everyone's flirting with you.'

'Well, they often are,' Sean said. 'But, no, definitely. I knocked his phone out of his hand and when I gave it back to him, he did this.' He picked up Anna's hand and ran his thumb across her knuckles. 'Flirting, no?'

Anna felt a flutter in her stomach and laughed at herself. 'Definitely flirting.'

'And then we went for coffee and he was really funny and encouraging and told me all these indiscreet stories about Hollywood. And he said we should have dinner.'

'Dinner?' Anna said. 'Wow. He's gorgeous.'

'I KNOW!' Sean said again.

'So that's it now?' Alfie asked. 'Charlie's out and Roman's in?'

'Charlie is definitely out,' Sean said. 'I saw him kissing his boyfriend outside college.'

'Shit,' Alfie said. 'Sorry.'

Sean shook himself. 'It's fine. I have traded up.'

'You can't go out with him, can you?' Alfie asked. 'If he's a lecturer, I mean.'

Sean rested his chin on his hand. 'I think it's a grey area. You know, cos he's just a guest lecturer.'

'I don't know . . .' Alfie said.

'I think it's fine,' Sean said. 'As long as no one finds out.'

Alfie burst out laughing. 'Yeah, that sounds like a plan.'

SPARKSLIFE: Zombied

by AnnaSparks 9,723 views
Published on 13 October

[Transcript of Anna's vlog]

So. Remember I was telling you about my housemates who are at the performing arts college? And they have this guest lecturer who's famous? Well, one of them is going out to dinner with him. He thinks he was flirting with him, but he thinks everyone is flirting with him, so I don't know. But how cool is that?

Anyway it made me think that I've never done that 'perfect dinner party' thing. So I was going to do it but then I couldn't choose five people. I know you can pick people dead or alive, but I got stressed out trying to pick alive people. So I thought I'd just pick dead people instead and make it a zombie apocalypse dinner party.

So then I started thinking about what you'd need at a zombie apocalypse dinner party and I got very distracted doing that. I mean, what do zombies eat? Is it just brains? Or do they only eat brains because they're easier to find than, say, pizza? If I made a really nice meal – a veggie curry or something – would they be thrilled or would they just, you know, eat my brain?

What if I did a Heston Blumenthal and made something that looked like brains. Maybe out of spaghetti or noodles or something. Would they eat that happily? And would they want pudding? What do zombies drink?

And I'm not sure about the conversation. Whenever I've seen zombies – granted only in films and on TV, I've never met a real one – they don't seem to be scintillating conversationalists. It's usually just a lot of groaning and some drooling. I'd need music to drown that out. So I started thinking about a zombie playlist. But again, would they want to listen to, like, morbid music or would they want cheering up? Should I be going with 'Happy' by Pharrell or something like 'Monster Mash'? (Maybe I could make monster mash to eat! But maybe they'd be offended to be called monsters.)

And what would we do after dinner? Party games? Pin the tail on the donkey, but with zombie body parts? Bobbing for apples and leaving their heads in the bowl? That one where you pass the orange between your necks? But they'd just be biting each other's necks instead. Do zombies even bite necks or is that just vampires?

I don't know.

I got quite stressed out thinking about it so decided not to bother.

Do you think maybe I need a holiday?

COMMENTS:

Sara Soprano: Awesome! How's the job hunt?

Daisy Locke: I don't think you can date a guest lecturer, can you? I mean, I know it's not you. But your friend?

Butterflyaway: This made me LOL so much. Can you check out my channel? It would mean a lot to me.

Lord Jim: U think ur funny.

Sara Soprano:
+ Lord Jim: Go away, troll.

Chapter 28

'Woah, you look hot!' Nina said, as Molly flitted around the living room looking for something. 'Where are you going? What've you lost?'

'Ooh, I know this one!' Sean said from the dining table. 'Is it . . . your virtue?'

'Not yet,' Molly said. 'Give me a couple of hours. Have you seen my bag? The little one with the baby cowboys on it?'

'No,' Sean said. 'But it sounds delightful.'

'Who are you going out with?' Nina asked. She was half lying on the sofa, where she seemed to be spending most of her time when she wasn't at work or with Jack. She was wearing her *42nd Street* T-shirt.

Molly rummaged through the plastic crate that served as magazine storage. 'A man I met at that gig Adam took me to.'

'He phoned?' Sean said. 'Took him long enough.'

Molly pulled a face at him. 'He's a busy man.'

'Way to play hard-to-get.'

'I thought about playing hard-to-get,' Molly said, 'but then I thought about getting him hard and . . .' She grinned. 'Where's my fucking bag?!'

'Isn't it more likely to be in that jumble sale nightmare you call a wardrobe?' Sean asked.

'Yeah,' Molly said. 'But I can't find it. I thought maybe I'd come in one night and just dropped it in here. I'll go and have a look.'

As she opened the living-room door, Anna appeared at the top of the stairs.

'You haven't seen a little white handbag with baby cowboys on it, have you?' Molly asked.

Anna frowned. 'Not that I remember, no.'

'Ooh!' Molly said. 'Have you got chips?'

Anna nodded, passing Molly and walking into the lounge. 'And fish. Perk of the job. One of the jobs.'

'Oh, thank God,' Nina said, climbing over the end of the sofa and crossing the room to the dining table. 'I'm starving.'

Molly chewed on her bottom lip. 'I'll just have a few chips. As a starter. Don't let me gorge myself.'

Anna put the paper-wrapped packages on the table and opened them, the smell of vinegar and batter filling the air.

'Where's Alfie?' Anna asked, sitting down and snapping the end of a piece of fish.

'Where d'you think?' Sean said.

'Work?' Anna said. 'God.'

'I don't know when he gets his uni work done,' Nina said.

'He does it during the night, I think,' Anna said.

'So when does he sleep?' Molly asked, blowing on the chip she was holding.

'He doesn't,' Sean said. 'I think he's bionic.'

'I can have a bit of fish, can't I?' Molly said. 'It's better if

I'm not too hungry so then I won't stuff myself and Michael will think I'm dainty and ladylike.'

'Good luck with that,' Sean said, snorting.

'Just this bit,' Molly said, shoving a piece of fish and batter into her mouth. 'And now I'm really going.' She stood up.

'Be good,' Sean said, as Molly left.

'Oh, don't worry,' Molly said. 'I'm going to be great.'

'How was work?' Nina asked Anna once Molly had gone.

'It was fine,' Anna said. 'It's pretty busy so it's not boring, it's just . . . I didn't expect to be working in a chippy, you know?'

'Has its benefits though,' Sean said, holding up a chip.

Anna smiled. 'Yeah. And the staff are nice and at least I'm doing something. It's just . . . Someone came in today and I thought it was a girl I was at school with and I thought . . . They all think I left and moved here for this fabulous theatre job and I really don't want them to know that I work in a fish and chip shop.'

'Just for now though,' Nina said. 'It's not for ever. And it's still a brilliant thing you're doing. You left home, you're making your own way, doing your own thing and all that.'

Anna nodded. 'I know. Thanks. It just doesn't feel like that when I'm burning my hands on the batter and people keep winking at me when they ask for a large sausage.'

Sean laughed so hard a bit of chip flew out of his mouth. 'Sorry,' he said. 'Gross. But, you know, olden but golden.'

'What about you?' Anna asked Nina. 'Are you planning to stay at the hotel?'

Sean blew out a breath and then pretended he'd been blowing on a chip.

Nina shook her head. 'I'm not planning to stay at the hotel for ever. But I'm not ready to leave yet either.'

'Where's Jack tonight?' Sean asked, poking about in the package for more batter.

Nina shrugged. 'Out with his mates, I think? We don't have to do everything together, you know.'

'No, you don't have to,' Sean said. 'But you do, don't you?'

Nina shook her head. 'Don't start.'

'I'm not starting anything,' Sean said. 'What are you doing now? You're planning to finish these chips and then crawl back down the sofa and watch *The Good Wife* or something?'

'Probably,' Nina said. 'I might have a bath.'

'Oh, I was going to have a bath,' Anna said. 'My hair smells of vinegar.'

'Bollocks to that,' Sean said. He pointed at Anna. 'You have a shower.' And then at Nina. 'And you go and get changed. And then we'll go and get a drink.'

Nina groaned. 'Sean, I'm tired.'

'We're all tired. But we're young and gorgeous and we need to get out and have fun. Even if it's only for, like, an hour. Come on. Live a little.'

'Sounds good,' Anna said, pushing the chips away so she wasn't tempted to eat any more.

'Just for an hour,' Nina said. 'OK?'

'Absolutely,' Sean said. 'Just an hour. Or two. Three at the most.'

'One hour,' Nina said, pushing her chair back and standing up. 'And not a minute more.'

'I'll set a reminder on my phone,' Sean said and rolled his eyes at Anna.

Chapter 29

Molly took a deep breath, straightened her dress, pulled her shoulders back and pushed open the glass door of the restaurant. To the left was a bar area – she glanced in but couldn't see Michael – and to the right was a reception desk. She turned and smiled at the man and woman standing there. The man had a tight smile, the woman was looking Molly up and down, slowly.

'I'm meeting a friend here,' Molly said.

The woman smirked.

'Perhaps you'd like to take a seat in the bar?' the man said.

Molly smiled a sarcastic 'thank you' and headed into the bar. She ordered a drink and perched on the edge of one of the large, uncomfortable, sofas. She wanted to look relaxed, but if she sat against the back of the sofa, her legs would be sticking straight out like a child's.

She drank her wine too quickly and looked around the bar. She knew Michael had chosen this place to impress her. Or to show her that he was rich and sophisticated, whatever. But she wished he could have picked somewhere about seventy-five per cent less snooty. Maybe when he arrived she could convince him they should go to Pizza Hut or something. She smiled at the idea of Michael in Pizza Hut and then heard him say, 'You look lovely.'

She looked up at him. 'You look fucking gorgeous.'

He laughed out loud and Molly wiggled forward on the seat before taking the hand he was holding out and letting him pull her up.

'These sofas are really uncomfortable,' she said.

'Thanks for coming,' Michael said. 'I wasn't sure you would.'

'Really? Why not?'

He shrugged. 'I thought perhaps you'd decide the boy at the pub was more you.'

Molly laughed. 'I don't know what's "me" yet.'

Michael smiled. 'I think our table's ready. Are you ready?'

Molly put her empty glass down on the pebble-shaped table in front of the sofa and let Michael guide her through to the restaurant, his hand in the small of her back, following the woman from the front desk. They were seated in a booth shaped almost like a clam shell and sheltered from the rest of the restaurant.

'Very discreet,' Molly said once the woman had left. 'Is this your first date place?'

Michael laughed. 'I don't have a first date place. It depends on the woman I'm dating. What's yours?'

Molly fiddled with the edge of the white cloth napkin folded in her place setting. 'I usually suggest coffee first, but I think we skipped past that step at the pub.'

She looked up at Michael from under her eyelashes and noticed the corner of his mouth quirk up.

'Then I'd usually suggest dinner, but somewhere more relaxed. Not somewhere like this. Not least cos I doubt I've ever gone out with someone who could afford somewhere like this.'

'I wanted to bring you somewhere you'd never normally go,' Michael said.

Molly laughed. 'Yeah, I'd never normally come here. And the woman at the front desk gave me a right look when I walked in.'

'Really?' Michael said, frowning.

Molly nodded. 'It's no big deal. You don't need to get her fired or have her killed or anything.'

Michael barked out a loud laugh. 'Who do you think I am?'

'I don't know,' Molly said, grinning. 'Who are you?'

Molly hadn't intended to order the most expensive things on the menu, but the things she wanted to try – the food she'd never eaten before and wasn't sure when she'd get a chance to eat again – turned out to be the most expensive.

Michael had said it was fine and Molly wondered what it would be like to not worry about it, to not even look at the prices, to know that when you put your card down to pay, the bill would be paid and no way would a waiter ever come back to the table looking slightly embarrassed and mumbling something about it being declined.

Michael had ordered the wine – something Molly had never heard of, so she assumed it probably cost more than the six pound-bottle she was used to. It tasted a lot better than the wine Molly was used to as well. Richer. Stronger. The first taste was almost unpleasant – sort of earthy – but then it became really easy to drink.

Molly asked Michael about his job – his company, as it turned out – but he said that was too boring and asked her what she did.

'I'm at performing arts college,' Molly said.

'Ah,' Michael said, smiling as he cut. 'That explains a lot.'

'Does it?' Molly said, pretend-affronted.

'It explains your confidence,' Michael said. 'You're very confident.'

'I've always been confident though,' Molly said. 'I wouldn't be there if I wasn't confident.' She stabbed at a prawn on her plate. 'Confident in my talent, at least.'

'It's interesting,' Michael said. 'It's not something I could ever imagine doing. I was painfully shy as a child.'

'You were not.'

Michael nodded. 'I was. I couldn't talk to anyone. I was one of those kids you see hiding behind their mother. I used to sort of cling to the back of her skirt. It drove her absolutely mad.' Michael smiled. 'By the time I got to high school, it was becoming a real problem. It made everything harder. I dreaded every day. And then one day I just decided to pretend to be confident. Even just a bit. I thought if I could do one thing each day with confidence then it would get easier and easier. And it did.'

'What was the first thing you did?' Molly asked. She'd put her fork down on her plate and was staring across the table at Michael.

'The first thing?' Michael said. He drank some wine. 'God. I don't know if I can remember.' He frowned.

Molly drank some wine. Stabbed a few more prawns. Buttered a piece of bread.

'The postman!' Michael said. 'I used to walk past him every morning on the way to school. He always said "Morning!" and I used to just . . .' Michael did a sort of embarrassed head dip. 'So I made myself say good morning back. It was basically a mumble the first time, but he . . .' Michael laughed, shaking his head. 'God, I'd totally forgotten this. He stopped dead and said, "He speaks!"'

Molly laughed.

He ran his hand back through his hair, still laughing. 'I can't believe I forgot that. I said good morning to him every day after that. I was almost shouting it a few weeks later.'

'I was never shy,' Molly said. 'My mum took me to a baby ballet class when I was only just walking and she couldn't get me out of there. I was up at the front, singing and twirling and shouting, "Look-a-me!" at everyone.'

Michael grinned. 'So you've always wanted to . . . Is it acting you're studying?'

Molly nodded. 'I take some dance classes too and we all have to do some singing, but it's mostly acting.'

'So what do you want to do when you graduate? TV, film, theatre?'

'I just want to work really,' Molly said.

Michael smiled. 'Come on.'

Molly grinned. 'Yeah, OK, I want to be hugely famous. I want to do a show on Broadway. I want to win an Oscar. That better?'

'Much,' Michael said.

They talked about their favourite films and shows and Molly mocked Michael for being one of those people who says they don't have a TV, but then just watches TV shows online instead.

They ordered dessert and coffee and Molly started thinking about what she was going to do after they – Michael – paid the bill. She'd told herself she wouldn't go home with him, but she really wanted to go home with him. When Michael went to the bathroom, Molly texted Nina 'Tell me not to go home with him' but she hadn't replied by the time Michael came back.

Over dessert they talked about school dinners and PE and exams and then they'd finished their coffee and Michael had given Molly the little wrapped Italian chocolate and paid the bill and then they were outside on the street and Molly felt nervous. She couldn't remember the last time she'd felt properly nervous on a date.

'How did you get here?' Michael asked as they walked along the side of the dock. Molly looked out at the lights reflecting in the water. It looked so pretty. Almost magical.

'Walked,' Molly said. 'It's not far.'

'Don't be silly,' Michael said. 'Get a cab.'

'I'm fine to walk, honestly,' Molly said.

Michael held her arm to help her over the cobbles.

'How are you getting home?' she asked him.

'Walking,' Michael said. 'I live there.' He pointed at a black, wedge-shaped building jutting out over the dock.

'Fuck off,' Molly said. 'Really?'

'During the week, yes. I've got a house as well. On the Wirral.'

'Right,' Molly said. She stopped and leaned against the carousel, which was covered over for the winter. 'Are you married?'

'Yes,' Michael said.

Molly nodded, feeling disappointment like a punch in the stomach. 'And now you're going to tell me that your wife doesn't understand you?'

'No,' Michael said. 'She understands me. She understands I have one life with her and another life here, in town.'

'And she's OK with that, is she?' Molly said.

'She accepts it, yes,' Michael said.

Molly shook her head. 'Maybe she can. I can't.'

Michael took a few steps towards her and said, 'I've had a really good time, Molly.'

Molly nodded. 'I did too. But you're married.'

Michael ducked his forehead against Molly's and she tipped her face up, almost involuntarily. His cheekbone slid against hers and she felt her breath catch in her chest. She bunched the canvas covering of the carousel in her hands behind her back.

One kiss. One kiss was OK. His wife was fine with it. One kiss and then she'd go home and never see him again.

Alfie lay back on his bed and stared up at the ceiling. He'd almost finished the outline for his project; he just wanted to find a few more references. He'd decided to make the Coffee Cafe idea his project and he felt good about the idea in general. He thought it could really work. He sat up and opened his laptop and stared at the screen. He thought about Ms Nguyen saying he should make sure to have a life and Molly and Anna telling him he needed to relax more. He closed the laptop again and headed out into the house to see who was around.

No one was around. The house was empty. Alfie went out on the terrace and picked up some bottles and a magazine someone had left out there, before collecting the various mugs that had been stashed all around the lounge. He took everything downstairs and loaded the dishwasher, before looking around the kitchen to see if anything else needed doing.

He was contemplating emptying the fridge to clean it – there was some sort of disgusting sludge in the bottom of the salad tray that made him wince every time he made a cup of tea – but then he stopped and said, aloud, 'What the hell are you doing?'

He slumped down on the sofa in the corner and then sat up again, pulling out a small white leather bag covered in pictures of little kids dressed as cowboys. Molly's. He took out his phone.

'Where are you?' he texted Molly.

His phone buzzed almost immediately with Molly's reply: 'Hot date!'

'Of course,' Alfie said out loud.

And then he texted Sean.

Chapter 30

'So this is nice, isn't it?' Sean said.

Anna and Nina laughed. The three of them were standing in the street outside the pub at the bottom of their road. They'd just been on their way in when everyone else had poured outside for some sort of fire alarm. And Sean had come distressingly close to stepping in a pile of vomit.

'We could walk down to Albert Dock, maybe?' Nina said.

Sean huffed. 'Too far. Especially if you don't want to be out long.'

'I don't know how far I can walk in these shoes,' Anna said, holding one foot out.

'They are gorgeous though,' Nina said. 'Totally worth it.'

Anna had bought them in one of the charity shops on Bold Street – they were like Dorothy's red shoes but gold and Anna was in love with them, but they definitely pinched a bit.

'Let's just go up to Marco's,' Sean said. 'We haven't been there for ages.'

'What's Marco's?' Anna asked.

'Little bar up near college,' Sean said, glancing at Nina.

Nina was biting on her bottom lip, her teeth making little white crescents against her dark pink lipstick.

'OK,' she said.

'Really?!' Sean said. 'God, I thought you'd say no way! Come on then!'

He grabbed both of the girls' arms and tugged them towards the cobbled street.

'Why did you think she'd say no?' Anna said. 'Nina?'

'We used to go there after college,' Nina said. 'Actually it was were I first got talking to Sean. He was trying to get people to do karaoke and he bugged the shit out of me until I agreed.'

'And she blew everyone away,' Sean said, dropping his arm around Nina's shoulders.

'Really?' Anna said.

'Yep. Nina has got A Voice.'

'But she doesn't like to talk about it,' Nina said. 'So shut up.'

'So after you did the karaoke you, what? Became friends?' Anna asked.

'And now Anna doesn't take any notice of me either,' Nina said.

'It's because you talked about yourself in the third person,' Sean said. 'No one takes any notice of that on principle. For a while we just said hello at college and stuff,' Sean told Anna.

'But then I fell out with the girl I was sharing a flat with and I was looking for another place to live and I got talking to Sean one day and he said there was a room in the house he lived in.'

'And the rest is housemate history!' Sean said. They stopped at the traffic lights on Berry Street.

'Talking of "housemate history",' Anna said. 'What happened with Harry? I've been wondering about him since I've got his room.'

Sean made a sort of strangled noise.

'Oh, it doesn't matter!' Anna said.

Sean laughed. 'No, it's OK. We were on the same course. Moved into Alfie's house and then he got a job and left. Left Liverpool, left the house, left me.'

'God,' Anna said.

'Right?' Sean said, grinning at her. 'I thought we were going to be like a gay musical theatre power couple, you know? That was the plan. But no. Turns out I was the broken-hearted first boyfriend he left behind. I'm over it now though. You know, mostly.'

They crossed the road and Nina said, 'We all used to go to Marco's a lot. Which is why we haven't been there for a while.'

'But I'm on a mission,' Sean said. 'To deal with my demons. Particularly any demon with curly hair and green eyes and dimples and a huge . . . voice.'

Nina groaned. 'It's OK for you. But I don't want to bump into people from college.'

They turned down a dark side street.

'You know how you were saying earlier about your friends knowing you work in a chippy?' Nina asked Anna. 'Well, I don't really want to see my college friends and know they all know I couldn't hack it.'

'That's not true,' Sean said.

'Except it is,' Nina argued. 'If I could've hacked it, I'd still be there, wouldn't I?'

'You're too hard on yourself,' Sean said. 'You had a bad time, yes. But you could totally go back. You know they'd have you.'

'Yeah,' Nina said. 'Maybe. Oh, look, we're here.'

Sean snorted and pulled open the plain black door. Anna would never have known it was a bar from the street, but inside it was dark and cosy and surprisingly busy.

'Are you OK?' she asked Nina.

Nina's eyes were wide, but she nodded and said, 'What do you want to drink?' with her mouth close to Anna's ear.

'These are on me,' Sean said. 'It was my idea. You go and grab a table.'

Anna followed Nina around a corner into an area with tables set into bare brick alcoves. They sat down and Anna kicked her shoes off under the table, stretching her toes out and feeling the bones pop and crack.

'How come you agreed to come here tonight?' Anna asked Nina. The music was loud, but not so loud that she had to shout.

Nina shrugged. 'It's been a while. And Sean was right – I've been spending too much time waiting around for Jack and not enough time with my friends. Or even doing stuff I like, you know?'

Anna nodded.

'And I miss this place. When I started at college and we started coming here . . . I just thought it was the most exciting thing. We always sat at the same table.' She swivelled on her chair and pointed to a big table in an alcove at the end of the bar. 'It felt like *Friends* or something. Like this was our place. I was doing exactly what I'd dreamed of doing and I had these great friends and it was all just . . .' She grinned.

Anna nodded again. 'That's kind of how I feel about the house.'

'I think . . .' Nina started, looking down at her hands on the table. 'It's just hard when something goes wrong. When you have all these expectations, you know? Well, you do know, don't you?'

Anna smiled. 'I do. But I also think we shouldn't let one thing going wrong be the end of everything. I've done that before. There was this thing at school . . . I had this one teacher who was really encouraging and he entered something I wrote into a competition. And . . . I don't know, I thought I was going to win. I mean, he thought I was going to win, he told me that. And then when I didn't win – didn't even come in the top three – I kind of thought, well, that's that then. No point trying again! But that's just stupid. I was fourteen! And you can always try again.'

Nina nodded. 'It's hard though.'

Anna smiled. 'Oh, yeah.'

Sean came back and put their drinks down on the table and then turned to Nina. 'Good to be back?'

'Yes, actually,' she said.

'And Alfie's texted,' Sean said. 'He's going to come and join us. It's a miracle!' He held his bottle up to Nina and Anna.

After a couple of lagers, Nina was less keen on going straight back home. She was surprised to find she was really enjoying herself. She'd also been pretending she was still at college. Imagining one of her old friends – one of the ones she'd lost touch with – coming over to say hello and Nina telling her all about the fantastic production she was in. Or that she was recording with someone amazing. Or that she was auditioning for the West End. Anything. Just something other than, 'I work as a maid in The Campbell, do you know it?'

It wasn't as if she hadn't thought about trying to go back to college. She thought about it a lot. She thought about it every time she turned left at the top of Bold Street towards the hotel, rather than heading straight up the hill to college. She thought about it every time she talked to her parents and one or the other asked her how it was going. She always made up detailed stories before phoning them, even though they generally seemed to be satisfied with 'great, thanks'. She thought about it every time she sang at work.

And she missed singing. Properly singing. Challenging herself and learning and feeling like she was developing and improving and really getting somewhere. She hadn't felt like that at all since she dropped out.

'Come on,' Sean said to Nina. 'I'll even go first, if you want.'

He stood up and Nina looked up at him. Why not? Why shouldn't she sing? She wanted to sing. She let him pull her to her feet. Sean pulled an exaggerated shocked face.

'Don't get too excited,' Nina said. 'I could still change my mind.'

Sean tugged Nina across the bar towards the karaoke machine.

'She's really good,' Alfie told Anna from the other side of the table.

Anna nodded. She watched Sean and Nina go and talk to a member of staff then stand waiting next to the bar. When the song playing over the PA finished, the screens around the bar flashed a karaoke logo and then Sean had a microphone and was singing 'Can't Take My Eyes Off You', leading everyone in the 'I love you, baby' bits and generally hamming it up, but he had a great voice – deeper and smoother than Anna would have expected. She'd love to hear him sing when he wasn't messing about.

When he finished, he handed the mic to Nina. Nina looked nervous and it made Anna feel nervous. She couldn't even imagine singing in a bar full of people. She reached for her drink. And then Nina started to sing and Anna just stared.

Nina looked completely different when she was singing, Anna thought. She was always pretty, but singing she looked beautiful. The way she moved, curling around the microphone stand, her body moving to the music . . . She looked more relaxed; older, sexier.

And her voice was beautiful – delicate and powerful at the same time.

'She's amazing,' Anna said. She looked at Alfie. He was looking back at her with an odd look on his face. A look that made her stomach twist with nerves.

'How come you decided to come out tonight?' she asked him, just for something to say.

'I realised I was stuck in a rut,' he said, smiling a little. 'I like routine; I'm not keen on change. But I realised tonight . . . I sometimes get too . . .' He held his hands up next to his eyes. 'Focussed. You know?'

Anna smiled. 'I can't really identify. But I'm glad you decided to come out anyway.'

'Me too,' Alfie said.

Nina felt almost dizzy with happiness. She'd sung again. In public. She didn't think she could do it, but she'd done it and it felt . . . it felt amazing. But she was bursting for a pee.

In the bathroom, she sat on the loo for slightly longer than she needed to – picturing herself back at college, trying again – and then told herself to get a grip. She was with her friends. She was having fun. She didn't need to worry about any of it tonight. She didn't need to worry at all.

When she came out of the loo, Jack was standing in the corridor that led back to the bar.

'Hey!' she said, grinning. 'What are you doing here?'

'I'm out with my mates,' Jack said. 'I told you that. What are you doing here?'

'Sean suggested a night out,' Nina said. 'We weren't going to stay long, but . . .' She shrugged. 'Where are you sitting? Come and sit with us?'

'Maybe,' Jack said. 'Just going for a piss.'

Nina reached up to kiss him, but he pushed past her. 'I'm bursting, here.'

'Oh, right, yeah. Sorry. See you in a bit.'

Jack was with Ali from the hotel, who Nina knew and liked, and another boy she'd never met before. Jack introduced him, but Nina missed his name. They all moved over to the big table – the one Nina thought of as the *Friends* table – and somehow Nina ended up on the bench seat between Ali and Sean, while Jack was across the table next to Anna.

Jack's friend went to get more drinks for everyone and Ali started telling Nina about something that had happened at work. Something about a customer losing something in one of the industrial bins and Janice, their boss, trying to get Ali to climb in and look for it, even though that was against health and safety.

She couldn't really hear him very well – at some point the music had been turned up – and she was wondering what Jack was talking to Anna about. His mouth was right up against her ear and Anna was frowning.

When Jack's friend came back with the drinks, Jack turned to talk to him and Sean started telling a story about how when he was a kid, his dad had caught him standing on his snooker table in the garage, pretending to be Robbie Williams and singing 'Angels'.

'He freaked out about the baize,' Sean said. 'And then he realised I was filming myself on his video camera and he really lost his shit.'

'He's all right now though, isn't he?' Anna said.

'I dunno,' Sean called back. 'He's in a bit of a bad way.'

'I meant about you being gay,' Anna said, leaning across the table. 'He's OK about that?'

'Oh, yeah!' Sean shouted. 'He's fine about that.'

Nina looked at Jack. He was looking at Anna's arse as she leaned over the table, she could tell he was. And then he looked straight at her and she felt her face flame. She picked up her lager and downed it.

'So Nina tells me you're a virgin,' Jack said, his mouth against Anna's ear.

Anna felt her breath go out of her. 'Um. Yeah, I am.'

'How's that happened then?'

Anna frowned and glanced across the table at Nina. 'It wasn't exactly a plan? I just . . . haven't met anyone I wanted to sleep with yet.'

Jack smiled, leaning forward and putting his lager on the table. 'That seems like a shame.'

Anna tipped her head back. Hair that had come loose from her ponytail was sticking to the back of her neck. She pulled the bobble out of her hair and slid it onto her wrist, before running both her hands through her hair.

'You look good with your hair down,' Jack said.

Anna pulled it back up into a ponytail and fasted the bobble on. She drank some of her lager and fiddled with the label on the bottle. She really had no idea what to say to Jack. Particularly since he'd asked about her virginity. And seemed to be flirting. Maybe. She wasn't good at recognising flirting; maybe he was just being interested.

'So have you any plans to do something about it?' Jack said.

'What?' Anna said. 'My—'

'Yeah.' He grinned. 'Your virginity.'

Anna shifted on the seat. 'No. I mean, I'm just going to wait until I meet someone.'

'It's good to do it with someone who knows what they're doing,' Jack said. 'The first time, I mean.'

Anna nodded. She'd peeled the label right off the bottle and rolled it up into a tight cylinder. She wanted to ask Jack to stop talking about it. To talk about something else. But she couldn't make herself do it. She thought about channelling AnnaSparks again, but the last time she'd done that Jack had called her 'sexy as fuck'. She wasn't taking that chance again.

Nina tried not to look at them. She could tell Jack was flirting with Anna and it made her feel sick. He was glancing over at

Nina every now and then, so she figured he was doing it for her benefit and she knew why. He must have seen her doing karaoke. She looked down at her hands on the table and when she looked up again, Anna was running her hands through her hair, sweaty strands stuck against the back of her neck. It made Nina want to slap her.

Ali had gone to the bar to get more drinks and Sean was reading the karaoke list, so Nina turned to Alfie. But Alfie was staring at Anna too, a muscle in his jaw jumping. For fuck's sake.

'Is he bothering you?' Alfie asked Anna quietly when Jack and then Nina went to the bar.

'No, no,' Anna said. 'It's fine. Thanks though.'

'You just looked a bit uncomfortable,' Alfie said.

Anna smiled at him. 'Did I? I think he was trying to make me uncomfortable, to be honest. He was asking me about being a virgin.' She'd thought she was OK to say it because she'd had a few beers, but she still felt her cheeks burn.

'Cheeky bastard,' Alfie said, glancing over at the bar. 'What's it got to do with him?'

'I think he was suggesting I might like to find someone who knows what they're doing and get it out of the way,' Anna said, staring at her hands, turning her beer bottle round and round.

'I bet,' Alfie said.

His voice sounded weird. Anna glanced up at him. He was looking down at her mouth. Anna looked down at his and wondered what it would be like to kiss him. She'd only need to lean forward a little bit and her lips would be on his. He knew nothing was going to happen with Molly, he'd said so, so why couldn't she just kiss him? It didn't have to mean anything. She could just do exactly what Jack had said – lose her virginity with someone who knew what they were doing. She assumed Alfie would know what he was doing. And even if he didn't, she'd like to lose it with someone nice, someone she liked, someone who wouldn't hurt her.

'Listen, I'm going to get going,' Sean said, sitting down next to Anna. She blinked at him. 'Or I'll end up staying out all night and I've got a seminar with Roman Lucas tomorrow. I need to get my beauty sleep.'

'I'm ready to go too,' Anna said.

Alfie stood up and they walked over to the table where Nina had sat down with Jack and Ali after coming back from the bar.

'We're off,' Sean said.

'OK,' Nina said, smiling. 'I'm going to stay, I think.'

Jack shook his head. 'This was meant to be a lads' night out. If these three are leaving, you can go with them.'

Nina frowned. 'But it's almost last orders anyway. I thought you could walk me home.'

'Nah,' Jack said, pulling his phone out of his pocket. 'We'll be going on somewhere else.'

'I could do that too,' Nina said.

Jack just shook his head.

'Right,' Nina said, standing up. 'See you at work in the morning then.'

SPARKSLIFE: Bullied

by AnnaSparks 9,116 views
Published on 19 October

[Transcript of Anna's vlog]

I don't think I've ever been bullied. I'm not sure. I think that I've always thought of bullies as behaving in a very specific way: making threats to hurt you or saying hurtful things. I never really thought that it can be more insidious than that. Or that it doesn't even need to be direct.

But then I went out with my housemates and one of them has this boyfriend and . . . I don't know. He said some stuff to me that made me uncomfortable – it's not the first time he's done that – and I think that's why he does it. He wants to make me uncomfortable. Is that bullying?

And then he wasn't very nice to her either. She sang karaoke for the first time in ages – she used to go to the performing arts college too, but something happened and she left, so it was a big deal for her to sing in public again, and he . . . I don't know, it seemed like it bothered him that she had. And that maybe he was messing with me to get to her? Is that bullying?

And it's funny, because this boy is incredibly good-looking and at first I was envious of her, but now I'm really not. And I feel like an idiot for thinking someone was nice or good just because of what they look like. If anyone should know that you shouldn't judge a book by its cover, it should be me. It seems to be a lesson that I need to keep learning.

COMMENTS:

Daisy Locke: That sounds like bullying to me, Anna. You should tell your friend to keep away from him and you should keep away from him too. Stay safe!

Mr Nice Guy: You girls are all the same. You say you want a nice guy, but you really all want bad boys. Good luck!

Melba Toast: How shallow are you? You thought he was nice because he was good-looking? You deserve everything you get.

Maria Rushton: Nothing like a vlog about bullying to bring out the bullies! Ignore the trolls above, Anna. I agree with Daisy – you should keep away from this dude and tell your friend too. Good luck (for reals).

Chapter 31

'Eh up, love!' Ted said, grinning at Anna over the counter.

She smiled weakly back. 'Morning.'

'Oh, aye? Bad head?' He laughed. 'I'll have a coffee and take one for yourself, eh?'

Anna made his cappuccino and tried not to think about how rough she felt. She hadn't been anywhere near as drunk as she had on the first night in the house, but she'd still drunk more than she should have and her stomach and head felt precarious.

From the look of Alfie, he wasn't feeling too great either. They'd walked to Bean together, but it was only a couple of minutes from the flat and since they'd opened up the coffee shop had been so busy they hadn't had a chance to talk. Once the pre-work rush was over, they both leaned back against the counter and Alfie said, 'I feel like shit.'

Anna laughed. 'Yeah. Last night wasn't our best idea ever, was it?'

'Nope,' Alfie said.

'I'm glad I went though,' Anna said.

And she was. Even though whenever she thought about Jack, she got a creepy feeling up the back of her neck. And when she remembered wanting to kiss Alfie . . . Anna stared at a pastry in the display case until her blush subsided. Jam. Icing sugar. Jam. Icing sugar.

'Have you had any luck with the Coffee Cafe idea?' she asked Alfie.

'Yes and no. I mentioned it to my dad yesterday. I thought he might know someone who might want to support it. I should've known better.'

Anna frowned. 'Why though? I thought he wanted you to learn business.'

'He wants me to learn his kind of business. He doesn't want me wasting my time with charity.'

'Right,' Anna said. 'What if you—'

She was interrupted by a customer coming up to order coffee and porridge. She got on with the porridge while Alfie made the coffee.

'What were you saying?' Alfie asked, once the customer had gone.

'I was thinking that if you put a business plan together, maybe? If you presented it to your dad like that? Then he'd see that you really have thought it out. He might see the value then?'

Alfie nodded. 'That's a good idea. I mean, there's still the issue that it's not for profit, that's his sticking point, but at least then he'd be able to see that I know what I'm doing.'

'Exactly,' Anna said.

'But I've talked to Malc about it and he thinks we should trial it anyway – just do a one-off evening, invite the local papers, show people the kind of thing we could do.'

'That sounds like a good idea,' Anna said. 'A lot of work for you though.'

'Yeah,' Alfie said. 'But I think it could be worth it. I'm doing it for my college project too, so it's kind of killing two birds, you know? And I was hoping you'd help?'

'Absolutely,' Anna said.

She reached for her cup of water on the counter just as Alfie reached out towards the till. Her hand brushed the back of his and she yanked it back, embarrassed.

'Sorry!'

Alfie smiled and shook his head. 'You're fine.'

'Remind me never to listen to Sean again,' she said. 'I'm a nervous wreck.'

Nina stripped the bed and dumped the bedding in her cart. She'd texted Jack when she got home the previous night, but he hadn't replied and he wasn't in work this morning. In fact, Janice had been really pissed off, so Nina was worried that if and when Jack did actually turn up, he might be out of a job. She smoothed a new mattress protector over the mattress and then lay down, curled on her side.

Nothing was turning out how she'd expected it to. She'd felt so great last night after singing, but then Jack had turned up and pissed all over it, flirting with Anna and then refusing to let Nina stay out to, what? Punish her? Punish her for singing? Why would he want to do that?

She remembered when she'd first met him, telling him about how hard she was finding college and how she'd thought about leaving and he'd encouraged that, hadn't he? She frowned, trying to remember. She couldn't remember him ever being encouraging, she mostly remembered him saying that if she was so unhappy there, she should just leave.

And then she had. She'd just left. But maybe she should have stayed.

She clambered up off the bed – the last thing she needed was to lose her job too and she was already behind since, between last night's beer and subsequent lack of sleep, she was working on about half power.

What if she'd stayed at college? What if she'd just pushed through feeling like she wasn't good enough? What if she'd just kept learning and improving? She took her phone out of her pocket and scrolled to her mum's number. What if she phoned her mum and told her exactly what had happened? Would she be horrified? Disappointed? Nina had always assumed that her parents would feel horribly let-down, but what if her mum understood and wanted to help?

She put her phone back in her pocket and carried on making the bed.

Molly waited for Sean for a while, but he didn't come out of college and he didn't reply to her texts, so eventually she left without him. She walked down the steps, through the car park and out through the ornate gates and there, on the other side of the road, was a black car with tinted windows. And leaning on the car was a tall, familiar and handsome man with silver hair.

'What's with the *Pretty Woman* bullshit?' Molly said, but her stomach was turning itself inside-out with excitement.

'I thought I'd come and sweep you off your feet,' Michael said.

Molly pulled a face. 'You're married. I told you, I'm not interested.'

Michael walked around the front of the car as Molly crossed the road and walked around the back.

'I know,' Michael said. 'And I respect that.' His eyes crinkled at the corners.

Molly rolled her eyes. 'Yeah, it looks like it.'

'I just wanted to take you out one more time,' Michael said. 'And then that's it. I'll never contact you again. If that's what you want.'

Molly glanced back at the Academy before opening the car door and looking inside. 'No flowers? No champagne?'

'I thought that would be too clichéd.' Michael said.

She stood up and looked at him over the top of the door. 'We're not just going back to your flat.'

'Absolutely not,' Michael said, a smile tugging at the corners of his mouth.

Molly thought about the two of them in the back of the car on the first night she'd met him. She had to press her thighs together at the memory. She wanted to go out with him. She wanted *him*. And just once more wouldn't hurt. He said his wife didn't mind. She rolled her eyes at herself. Of course he said that. She really should just shut the door and head home.

'Just this once,' she said instead.

Michael leaned across the top of the door and kissed her. And she'd forgotten what a fucking incredible kisser he was. She'd been out with boys who knew what they were doing kiss-wise before, of course, but Michael's kissing was another level. It wasn't just the confidence – although that helped – it was how she could feel that he wanted her. He'd come here to take her out again. And, yes, it was a bit wanky that he'd just turned up and hadn't called, but it was exciting too. Here he was, a grown man, with a flash car, waiting for her and kissing her and wanting to take her out. It wasn't some spotty boy groping her in a pub. She pressed against the car door and felt her fingers digging into the top of the frame.

'Shall we go?' Michael said, pulling back and smiling at her.

'Where?' Molly asked, reaching up to rub her thumb across his bottom lip.

'Where do you want to go?'

Molly tipped her head back and looked at the bright blue sky.

'Surprise me,' she said.

Roman Lucas shut the door and dragged the nearest exercise bike across in front of it. One-handed. Sean knew from experience that those things were heavy and took a moment to admire the bulge of muscle in Roman's bicep before looking around the rest of the room. It was set up like a small gym, with a treadmill at the far end and then a Pilates machine that looked like some sort of medieval torture device. Sean really hoped that wasn't why Roman had brought him in here. He'd only just finished that thought when Roman put his hands on Sean's shoulders and guided him back a few steps until he stopped with his shoulders against the mirror that covered the entire wall.

'I've wanted to do this since the first time I saw you,' Roman said. And then he kissed him.

Sean held on to Roman's upper arms, feeling the muscles he'd just been admiring, as Roman's tongue slid along Sean's bottom lip.

Sean had known, obviously, that this was why Roman had brought him to the workout room, that this was exactly what was going to happen, but he still couldn't quite believe it. Not just because Roman was so fucking hot, but because they were at college. And Roman was a guest lecturer. And a Hollywood film star. He really shouldn't be doing this. Neither of them should be doing this. But it was so long since Harry had left and although Sean had had a couple of one night stands, he wanted more, needed more. And this was more, wasn't it? For now, at least.

He tilted his hips up and ground against Roman and heard Roman groan against his mouth.

'What do you want to do?' Roman said, dropping his head down to run his tongue along Sean's collarbone.

'Whatever you want,' Sean said. He felt boneless, like he would just slide down the mirror onto the floor. He wanted to do whatever Roman wanted to do and he wanted to do it immediately.

'OK,' Roman said. 'I haven't got a lot of time.'

He started undoing Sean's jeans and Sean reached for Roman's belt. Once he'd popped the top two buttons of his fly, he slid his hand inside and groaned. Roman pressed his mouth to his again, Sean's head banging lightly against the mirror. He wanted to turn around so he could see them reflected, but his legs were too weak and Roman had pulled his jeans halfway down his thighs and pressed his palm flat against Sean's erection.

'Shit,' Sean said. 'I want—'

'I know,' Roman said. 'I do too.'

Chapter 32

'Where are we going?' Molly asked Michael.

He was wearing sunglasses. Expensive-looking sunglasses. They suited him, made him look younger. He glanced over at her and smiled and Molly felt her stomach curl slightly. He was so gorgeous. But she kind of wished she knew where they were going.

Michael turned off the dual carriageway they'd been on for a while and down a narrow road that seemed to be in the middle of a golf course.

'You'd better not be taking me to play golf,' Molly said.

Michael laughed. 'I am absolutely not taking you to play golf.'

'Where are you taking me then?'

'You'll see,' he said. 'I think you'll like it.'

At the end of the road they seemed to be in a housing estate, the streets winding between executive townhouses with expensive cars parked outside, but no one actually around. Molly thought about how she really didn't know anything about Michael at all and he could be bringing her there for all manner of nefarious reasons. And not sexy ones either.

'Are we nearly there?'

Michael smiled. 'God, you really are young, aren't you?'

'Shut up,' Molly said. 'I just want to know where we're going. And that you're not to stop at one of these houses, kill me and poke my parts down the drain.'

Michael glanced at her, a line between his eyebrows. 'I'm sorry. I didn't think. This must look a bit dodgy.'

'Little bit,' Molly said, shifting in her seat so her legs were closer to the gearstick and her back was against the car door.

'I can promise I'm not going to kill you,' Michael said.

'But you might poke my parts?' Molly said.

Michael laughed again and ran his hand quickly along her thigh – which is exactly what she'd had in mind when she'd moved – before putting it back on the gearstick. They were out of the housing estate now and driving along a tree-lined road that ran alongside a river.

'Is that the Mersey?' Molly asked.

'Of course,' Michael said.

'Don't "of course" me,' Molly said, laughing. 'I don't know where we are. I haven't been here before.'

'But you only live just over there,' Michael said.

'I know. I can see my house from here.' She sat up straighter in her seat. 'Actually we might be able to see your house from here, hey? Your flat, I mean.'

Molly slumped back in her seat. She didn't want to think about his house. Somewhere near here, presumably. Or not. Far enough away that he wouldn't see anyone he knew.

'Bit further along, I think.' He pulled the car around into a car park and stopped.

'What's this?' Molly asked.

'Eastham Woods,' Michael said, undoing his seatbelt. 'I used to come here as a kid. I came for a teddy bear's picnic once.'

Molly grinned. 'I can't imagine you having a teddy bear.'

Michael took off his sunglasses and Molly was struck by how beautiful his eyes were, dark with stupidly long eyelashes. 'I had two,' he said. 'Rupert was blue with a pink neckerchief, and Big Ted. He was a pyjama case, really.'

Molly stared at him, still grinning. 'Wow.'

'Have I killed it now?' Michael said. 'Are you never going to have sex with me again?'

'I might have sex with you now,' Molly said, lifting her right leg and dropping it into his lap. 'Tell me more about Rupert's neckerchief . . .'

Michael snorted and ran his hand along her leg. Molly leaned back against the door.

'After dinner,' Michael said.

'Spoilsport.' Molly sat up and pulled her leg back. She was about to open the door when Michael said, 'Wait.'

When she turned back, he leaned over to kiss her, his hand pushed into the back of her hair, cradling her head.

'Let's skip dinner,' Molly said, against his mouth.

'No, I've brought you here especially,' Michael said.

'We're not staying for dessert then,' Molly said.

'No,' Michael agreed. 'We can have that back at my flat.'

'That's very presumptuous of you,' Molly said.

'I'm quietly confident,' Michael said, pulling away and opening his car door.

Molly climbed out of the car and waited for Michael to come round to her side. He slid his hand down her arm and took her hand and she followed him through the car park towards a cafe set slightly back and with chairs and tables outside. They walked through a small building lit with fairy lights and decorated with mirrors, and then out into an outdoor cafe: mismatched chairs and tables set under multicoloured gazebos with jewel-coloured chandeliers and wrought-iron birdcages; an archway out to the park beyond had a disco ball hanging from it.

'Oh, this place is amazing!' Molly said.

'Last time we had dinner you said the restaurant wasn't very "you",' Michael told her, steering her through to a table with curly wrought-iron chairs and a stained-glass window leaning up against the hedge behind. 'I thought this place might be more you.'

Molly grinned as she looked around. It was all a bit haphazard and untidy and more than a bit eccentric – there was a small garden full of random garden gnomes and statues, kids' toys, fake flowers and shells.

'I love it,' Molly said.

SPARKSLIFE: Caffeinated

by AnnaSparks 10,995 views
Published on 16 October

[Transcript of Anna's vlog]

One of my housemates is launching a charity initiative tonight. It's so exciting because I was there when he had the original idea and now it's actually happening.

It's all come together really quickly because he's incredibly ambitious and works really hard, and pretty much everyone wants to support him – including me – but it's made me think about how I could be more proactive about getting my own things back on track.

Yes, I had a knock-back as soon as I moved to Liverpool and that was hard to deal with, but I don't need to let that be the whole story. I could take myself round to other theatres and introduce myself. I could do some voluntary work there to get my name known and to make sure I'm the first person they think of when a paid position comes up.

I meant to go back to the woman who offered me the job in the first place and then took it away [Cut to: shot of Anna pretending to weep] but I told myself that I'd made a fool of myself and it would be embarrassing to ask her for help. But everyone has to ask for help sometimes and there's no shame in it. Plus, she *told* me she would help me. But I went [shot changes to one from up above, with Anna looking up, all sad eyes] 'No, that's OK, I can make it on my own . . .'

Well, no one makes it on their own. Or maybe if they do it's because no one likes them. People need other people and that's fine. Other people often want to help. You just have to ask. And I'm going to ask.

COMMENTS:

Martha Brick: Good luck! This sounds exciting. It's hard when you get a knock-back, but it sounds like you need to get back on the horse.

Daisy Locke: What horse? ;) Hope your friend's thing goes really well and you find something perfect for you. Am sure you will. You work really hard.

Mr Nice Guy: Get off your arse. The world doesn't owe you a living.

Butterflyaway:
+ Mr Nice Guy: Charming! Good luck, Anna! xx

Chapter 33

As she stood in front of her wardrobe trying to decide what to wear, Anna's stomach was flipping with nerves, so she was sure Alfie must be terrified. He seemed pretty calm, but then he always seemed pretty calm. He was probably the most unflappable person Anna had ever met.

She pulled out her jeans and an old long-sleeved black V-neck top, but then saw the dress Molly had made her buy and decided to try it on again. She stripped down to her bra and knickers and dropped the dress over her head with her eyes closed. Only once she'd fastened the belt and pulled at the shoulders until she thought it was fitting properly did she open them. And Molly had been right – it really suited her. The V-neck was a bit low so she'd have to wear a vest top under it and she didn't really want to show her legs either, but she could wear tights . . . Apart from that it looked great. It made her look older and like she'd actually tried, rather than just put on the first thing she could find.

Once she'd added the tights and vest, she stepped into a pair of red ballet pumps that picked out the red of the birds on the dress and knocked on the door of Molly's room.

'Oh, wow!' Molly said, grinning. 'That looks *amazing*! I told you, didn't I?'

Anna felt slightly sheepish, but she couldn't stop smiling. 'I really like it,' she said.

Molly stepped back and looked Anna up and down. 'I'm not sure about the shoes though. Have you got any boots?'

Anna shook her head. The only boots she had were some knock-off Uggs that she wore around the house like slippers.

'What size are you?' Molly said, turning back into her bedroom.

Anna loitered at the door for a second, then followed her in. Molly's room was a complete tip, but it somehow seemed so totally Molly that Anna liked it.

'I'm a five,' Anna said.

'Ooh!' Molly said, pulling open her wardrobe doors and getting down on her hands and knees to rummage through the pile of crap at the bottom of the wardrobe. 'I bought some Docs that were too small for me. I bet they'd fit you.'

'I don't think Docs are very me,' Anna said, perching on the edge of Molly's bed.

'Bullshit,' Molly said, head still inside the wardrobe. 'Docs are for everyone. That's why they're a classic.'

'My mum . . .' Anna started to say and then stopped herself. She'd been about to say that her mum hated them, thought they were unfeminine. But Anna was eighteen. She'd left home. Why was she still worrying what her mum would think?

'Here!' Molly said, holding out a pair of dark-red lace up Doc Marten boots. They looked practically new.

'Have you even worn them?' Anna asked, kicking off

one of her ballet pumps and poking her foot inside one of the boots.

'I think I wore them once,' Molly said. 'I bought them in a sale and I knew they were probably too small, but I couldn't resist. I kind of hoped they'd stretch, but instead, well, let's just say there might be some of my DNA in there.'

Anna winced and then grinned. The boots fitted her perfectly.

'Here,' Molly said, crawling across the room and kneeling in front of Anna. 'I'll do them up for you.'

'I feel like Cinderella,' Anna said, looking down at Molly's pink hair.

Molly snorted. 'And you shall go to the ball. And by "ball" I mean Alfie's charity coffee evening. Still might meet Prince Charming though . . .'

Anna's cheeks flushed and she hoped Molly wouldn't look up and see, but of course she did.

'Still like him, eh?' Molly said.

'We're friends,' Anna said.

'I know you are. But that doesn't mean he doesn't make your nipples harden.'

'Oh, my God,' Anna said.

'Sorry.' Molly grinned. 'Totally just said that to see how red I could make you go. So you're really not going to say anything to him?'

'No,' Anna said. 'I mean . . . I don't think so.'

'Why not, again?' She'd finished lacing the second boot and stood up, looking down at Anna with her hands on her hips.

'Too complicated,' Anna said.

Molly shook her head. 'I don't get it. Life is short. If you like someone you should tell them. If you fancy someone, you should fuck them.'

'No matter what?' Anna said, frowning.

'No matter what,' Molly said. 'Stay while I get dressed? I'll only be a min.'

She turned and pulled her own dress over her head. She was wearing knickers but no bra. Anna looked down at her boots.

'Really though?' Anna asked without looking up. 'What if what you want might hurt someone else?'

'Well, obviously I don't mean do what you want and fuck the consequences,' Molly said. 'Although sometimes that's OK too. I mean . . .' She wriggled into a pair of jeans that seemed to be more rips than denim, looked at herself in the mirror and wriggled out of them again. 'I think people worry too much about what might happen, what could go wrong, you know? And I think—' She crossed the room and pulled open the middle drawer of her chest of drawers. 'I think sometimes you have to take a chance.'

She pulled on what looked to Anna like a slightly long, white T-shirt and then went back to her wardrobe for boots and a leather jacket.

'What's the worst that could happen if you told Alfie how you feel and he wasn't interested?'

Anna frowned as she watched Molly applying bright red lipstick in the mirror.

'I'm too humiliated to see him any more. I have to move out of here. My parents won't have me back. I end up on the streets.'

'Yeah,' Molly said, turning round and grinning a red-lipstick grin. 'But he's totally going to be interested, right?'

* * *

'Are you OK?' Anna asked Alfie.

He'd been opening and closing the cupboards behind the counter, checking and rechecking the machinery for five minutes. Anna had noticed his hands were shaking slightly too. So much for him being unflappable.

'Everything's fine,' Anna said, not for the first time. 'You're ready.'

Alfie stopped opening a box of sugar sachets and looked at her. 'You look fantastic.'

Anna blushed. 'Thank you.'

'Thank you for all your help with this,' Alfie said. 'I couldn't have done it without you and Sharda.'

Sharda was almost as nervous as Alfie. She was wiping over the tables for the second or third time.

'You totally could've,' Anna said. 'But I've enjoyed it. And it's going to be fine. Just relax.'

Alfie nodded and put the box of sugar back in the cupboard. 'Did I tell you a journalist's coming from the *Echo*?'

Anna nodded. He'd told her at least five times.

'And there's a blogger coming to interview me and take photos.'

He'd told her that too.

'And someone from *The Big Issue* said they might pop in too,' Sharda called from the other end of the room.

'What?' Alfie said, almost pushing past Anna to get to Sharda. 'You didn't tell me that!'

Anna carried on setting up the coffee machine so they'd be ready to serve as soon as the doors opened.

Chapter 34

Half an hour later, the cafe was crammed with people. Anna went through collecting cups and had to almost push her way through the crowds. At the front of the room, a local duo called Finch and the Moon were playing guitar and singing and everywhere else Anna looked, people were laughing and chatting and drinking and eating.

When Anna had told Tony what Alfie was doing, he'd offered to provide food for free. Anna waved at him now, standing behind a table of mini fish and chips in cones. While working in a fish and chip shop certainly wasn't her ideal job, she'd lucked out with Tony as a boss.

Alfie was sitting right at the back of the room, deep in conversation with a blogger – or maybe it was the journalist from *The Big Issue*, Anna wasn't sure.

'Hey!' Molly said, grabbing Anna's arm as she made her way back behind the counter. 'How cool is this!'

'I know,' Anna said, smiling. 'It's brilliant. So busy though! I had no idea.'

'Can I help?' Molly asked. 'Alfie probably wouldn't want me to since he thinks I'm a walking disaster as a barista, but—'

'No, thanks, it's fine,' Anna said. 'I think everything's under control.'

Molly laughed. 'Did Alfie warn you not to let me anywhere near anything?'

'Of course not!' Anna said. He'd just said if they could manage without Molly's help, that would probably be better.

'Are Nina and Jack here?' Anna asked Molly, as she wiped the counter over again.

Molly shook her head. 'Nope. No Sean either.'

'They are coming though, aren't they?'

'They said they were,' Molly said. 'Don't worry. It's still early. Lola's not here yet either and you know she wouldn't miss it.'

Anna was collecting cups and plates when a strange hush seemed to fall over the room. At first Anna thought Alfie was making a speech or something, but when she turned she saw exactly what had caused it: Sean had just walked in. With Roman Lucas.

'Holy shit,' Molly said, suddenly next to Anna. 'He didn't tell me he was bringing him.'

Sean looked slightly too bright-eyed and Anna could tell he was nervous. Roman Lucas looked utterly relaxed and ridiculously handsome. He was already smiling widely and shaking hands with everyone in his path.

Molly waved at Sean and Anna saw him touch Roman Lucas's arm and then he was crossing the room towards them.

'What the fuck, Sean?' Molly said, standing on tiptoes to kiss him hard on the mouth.

'Thanks,' Sean said, grabbing a paper napkin off the nearest table so he could wipe off Molly's lipstick. 'I thought it might be good press.'

The three of them turned to look at Roman Lucas. He was talking to someone Anna recognised but couldn't quite place. It was only when the other man laughed and Anna saw how many teeth he was missing that she realised it was Orville.

Roman Lucas, however, had all his teeth. Perfect white – probably whitened, and capped – Hollywood teeth. He must have sensed them watching because he glanced over, grinned, and winked at Sean.

'He said he was going to work the room,' Sean said.

'So what's the deal?' Molly asked. 'If you're not doing him, what's he doing here?'

'I mentioned it when we were talking after class and he said he wanted to come along. He does a lot of stuff for charity.'

'Oh, Christ,' Molly said.

'Have you seen Orville?' Alfie said, joining Anna behind the counter, where she was adding mini Eccles cakes to the coffee saucers. 'He looks fantastic!'

Anna nodded. Orville had told her earlier that he'd wanted to get dressed up and support Alfie, so he'd gone to the hostel and borrowed a suit from a friend who'd been given it for job interviews.

'There's all this support that I never knew about,' Anna said. 'It's fantastic.'

Alfie nodded. 'Yeah, there's a lot of people doing good stuff, but they can't help everyone.'

'This will help,' Anna said.

'I hope so.'

'It will. It's a fantastic thing you're doing.'

Alfie stopped opening the carton of milk he'd been fiddling with and turned and looked at Anna. Anna's stomach flipped like a fish and she forced herself to look back at him, even though it would have been so much easier to look away.

'Thank you,' Alfie said. 'Thanks for helping me set it up. Thanks for not laughing when I first told you about it. Thanks for being here tonight.'

Anna nodded. She didn't trust herself to speak. Either her voice would come out as an embarrassing squeak or she'd say something she'd regret or both. She thought about Molly telling her to tell Alfie how she felt, but when she looked at Alfie, his face so open and happy and proud, there was no way she could do it.

'Hey, Lola's here!' Alfie said.

'Oh . . . great,' Anna said. 'I just need to . . .' But Alfie had already gone to greet his sister, leaving Anna fiddling with the coffee machine, pointlessly.

She wiped the machine and then the counter again. And then she counted to ten and headed back out into the cafe. She wanted to approach Lola; she didn't want Lola coming to find her. She wanted to walk right up to her and tell her everything was fine, no regrets.

'Anna!' Lola shouted when Anna was still a few metres away. As Anna reached her, Lola threw her arms around her and squeezed. 'How are you?'

Anna felt all the nerves, all the disappointment, all the worry about seeing Lola again drain right out of her. She'd totally forgotten how much she liked Lola, how much fun she'd had working for her, how Lola had been the first – maybe the only – person to believe in Anna. To believe in the real Anna, not the Anna her parents and teachers and even her friends – her home friends – thought they knew. For a second, Anna was worried she might cry, but then she squeezed Lola back and said, 'I'm absolutely fantastic. Thanks.'

'So, that couldn't have gone much better,' Molly said.

Almost everyone had left – the guests, the journalists, the musicians, the photographers and bloggers. Only Sharda, Lola, and the housemates apart from Nina were still there. They'd all helped tidy the cafe and then flopped down on the sofas at the front of the room.

'Thank you,' Alfie said. 'I couldn't have done it without you lot.'

'You totally could,' Anna said. 'But it wouldn't have been as much fun.'

'And of course Sean brought a fucking Hollywood superstar,' Molly said.

'Yeah, that was pretty damn cool,' Alfie said. 'The journalist reckoned that might get us on the front of the paper instead of in the worthy society/charity events bit, so . . .' He pretended to tip an imaginary hat.

'Has anyone heard from Nina?' Alfie asked.

No one had.

'She'll be off somewhere shagging Jack,' Molly said.

'Not like her to just not turn up though,' Alfie said.

Molly shook her head. 'She forgets about everyone else when he clicks his fingers.'

'You don't like him?' Lola asked Molly.

Molly tipped her head back and stretched, and Anna watched her T-shirt ride up her thighs. She glanced at Alfie. He was watching too.

'I don't really know him that well,' Molly said. 'I just . . . I don't like the way she gets when she's around him, you know? I don't know. I've just never been one of those girls who dumps her friends when—'

She didn't even get to finish the sentence because Sean was laughing so hard. 'You totally are!'

'I'm not!' Molly said.

'Oh, please. When you first hooked up with Adam, I don't think I saw you for a fortnight.'

Molly laughed. 'Yeah, OK. But that was different.'

'How?!'

'I really, really fancied him.' She burst out laughing.

'And where are you going now?' Sean asked her. 'I've seen you checking your phone.'

'Shut up,' Molly said. 'You're in no position to talk, bringing Roman fucking Lucas as your date.'

'That was a totally selfless act,' Sean said. 'All about press for Alfie.'

'Yeah, right,' Molly said.

'Whatever your reasons, I'm very grateful,' Alfie said. 'But I think I'm going to have to sleep here. I can't get up.'

'Come on,' Sean said, standing and reaching out to pull Alfie to his feet. 'Let's get you home to bed.' He waggled his eyebrows suggestively and Alfie laughed.

They all stood up, but then just stood there, as if they didn't want to go; they didn't want the evening to end. Even though most of them were going back to the same house.

'It's been such a great night,' Anna said.

'I just hope Malc's pleased with it,' Alfie said. 'Then we might get to do more.'

'If it gets Bean on the front of the *Echo*, he can't not be pleased,' Sean said.

Alfie bumped him with his shoulder and Anna smiled and pushed past them to go and get her coat from the staff room next to the loos. She was still thinking about Alfie and Sean and Roman Lucas when she pushed the door open and saw Lola. And Sharda. And they were kissing. They stepped apart as soon as they realised Anna was there.

'Don't say anything to Alfie,' Lola said, one arm still around the other girl. 'Not yet.'

'I won't,' Anna said. 'Of course.'

'It's just . . .' Sharda leaned slightly against Lola and then looked back at Anna. 'It's pretty early days and we don't really know . . .'

'No,' Anna said, again. 'I won't say anything.'

'Because Sharda works with him and—'

Anna laughed. 'Don't worry, honestly. I won't say anything!'

'OK,' Lola said. 'Thanks. OK.'

Anna smiled at them. They both looked really happy. Slightly flushed and giddy. Anna reached up and lifted her coat and Alfie's coat off the hooks. 'I'll just get these and then, um, go.'

'No worries,' Lola said, smiling. 'Oh, hang on. Anna?'

Anna stopped at the door and turned back. 'Have you had any luck with theatre work?'

Anna shook her head. 'Not yet, no.'

'OK, give me a ring in a couple of weeks and there might be something. It's not much and it's not glamorous, but it's something.'

'I definitely will,' Anna said and left, pulling the door shut behind her.

Anna cleaned her teeth, took off her make-up and got into her pyjamas. She lay down and tried to sleep, but she was excited about how brilliantly the evening had gone and suddenly desperately thirsty and knew she wouldn't be able to sleep without getting a drink first. She tiptoed downstairs – the house was quiet – and into the kitchen. She got herself a glass of water and was just about to go back to bed when Alfie came in.

'I thought it was you,' he said, smiling. He was wearing pyjama bottoms and a white T-shirt and looked, as always, tired but gorgeous.

'Thirsty,' Anna said, holding up the glass of water.

'Me too,' he said.

Anna stood there awkwardly while Alfie got his own drink.

'It went so brilliantly tonight,' Anna said. 'I'm too excited to sleep.'

Alfie closed the fridge and grinned at her. 'Me too.'

They stared at each other and Anna felt the atmosphere change. Her stomach clenched with nerves and she wondered if she should say something, do something, but she just stood there.

'Anna,' Alfie said.

She felt her breath catch in her chest and then he was right in front of her. She hadn't even seen him move. He ducked his head down to hers and she tipped her face up and then they were kissing. She wasn't sure what to do with her hands, so she held on to his arms until she felt him press her back against the kitchen cupboards and she slid her arms around his waist and up his back.

'I wanted to do that before,' he said, against her mouth. He tasted like beer and toothpaste.

Anna shook her head. She didn't want to talk about it. About anything. She just wanted to kiss him again. She reached one hand up to the back of his neck and pulled his mouth down on hers.

A couple of minutes later, they moved across the room and flopped down on the sofa in the corner, Anna half on Alfie's lap. She felt his hand in her hair, pulling at her bobble and she reached up and pulled it out.

'You should wear your hair down more,' he said, kissing just under her ear. 'It suits you.'

'I will,' Anna said. She pushed him back against the cushions and moved her legs so she was almost straddling him, her hands on his chest. She felt his hands slide up under the back of her T-shirt and she shuddered against him, remembering she had nothing on underneath it.

'Is this . . . ?' Alfie said, his mouth sliding across her collarbone.

She nodded, dipping her head and rubbing her face against his, like a cat.

He turned his face back up and she pressed her lips to his again. She couldn't stop kissing him. She didn't want to stop kissing him ever. She hadn't kissed many boys before – a couple at school discos and a man on holiday who she thought was probably way too old to have been kissing her – and it had been OK, but nothing like this. This felt completely natural and completely right. Their mouths seemed to fit together and she just wanted to touch him.

Alfie laughed and swung her around so he was half on top of her. Anna could hear herself breathing. She wanted to ask Alfie if she could go back to his room. Or if he wanted to come up to her room. She wanted to carry on doing this, but she didn't really want to do it in the kitchen where anyone could walk in. She hooked one leg around his and he groaned against her neck.

'I need to . . .' Alfie started to say.

Anna bit gently at his bottom lip, curving her body up towards his.

'I need to get to bed,' Alfie said.

'OK,' Anna said. She slid her hands up under his T-shirt, feeling the muscles moving in his back.

'No,' Alfie said. 'I don't mean . . . I mean . . .' He lifted himself away from her and Anna felt suddenly cold.

'It's OK,' Anna said. 'I want to.'

'I'm sorry,' Alfie said. 'I don't think . . .'

He couldn't look at her, Anna realised. And she was holding onto his T-shirt. She let go. And he stood up.

'I'm really sorry,' he said. And left.

Chapter 35

'Is everything all right?' Anna asked Nina, who was sitting at the breakfast bar in the kitchen. 'You didn't make it to Alfie's launch?'

Just saying his name made Anna feel hot with embarrassment. She tried not to look at the sofa, tried not to picture the way she'd been straddling his lap there just a few hours before.

Nina didn't look up. 'Yeah. Sorry. Something came up.'

Anna wanted to ask what, but Nina clearly didn't want to talk about it and Anna wasn't in the best mood either, so she just got some milk out of the fridge and got on with making herself a cup of tea.

'Have you seen Molly?' Nina asked Anna after a couple of minutes.

Anna put the milk back in the fridge and shut the door. 'Yeah, she just popped out. She said she wouldn't be long.'

'OK,' Nina said, folding her arms and resting her head on them. 'Good.'

'Are you sure you're OK?' Anna asked. 'Do you want a cup of tea?'

'No. Thanks.' Nina tipped her head on one side. And then sat up again. 'Actually, yes. Can I have one, please?'

'No problem.' Anna filled the kettle and while she waited for it to boil, rinsed out all the mugs she'd collected from around the lounge.

'Do you have sugar?' Anna asked Nina, once the kettle had boiled. 'Sorry, I can't remember.'

'I don't usually,' Nina said. 'But can I have one now?'

'Course,' Anna said. She put a heaped spoonful in Nina's mug and put it down on the breakfast bar.

'Did you shag Jack?' Nina asked her.

Anna jerked back as if she'd been slapped. 'God! No! Why? Did he say—'

Nina shook her head. 'He didn't say anything. I haven't even spoken to him since that night in Marco's. I know he was flirting with you. He's not answering my texts. He hasn't been in work. I thought that was maybe . . . Fuck.'

Anna chewed on her lip. She didn't know how much she should tell Nina about what Jack had said. He hadn't done anything and that was more important, wasn't it? Flirting wasn't that big of a deal. She thought back to the vlog she'd recorded after that night and changed her mind.

'He was flirting. And he said some stuff to me that made me . . . uncomfortable.'

Nina looked at her and Anna noticed how pale she was, the dark smudges under her eyes.

'I mean,' Anna said, 'I don't have a lot of experience with boys, men. So maybe it's not that big a deal. I just . . . I didn't feel good about it.'

Nina nodded, picking up the tea and blowing on it. 'OK. That helps. Thanks.'

Anna wondered if she should say that she thought he'd done it to get back at Nina, but she didn't think that would be particularly helpful, so instead she drank some of her tea and fiddled with her phone for something to do. She was relieved when she heard a key in the door and then Molly came bursting into the kitchen with a Tesco's bag and a copy of *The Big Issue*, both of which she plonked down on the breakfast bar.

'Hey, Nina!' Molly said. 'You OK?'

And Nina burst into tears.

'It's only very faint though,' Molly said, looking at the line on the pregnancy test. 'I think you need to do another one to make sure.'

They were up in Nina's room. Anna hadn't been in it before and it was the complete opposite of Molly's. Where Molly's room was filled with her personality (and mess), Nina's room was more like a boutique hotel room – or what Anna imagined a boutique hotel room would be like, anyway. The walls were painted a soft dove grey, there was a blue-and-white patterned rug on the floor and fairy lights wound around a small, glossy, white bookshelf with an old-fashioned record player on the top. But there were no pictures on the wall and not a single thing out of place. Anna felt like she was messing it up just by sitting on the end of Nina's bed.

Nina was at the other end, leaning against the headboard, with Molly next to her, her arm around Nina's shoulders.

When she'd burst into tears in the kitchen, Molly had grabbed her and steered her up the stairs to her room, so quickly that Anna had been left in the kitchen, wondering what to do. Finally, she'd grabbed the two teas and followed them up.

She'd worried that Nina might ask her to leave, that maybe Nina didn't feel like she knew Anna well enough to share this with her, but when Anna knocked and then took in the tea, Nina had given her a watery smile and said, 'Sit down. I need all the help I can get with this one.'

'I think sometimes they can say you're pregnant when you're not,' Anna said. 'Especially if it's early?'

'I don't think that's a thing,' Molly said. 'It's the other way round – if it's too early you can get a negative when it should be positive. Did you follow the instructions exactly?' Molly asked Nina.

Nina shook her head. 'I don't know. Maybe not. I was kind of losing it a bit.'

'Maybe you should buy another one and try again?' Anna suggested.

She felt completely out of her depth. This felt real and scary and way too grown up. Anna felt ashamed that one of her first thoughts had been that this was something they needed to find an adult to deal with. And then she realised that she was an adult now. She was filing that one away to think about when she had more time.

'They're really fucking expensive,' Nina said.

'Don't be stupid,' Molly said. 'We can go and get another one right now.'

Nina shook her head. 'I know it's real. I feel different. I can't explain it.'

'Does Jack . . . ?' Molly said, gently.

'No,' Nina said. 'God, no. I haven't even seen him much. I will need to tell him though. Obviously.'

'Do you know when . . .' Anna started and then faltered, unsure of how to ask. '. . . it happened?' she finished.

'In Whitby,' Nina said. 'It must've been. We haven't had sex since then.'

Anna noticed Molly's eyebrows quirk up and assumed that must be unusual.

'I think I did something to piss him off,' Nina said. 'He was great when we were there, and his mum was amazing, but then since we've been back . . . I don't know.'

'What are you going to do?' Anna asked Nina.

'I'm going to go and see him,' Nina said. 'It's worse not knowing what's going on.' She rubbed her face with both hands. 'I think.'

'Does he ever . . . ?' Molly started and then glanced at Anna. 'He doesn't ever . . . hurt you. Does he?'

Nina shook her head. 'No. I mean, sometimes he's a bit rough. And he likes –' she glanced at Anna – 'quite rough sex. But, no. What made you ask that?'

'The bruises you had when we were in Talia's,' Molly said. 'I just wanted to make sure you were OK.'

'Oh,' Nina said. 'Yeah. I didn't actually get them at work, they were from Jack. Well, I got them from Jack at work. But, yeah, they were a sex thing.'

'I thought you hadn't had sex since Whitby,' Anna said.

'We haven't had proper sex,' Nina said. 'We do other stuff at work sometimes.'

'Right,' Anna said.

'But you're OK?' Molly asked. 'Do you want us to come with you when you go and see him?'

'No,' Nina said. 'Thanks, but no. There's no need. It's fine.'

SPARKSLIFE: Scared

by AnnaSparks 10,481 views
23 November

[Transcript of Anna's vlog]

Remember when I talked about bullying and how I thought my housemate's boyfriend was a bully? Well, she hasn't heard from him for a while. They went away together, when they got back he went a bit cold and now he's basically disappeared. And she's just found out she's pregnant.

I don't know what she's going to do, but it just seems so scary to me that she could get pregnant so easily, you know? It feels like it's such a big, life-changing thing that you should have to fill out a contract or get signed permission or something. It doesn't feel like it should be something that can just happen to you.

And I've never really known anyone get pregnant before. Not my age, anyway. There were some girls at school, but I didn't know them well. I just knew that they were off for a bit and then they'd come to meet their friends and they'd have a pram with them. I can't imagine it.

So now I'm trying to think of the best ways I can support her, whether she decides to have the baby or not, and that just seems like such a scary thing. If anyone's got any advice, I'd love to hear it. But no judgement or abuse – I don't say this often, but I will block you.

COMMENTS:

Martha Brick: Oh, your poor friend, that's so hard. I hope it's been a misunderstanding with her boyfriend and he turns out to be supportive, but she's lucky to have a friend like you.

[Comment deleted]

Daisy Locke: You sound like a good friend. Better than your friend deserves.

Martha Brick:
+ Daisy Locke: How would you even know that?! Anna said no judgement, so maybe back off, OK?

[Comment deleted]

Chapter 36

Jack's flat was in Albert Dock. Nina had got the address from work, sneaking into Janice's office when she knew she was busy elsewhere. Nina tried to remember what Jack had ever said about where he lived and she couldn't think of any details, but he'd certainly always given her the impression it was a bit of a shithole. That was why she never went to his place, why he always went home with her. But she was standing looking up at the red-brick building and it was anything but a shithole.

His flat was on the top floor and in the lift she rehearsed what she was going to say. She assumed he'd probably be pissed off with her for coming to the flat, but he hadn't been at work and he wasn't returning her messages and she needed to talk to him. So what else could she do?

Her stomach churned with nerves as she waited for the door of the flat to open. She hoped Jack was in on his own. She didn't know what she'd do if Ali was there, or the guy she didn't know, the one who'd been at Marco's.

The door opened and Jack stood and stared at her.

'What are you doing here?'

Nina shook her head. She didn't want to tell him. She didn't want to have this conversation. She wanted to go home. She wanted to sit on the sofa with Anna and Molly and cry while they told her she was better off without Jack and that they'd support her with whatever she wanted to do.

'I need to talk to you,' Nina said. 'Can I come in?'

Jack shrugged and stepped back to let her in the flat. It was huge and bright with wooden floors, bare brick walls and an enormous window overlooking the dock.

'Wow,' Nina said.

'It's my dad's,' Jack said from behind her.

'I thought . . .' Nina said. 'You never have a good word to say about your dad. I didn't know you were even in touch with him.'

Jack shrugged. 'He's an arsehole. But he's a rich arsehole so, you know . . .'

Nina stared at Jack. Who even was he?

He stared back. 'What's up?' he said eventually.

Nina frowned. 'You're always skint . . . This just doesn't—'

'This is my dad's place,' Jack said again. 'It doesn't mean I don't have to work.'

Nina nodded. It didn't. But it did help her understand why he was never that bothered about his job. He was coming home to this no matter what.

'You've not been at work,' she said.

'Is that why you're here?' Jack said. 'To find out why I haven't been at work?'

'No. But . . . I haven't heard from you. Since Whitby, you—'

Jack ran one hand back through his hair. 'I knew that was a mistake.'

'What?'

'Taking you to Whitby with me.'

'It's nothing to do with that,' Nina said.

'I don't . . . I'm not interested in a girlfriend. We've had fun, but—'

'I'm late,' Nina said, the words coming out broken in the middle as they caught in her throat.

'For what?' Jack said, which is exactly what Nina had thought Jack would say when she'd rehearsed this in her head and exactly why she'd intended to say 'my period's late' but then she'd forgotten.

'My period,' she said. Her hands were shaking. Her legs were trembling. She wanted to sit down, but Jack hadn't offered and he was still standing.

'Your what?' Jack said.

She didn't say anything, since she knew he knew exactly what she'd said. She could see a little muscle flickering in his jaw.

'When?' he said. 'Whitby?'

'I think so.'

He nodded. 'But we've used condoms.'

'Yeah, I don't know. Maybe one came off or something, I don't know.'

'Wouldn't you know if it came off?'

'Probably not, no. Cos you usually take it off and—'

'Are you saying this is my fault?'

'No! I just . . . You didn't ever notice if—'

'I didn't want to use them in the first place. I wanted you to go on the Pill.' He stood up and walked towards the door then turned back to Nina. 'You're getting an abortion, right?'

'I . . . I haven't really thought that far yet. I mean—'

'I'm telling you. You are. I'm not having a kid.'

Nina stood up. 'That's not your decision. I just wanted you to know in case . . .' She crossed the room towards him, but he was heading towards her. She actually saw his arm moving and thought for a second he was going to pull her into a hug but then his fist hit her under her eye and she staggered backwards. She couldn't believe the pain; it felt like her eyeball was receding through her head. She was actually seeing stars. She'd never known that was literally true, but there were little bursts of light in the blackness.

She dropped onto the floor, still holding her face. She was scared to look at her hands in case she was bleeding. She felt like something was broken. Her cheekbone maybe. Or her eye socket. She needed to get up and check, but when she tried to stand her legs collapsed under her. She shuffled across the carpet as far as the sofa and leaned back against it, her hands still over her face. She thought maybe her nose was bleeding so she tipped her head back but that made the pressure in her face much worse, so she leaned forward again and rested her forehead on her knees. She could feel the tears running down her face now. They were hot.

'Fuck,' Jack said. He crouched down next to her. 'Neen, I—'

'Get away from me,' Nina said. She used the sofa to clamber up from the floor and held her hands out in front of her. Jack looked scared and she was glad.

'Sorry,' he said. 'I didn't mean to do that. You just . . . It was just a shock, you know?'

'No,' Nina said, shaking her head. 'I don't know. And I don't know what I've been doing with you all this time. I must've been out of my fucking mind.'

She picked up her bag – she hadn't even realised she'd dropped it – and walked out of the flat. Jack didn't follow her and she was glad.

Sean needed a coffee. He was tired and struggling to concentrate and he needed a coffee. He definitely wasn't looking for Roman Lucas.

At first glance he thought the canteen was completely empty, but then he saw Charlie, sitting at the end of one of the bench seats right next to the door. Sean's instinct was to pretend he hadn't seen him, but then Charlie looked up, smiled and said, 'Hey.'

'Hey,' Sean said.

'You OK?' Charlie said, closing the book on the table in front of him.

'Yeah,' Sean said. 'Just looking for someone. But he's . . .' He glanced around the canteen pointlessly. '. . . not here.'

'Nope,' Charlie said. 'Just me. Do you want to sit down?'

Sean smiled. 'You really don't want to work, do you?'

Charlie laughed. 'I really don't. Have you done your essay?'

'Pretty much,' Sean said, pulling out the chair opposite Charlie and sitting down. 'It's about Beyoncé so it wasn't actually that bad.'

Charlie shook his head. 'That's genius. I should have chosen something I'd enjoy writing about. Instead I'm stuck with—' He shook his head. 'Nope, I don't even want to talk about it. I'm just going to ignore it and hope it writes itself.'

Sean peeled back the lid of his coffee and watched the steam rise into the air. 'Your boyfriend can't help you with it?' he said, without looking up.

Charlie laughed again. He had a nice laugh, Sean thought, low and sexy.

'Smooth,' Charlie said.

Sean glanced up, picking up his coffee to hide his grin. 'That's me.'

'We split up.'

Sean looked up properly then. 'Ah shit. Sorry.'

'Nah, it's OK. It wasn't serious. And we didn't have much in common really. It was mainly that we were both here. And both gay.'

'And both hot,' Sean said before he could stop himself.

Charlie laughed. 'How about you? Seeing anyone?'

Sean looked at the door. 'No. I mean, I guess I kind of was, but . . . no.'

'That sounds complicated.'

Sean winced. 'It was kind of a rebound thing. An inappropriate rebound thing. I got my heart broken a bit last year and . . .' He shook his head. 'And I can't make myself shut up when I'm nervous.'

'You're nervous?' Charlie said. 'Why are you nervous?'

Sean drank some coffee, took a deep breath and said, 'I've had a crush on you for ages.'

Charlie smiled. 'Really?'

Sean peered at him over the top of his cardboard cup. 'You knew?'

Charlie grinned. 'I suspected.'

'Seriously? I thought I was very subtle.'

'Oh, you were,' Charlie said. 'Until that day you stared at me in the canteen for about half an hour then followed me to work. And bought a . . . Furby, was it?'

'Shit. You knew about that?'

'You should never consider becoming a spy. Or a ninja.'

Sean nodded. 'Good to know. And I still need to get a refund on that Furby. It cost a fucking fortune.'

'I can make it worth your while,' Charlie said. 'Want to go and get a coffee?'

'Oh, yeah?' Sean said.

'What was it, sixty quid?'

'More, I think,' Sean said, smiling. 'About a grand.'

'In that case we'd better get dinner,' Charlie said.

'Now?' Sean asked.

Charlie laughed. 'I mean, it's a bit early, but I think we can make it work.'

As they stood up to leave, Sean's phone rang. Sean was about to turn it off, but it was his Aunty Jan.

'Sorry, I need to get this,' he said.

Charlie held one hand up as if to say 'no problem' and Sean smiled at him. He couldn't believe he was actually about to go on a date with Charlie.

As soon as he'd taken this call.

Nina's nose wasn't bleeding and nothing was broken, she didn't think. She just had a hell of a bruise under her eye. She stared at herself in the mirror in the bathroom at home. She couldn't believe it had happened. Couldn't believe Jack had actually hit her. He'd always had that bad-boy thing going on. She'd always liked that she never really knew where she stood with him, could never take him for granted. She'd actually found it sexy. Friends who had reliable, safe boyfriends were boring, she thought – there was plenty of time for safe and reliable, but surely in your teens you wanted excitement. But she hadn't wanted this. Nothing like this.

She splashed cold water on her face again. For some reason she thought that would make the bruising go down quicker, because that was the other thing: she looked like a girl who'd been hit in the face. There was no way she could get away with 'I walked into a door' or anything like that. She just looked like she'd been punched. She was both repulsed and fascinated by it. She'd never seen her face looking like this.

She walked her fingers over the bruise and saw her reflection wince. Then she pulled her jeans down and sat on the loo. And saw that she'd got her period.

Chapter 37

'Pardon?' Anna said into her mobile. She'd heard what the woman on the other end had said, but she hadn't understood it.

'I said,' she repeated. 'Would you like to talk to me about Sean Hart and Roman Lucas?'

'I don't . . .' Anna started and then stopped. She looked back over her shoulder into the living room, relieved she was out on the terrace, relieved she was on her own. 'I don't know what you mean.'

The woman laughed. 'It's nothing to worry about. I just want a bit of background. For the article.'

'What article?' Anna said. She tried to think if Sean had mentioned an article, but she couldn't think of anything. He certainly hadn't told Anna to expect a phone call.

'The article I'm writing about Roman Lucas,' the woman said. She'd started to sound slightly exasperated, as if she was tired of explaining it to Anna. But Anna still couldn't work out what she wanted or why she'd phoned her.

'Where did you get my number?' Anna said.

'Would it be easier for us to meet?' the woman said, ignoring the question. 'I could be with you in about ten minutes. I'm only at The Campbell.'

'I'm sorry,' Anna said. 'I just don't understand why you want to talk to me. I don't know anything about the article. I barely even met Roman Lucas.'

'You met him at Bean, is that right? At the launch of Coffee Cafe night before last?'

Anna opened and closed her mouth. 'Yes. But only for a minute.'

'And Sean Hart is one of your housemates, yes?'

'Yes,' Anna said. 'But—'

'And you've talked about Sean Hart and Roman Lucas on your vlog. Vlog. That's how you pronounce it, yes?'

Anna felt like she'd been punched. She actually curled over slightly. She couldn't catch her breath. Her vlog.

'You said, um, let me just find the transcript . . . Right, here we are.' She started reading and she actually changed her voice a bit, made herself sound younger and excited. '"So. Remember I was telling you about my housemates who are at the performing arts college? And they have this guest lecturer who's famous? Well,one of them is going out to dinner with him. He thinks he was flirting with him, but he thinks everyone is flirting with him, so I don't know. But how cool is that?" Remember that?'

'Yes,' Anna said. She wondered if she should have hung up already. She probably shouldn't have started talking to this woman in the first place. But maybe now she should find out exactly what she had planned.

'How did you even find my vlog?' Anna said. 'How do you know I was talking about Roman Lucas?'

The woman laughed. 'I have a teenage daughter who is obsessed with vloggers. She was telling me what you'd said on yours. You talked about moving to Liverpool, the performing arts school . . . You really should be more careful with the identifying details. And then Sean Hart turned up at Bean with Roman Lucas and it was on the front of the *Echo*. It really wasn't hard.'

Anna closed her eyes. She couldn't believe this was happening.

'So are you ready to come and meet me now?' the woman said.

'I don't think so,' Anna said. 'What was your name? Where are you calling from?'

The woman laughed. 'My name's Maria Caldwell. And I'm freelance.'

Anna stared at a spot of pigeon shit on the floor of the terrace. 'So you're not writing this for a paper?'

'Oh, yeah, it's for a paper, but I don't know which one yet. Listen, I know you're worried this is going to be a stitch-up or something, but I promise you it's not. I just want a bit of background to fill the story out properly.'

'And what is the story?' Anna said.

'It's about how Roman Lucas does exactly what you said in your vlog. Takes people under his wing. Mentors them. It's honestly nothing to worry about. I don't even need to speak to you, of course; I can just quote your vlog, I just thought you'd prefer to—'

'Can you do that?' Anna asked. 'Can you quote me without my permission?'

'It's in the public domain,' the woman said.

'I think I need to talk to Sean first,' Anna said.

'Of course. You do that and then call me. You've got my number.'

'OK,' Anna said. Her hands were shaking.

'Tell your friend Sean he's not the first,' Maria Park said.

'What?' Anna said. She looked up at the sky. It was almost entirely blue, just one cloud lazily drifting past.

'Tell him he's not the first and he won't be the last.'

SPARKSLIFE: Fucked

by AnnaSparks 10,236 views
Published on 25 November

[Transcript of Anna's vlog]

[Anna isn't on camera; instead the camera is pointing down at the street from Anna's bedroom window.]

I'm sorry. I don't usually swear in these vlogs, I just . . . Do you know when you feel good about everything and happy with the way things are going and then it all just falls apart? I did something that may have ruined everything. And I feel like shit.

[Comments are closed]

Chapter 38

Alfie counted his breath as he waited for his dad to open the door. In, two, three; out, two, three. He was nervous, which was ridiculous. It was his dad. It wasn't a business meeting, it wasn't a job interview, he just wanted to ask his dad's advice about something.

He shifted the binder under his arm. He had all the information, everything his dad could possibly need to know. And it all made sense. It was a good business plan. Malc had read it and had been impressed. He'd told Alfie he'd invest himself if he could. The launch had been on the front page of the *Liverpool Echo*. His dad had to see the value of that, didn't he? He had to.

And it's not as if he even wanted his dad to invest; he just wanted him to point him in the right direction. That wasn't too much to ask, was it? Of course it was all academic if he wasn't even going to open the door.

Alfie knocked again. He heard his dad's voice and then he heard a woman's voice. Laughing. It wasn't his mum. He knew it wasn't his mum because he'd spoken to her on the phone before he came over. It hadn't even occurred to him that his dad would have a woman at the flat. It should have done, but it hadn't.

He had to leave. He had to leave before his dad opened the door. But he couldn't seem to make his feet move. He wanted his dad to know he knew. That he wasn't quite as clever as he thought he was. That even if his mum knew and let him get away with it, Alfie wasn't going to let him get away with it.

So when his dad opened the door, his face going slack at the sight of Alfie, Alfie pushed straight past him and walked into the flat.

And saw the woman. But it wasn't the blonde woman from the car.

It was Molly.

'What's wrong?' she said. She looked young. And scared. 'How did you know where to find me?'

Alfie felt all the fury go out of him. He wanted to drop on the floor, hug his knees to his chest and rock. He wanted to go home, crawl into bed, pull the duvet over his head and stay there. Maybe for ever.

'You know each other?' his dad said, frowning.

Alfie saw the look of confusion on Molly's face as she looked from him to his dad and back again.

'Alfie?' his dad said.

'Don't tell me it's not what it looks like,' Alfie said. 'I know what it is. I know exactly what it fucking is.'

'What's going on?' Molly said. 'How do you two know each other?'

'Alfie's my son,' Michael said.

'Fuck,' Molly said. 'Oh, my God. Fuck!' She almost ran out of the room, towards what Alfie assumed was the bedroom.

'I can't believe you're fucking my friends now,' Alfie said.

He hadn't realised he'd done it, but at some point he'd backed up against the living room wall and now he was pressing his hands flat against the plaster.

'I didn't know she was your friend,' Michael said.

'She lives in the house, Dad! She's fucking nineteen!'

His dad nodded and Alfie could see the muscle in his jaw working. 'I didn't know you knew her. If I had, I never—'

'You what? You wouldn't have shagged her? You would've just shagged some other nineteen-year-old? I don't suppose there's an option where you don't cheat on Mum, is there?'

'Your mother and I—' his dad started to say.

'I don't give a shit!' Alfie said. 'I don't care if you've got an "arrangement". I didn't care when I was little and saw you kissing Aunty Jasmine and I don't care now. It's your business, I know it is. It's nothing to do with me. But it makes me fucking sick. I want to do good things. I want to make a difference. I came to see you today because I wanted to show you my business proposal.' He realised he wasn't holding the folder any more and looked around until he spotted it on the floor in the entrance hall. Some of the pages had fallen out and were spread out across the marble tiles. 'I wanted you to be impressed. I wanted to . . . I think maybe I wanted you to see that I could do something in business that was also ethical. Because that's what I want to do. That's what drives me. It's not the thought of working with you. I don't want to work with you. I could never do what you do. Not in business. Not anywhere.'

He shook his head. He felt like he might faint. He pressed harder against the wall.

Molly reappeared, this time fully dressed and with an overnight bag over her shoulder.

She passed Alfie and crouched down to pick up his folder, tucking the papers back inside, before holding it out to him.

He took the folder from her without looking at Molly or at his father. And then he turned and left.

Outside on the street, Alfie wasn't sure which way to turn. He didn't want to head home because he thought Molly might come after him and he wasn't ready to talk to her yet. Instead, he crossed the road towards Albert Dock. By the time he reached the river he'd started to feel calmer. Not calm, but definitely calmer. He no longer felt like he wanted to punch someone. Or, more likely, something. His breathing had slowed and he could actually see what was in front of him rather than the shadow image of Molly standing in the living room of his dad's flat.

He dropped down on a bench and stared out over the water. 'Fuck.'

'I didn't know!' Molly said. 'I'm so, so sorry.'

She was waiting in the kitchen when he got home. She looked tired and pale and nervous and his first instinct had been to tell her it was OK. But it wasn't OK. How could it be?

Alfie shook his head. He couldn't think of anything to say. He felt like his insides had been scooped out.

'Alfie,' Molly said. 'I promise you I didn't know. How could I have known?'

Alfie leaned back against the cooker and Molly reached out and grabbed his arm.

'I didn't even know your dad was white!'

Alfie looked at her. 'Do you believe in love?' he asked.

'What? Of course I do!'

'Are you in love with my dad?' He felt himself wince as he asked.

Molly took a breath. 'No. I'm not. But I . . . I feel like I could be. Or could've been. It wasn't nothing, Alfie.'

Alfie nodded. 'I walked down to the river. After I left Dad's. Have you seen that there's those love lock things on the railings? You know where people put padlocks with their initials on and then throw the key in the river?'

Molly nodded.

'I've had a crush on you since we first met,' Alfie said.

'What?' She blinked at him.

'You never knew?'

She shook her head. 'I had no idea. You never said. Why didn't you ever say?'

'I don't know. I should have done. Obviously. But I didn't want to ruin our friendship. And then Anna moved in and—'

'You forgot about me and started fancying her instead?' Molly smiled.

'Not quite,' Alfie said. 'But, yeah, I kind of started to realise that she was more . . . That you and me wouldn't . . .' He groaned. 'I'm so crap at this. I realised that a lot of it with you was because I knew it would never happen.'

'It's a lot safer that way,' Molly said. 'Much less likely to get hurt.'

Alfie turned towards her, but couldn't quite look at her. 'Exactly. But then I almost slept with Anna and I—'

'You almost slept with Anna?' Molly said, tugging on his arm again.

Alfie rubbed his hands back through his hair. 'Yes. And I wanted to. But I stopped. I've got so much going on. My head is just full of shit. And I felt like I needed to . . . get rid of something before I could really focus. On Anna.'

Molly shook her head, smiling. 'You're a one-off. I hope you told Anna that?'

'No. I just said I couldn't do it. So she probably hates me now. I just thought that if I got my dad's backing for the cafe idea then I could stop worrying about that, be able to shut that door. I just . . . I want him to be proud of me. For me. For who I really am, not who he wants me to be. And I thought, even if he said no, even if he thought it was a shit idea, then I could still close that door. I could stop trying to please him because I would know that I couldn't. That nothing would be good enough. And I just felt like I needed to deal with that before . . . taking on something else.'

'Alfie,' Molly said. 'Anna's not another project to add to your timetable. She's a person. A person who really likes you. And, I don't know, you like her too, right?'

'I do!' Alfie said. 'I really do. And you're right. But when I get overwhelmed my brain works in . . . spreadsheets.'

'So romantic,' Molly said. She moved to stand next to him and nudged him with her shoulder.

He smiled. 'You wouldn't understand. You just do exactly what you want to, Mol, you always have. And that's what I liked about you. What I like about you. You know? You're fearless. And I'm scared all the time.'

'Bollocks,' Molly said. 'You're the most together person I know.'

Alfie laughed. 'I'm not. I'm really fucking not. It takes so much work. I work all the time – at Bean and on college stuff. And I hardly ever sleep. I'm always tired. Like I could lie down and sleep right now. But I can't seem to stop.'

'Jesus,' Molly said. 'You do so much. You take care of us all. You look after the house. You're at college and you work and you have all these plans. You need to give yourself a break. And you know there's nothing wrong with asking for help.'

Alfie put his head in his hands. 'Now I've fucked everything up.'

'Of course you haven't,' Molly said. 'Anna will understand.'

Alfie looked up at her. 'My dad won't though.'

Molly shrugged. 'I think maybe he will too. And if he doesn't . . . well, you told him how you feel. That's a good thing.'

Alfie nodded. 'It doesn't feel like a good thing.'

Molly draped one arm around his neck and hugged him against her. 'I really am sorry. If I'd known, I never would have—'

'You knew he was married though,' Alfie said, quietly.

Molly nodded, her head against Alfie's shoulder. 'I did. But he said his wife was OK with it and I just . . . I mean, I know that doesn't make it OK.'

'She is OK with it, I think,' Alfie said. 'That's the fucked-up thing. I can't get my head round it.'

'I know,' Molly said. 'I'm struggling a bit myself.' She smiled. 'I mean, seriously. What are the chances?'

Alfie snorted out a laugh. 'Jesus.'

Molly's phone rang.

'Don't answer it if it's him,' Alfie said.

Molly looked at the screen. 'It's not,' she said. 'It's Anna.'

Chapter 39

Anna stayed out on the terrace until she heard the others coming home. She was hungry and thirsty and tired, but mostly she felt completely freaked out by the phone call. She'd Googled Maria Caldwell on her phone and had found a bunch of stories she'd written. She wrote for tabloids and seemed to specialise in celebrity exposés or simply tearing celebrities to pieces – there'd been a story about a young gay singer that didn't seem to have any sort of news hook or story at all, just a lot of innuendo and suggestions that he had shagged his way to success.

Reading them and thinking that Sean was going to be the subject of one made Anna feel sick. But if she was going to warn Sean – and she had to warn Sean – then she'd have to tell Sean it had been her fault. She'd have to tell him, all the housemates – about her vlogs. She tried to think of what she'd said about them, how much she'd revealed. She thought about getting up and getting her laptop, but she couldn't stand the thought of it. She couldn't even remember talking about Sean and Roman Lucas – if someone had asked her, she wouldn't have thought she'd mentioned them – but as soon as Maria had started quoting her, it had come back. What else had she said?

And why had she ever assumed that just because she didn't use their names, no one would know who she was talking about? She couldn't believe she'd been so stupid.

Maybe it wasn't so bad. Maybe Sean hadn't been sleeping with Roman Lucas and it was a misunderstanding and everything would be fine. But she still had to tell them about the vlogs.

'You will not believe the day we've had,' Molly said, coming in with Alfie.

Anna glanced at Alfie and then looked away. She'd been worrying about how they'd be in the house together after what had happened, but the phone call had totally replaced that worry. She assumed she'd be moving out after she told them all what she'd done anyway.

'What's happened?' Alfie said.

'I think it's probably easier if I wait till everyone's here,' Anna said. 'Do you know where Sean is? I texted him, but he hasn't replied.'

Molly tugged Alfie along behind her and they both slumped down on the sofa. 'I haven't heard from him, sorry,' Molly said.

Anna looked at her phone again. She'd been looking at it almost constantly since she'd spoken to the journalist. She was scared that she'd phone again. She was even more scared that she wouldn't phone again, but would just write the article, featuring Sean and quoting Anna, and she felt faint at the thought.

'Is Nina in?' Molly asked.

'Upstairs,' Anna said. 'She said she'd be down soon. Are you both OK? When you came in you said—'

'It's fine,' Molly said. 'We can talk about it some other time. I've just texted Sean too. I'll let you know if he replies.'

Anna nodded and went back out onto the terrace to wait.

'What happened?' Anna heard Molly say. She sat up from where she'd been slumped down on the table, trying not to cry. She could see Nina in the lounge and Molly and Alfie had both stood up. Anna headed inside and saw Nina, looking pale, an enormous bruise around one eye and down her cheekbone.

'Did Jack do that to you?' Molly said. She reached out to Nina, but Nina stepped away from her, shaking her head.

'Nina!' Molly said.

'It doesn't matter,' Nina said. 'I'm fine. I'm not pregnant.'

'You're pregnant?' Alfie said. 'What?'

Nina shook her head. 'I'm not pregnant. I thought I was, but I'm not. I just got my period.'

'You told Jack and he fucking *hit* you?' Molly said.

'It doesn't matter,' Nina said. 'It's over. I don't know what I was thinking.'

'Where is he?' Alfie said. 'I'm going to fucking kill him.'

'No, you're not.' Molly said to Alfie. She put her arm around Nina and Nina let her. 'Are you OK? Really?'

Nina nodded. 'I've just been sitting there thinking about it all. About how I let him treat me. I think he convinced me to leave the Academy . . . I mean, I know it was down to me, I could've stayed if I'd wanted to, but I lost my confidence and he . . . he encouraged that.'

Molly guided Nina over to sit down at the dining table.

'It's not your fault,' Molly said.

'I can't believe I let it happen,' Nina said. 'I keep thinking of more and more things. How he got pissed off that night when I did karaoke. The way he was with Anna.'

Anna saw Alfie look over at her and she wrapped her arms around herself. Maybe she didn't have to tell them. Maybe she could convince Maria Caldwell not to run the story. She looked at her phone again. Nothing from Maria Caldwell, but nothing from Sean either.

Anna took a deep breath. She couldn't wait for Sean. She needed to tell them now. Before she lost her bottle completely.

'I've got . . .' she started to say, but her voice didn't come out loud enough for anyone to hear. She cleared her throat and tried again. 'I'm really sorry. I've got some more bad news.'

She showed them the vlogs. All of them since she'd moved to Liverpool. Every single time she saw herself start to talk about something in one of the housemates' personal lives, she felt something like pins and needles run up and down her arms. It was the most mortifying experience of her life so far. Worse than losing the job at the Phoenix, worse than throwing up on her first night there, worse than finding out her parents had sold her childhood home.

The others were mostly pretty quiet. They seemed almost stunned, but every now and then Anna would hear a sharp intake of breath or someone would mutter something and her eyes would fill. She was trying really hard not to cry – this was all her fault; she didn't want to be the one sitting there weeping as if she expected them to feel sorry for her – but every now and then a tear sneaked out and she brushed it away.

'I just don't understand why you talked about us at all,' Alfie said, a few videos in. He was sitting on the floor, leaning back against the wall, separate from the rest of them and it made Anna's heart hurt.

Anna shook her head. 'I don't know. I didn't mean to. I mean, I didn't plan to. I don't usually have much of a plan before I start filming. Sometimes there's something I want to talk about or a question I want to ask, but mostly I just talk about my life – what's happened that day, you know. I mean, they're called "day in the life" videos. And since I moved here . . . you've all been such a big part of my life. The main thing in my life, really.'

'Didn't you think you should've asked us before talking about us?' Molly said.

'I do now, obviously,' Anna said. 'I wish I had. But I honestly didn't think of it. It's not like I decided to do it without telling you, without your permission; I just didn't think of it. I know that's hard to believe, but it's true. I've just been really stupid.'

'Was it because it was anonymous?' Nina said. 'Because you don't use your own name, I mean?'

'That's probably part of it,' Anna said. 'I mean, that's what I love about it. That I can talk about anything. That's why I feel much more like myself when I'm vlogging than when I'm doing anything else.'

'So that's you?' Molly said, pointing at the screen.

Anna nodded. 'I think so.'

'So who is this then?' She pointed at Anna.

'This is me too,' Anna said. 'Now. Before I moved here . . .' She paused to rub her face. 'Before I moved here, the video me felt like the real me. Like the me inside, but I couldn't make my outside match. The first time I started to feel like . . . *her* was on work experience. And then when I moved in here and met all of you.'

Molly frowned. 'How did she get your number? The journalist?'

'It's easy enough,' Alfie said. 'It's probably on Facebook or something.'

'But how did she find out who Anna was really?' Nina said.

'Do we know who Anna is really?' Molly said.

'Come on,' Alfie said. 'That's not fair.'

'I'm so sorry,' Anna said.

'Sorry's not really good enough though, is it?' Molly said. 'Do you know what this could do to Sean?'

'What what could do to Sean?' Sean said, walking in. They all looked at him. 'Sorry,' he said. 'I got your messages, but . . .'

'Are you alright?' Molly asked, standing up and crossing the room.

He shook his head. 'No, not really. My dad died.'

Chapter 40

It wasn't really warm enough to be on the terrace, not so early anyway, but it was the only place Anna really wanted to be. Inside the house, she felt like she couldn't quite catch her breath properly. Also, she'd hardly slept, so she thought the slightly chilly air might wake her up.

She'd drunk a cup of tea with one of the metal chairs pulled up to the railings, while she looked down at Bold Street waking up. She still loved it. She loved watching the litter and grime of the previous day being cleared away and then the street slowly coming alive.

She'd moved over to the picnic table, where her laptop was waiting for her. She'd logged into YouTube and planned to watch her old videos before deleting each one. She couldn't stand the idea of carrying on with vlogging, not after what had happened, what she'd done, but she wanted to watch them first as a sort of goodbye. She'd originally been going to just delete the channel in one fell swoop, but the idea of it made her want to cry, so she'd come up with a new plan. She put her headphones on and clicked 'play' on the first video she'd recorded as AnnaSparks.

She was surprised at how much younger she looked. And how nervous she'd been; it made her nervous to watch it. But by the end of the video, she could already see herself growing in confidence. She dropped her headphones down around her neck and tipped her head into her hands. She remembered how it had felt to realise she could become someone else. Or not even someone else, just more herself. The person she wanted to be.

She deleted the video and then played the next one with her headphones still round her neck. She felt more like AnnaSparks than Anna Parkes now, she realised. Anna Parkes belonged in Meadowvale, hanging out with Eleanor and spending Saturday nights in her room because she hadn't been invited to the party everyone had been talking about at school all week. AnnaSparks lived in Liverpool. In a cool house on Bold Street. With friends she'd let down horribly, but who seemed as if they could forgive her. She really hoped they'd forgive her.

'Hey,' Alfie said, stepping out onto the terrace.

Anna jumped and automatically went to shut the laptop, but then realised there was no need. He knew now. They all knew.

'You OK?' he asked, sitting down opposite her.

Anna nodded. 'Yeah. Thanks. Are you?'

Alfie smiled wryly. 'Yeah, I think so. I still can't believe that Molly and my dad . . .' He shook his head. 'But I'm just going to try really hard not to think about that. Ever.'

'Have you spoken to him?' Anna asked.

Alfie shook his head. 'I'm going to leave it a bit. And then I'm going to go home and talk to them both. My mum and my dad. Lola's going to come too, I talked to her last night.'

'Right,' Anna said. 'Good.'

'What are you doing?' Alfie asked.

'Oh!' Anna said, suddenly realising how it might look. 'I wasn't filming, I—' She reached up and realised her hair was down and started to fasten it back up.

'It looks nice down,' Alfie said. 'Your hair.'

Anna didn't know what to say. The last time he'd said that, his hands had been inside her clothes. She looked at the table. And then remembered how she'd just been thinking she was AnnaSparks now. She looked back up at Alfie.

'What happened? The other night?'

'God,' Alfie said. 'I'm so sorry. I just . . . freaked out. It wasn't about you, honestly. It was about me being a control freak. I talked to Molly about it and—'

'You talked to Molly about it?' Anna said. 'But—'

'I know,' Alfie said. 'I told her I'd had a crush on her. But I don't any more. I mean, I didn't anyway, but . . . shit, I really wouldn't now, would I?'

Anna smiled.

'I like you,' Alfie said. 'I'm sorry if I made you feel . . . that I didn't. Or that I didn't enjoy . . . That I wasn't enjoying . . . God, I'm terrible at this.'

'You're not so bad,' Anna said.

Alfie smiled. 'I'd love to take you out. For dinner, not another documentary. Do you think you might want to do that?'

'I would love to do that,' Anna said.

They smiled at each other across the table.

'What were you doing?' Alfie said, nodding at the laptop.

'Oh,' Anna said. 'I'm deleting my videos.'

Alfie shook his head. 'No. No, that's not right. Those videos were you. You said you felt more yourself on the videos than in real life, right?'

'Yes,' Anna said. 'But I don't think I do any more and they caused so much . . . I've made such a mess.'

'You made a mistake.' Alfie said. 'We all make mistakes. God knows I have. And Molly. And Nina. And the reason that journalist contacted you was because she was writing about Sean's affair with a teacher, basically. That should never have happened. Yeah, it would have been better if you hadn't talked about it, but Sean shouldn't have done it. He knows that.'

Anna looked at the laptop screen. The next video had auto-played and she saw herself. Her hair down, make-up on – talking animatedly about she didn't know what. She didn't want to delete it, she realised. But she still wasn't sure she could go on and make more videos. Not the way she had been, anyway. She shut the window and then closed the laptop.

'I won't delete any more yet,' she told Alfie. 'I need to think.'

'Good,' Alfie said. 'If you love it, you should keep doing it. You just need to find a way to do it—'

'Ethically?' Anna said.

Alfie smiled. 'Yeah.'

'Why are you out here?' Molly said, stepping out onto the terrace. 'It's cold.'

She was wearing the hoodie Anna had seen Alfie smelling. That seemed like a long time ago. The sleeves were hanging down over her hand and she pulled the hood up as she shivered against the cold.

'Just getting some fresh air,' Alfie said. 'How's Sean?'

'He's OK,' Molly said. 'He was with him when he died and I think that helped.'

'And Nina?' Anna asked.

'She's OK too,' Molly said. 'Freaked out about how it all went so far, you know? But we talked about how easy it is to be taken in by someone like that. Sean had some thoughts too.' She pulled a face. 'She's talking about coming back to the Academy, so that's good.'

Molly stretched and said, 'I'm meant to be making coffee. So I'll leave you two . . . to it.'

'Molly,' Anna said. 'I'm really sorry. You've all been so amazing, you especially. I thought you were going to ask me to move out and I—'

Molly shook her head, the hood falling back and revealing her red hair. 'Don't worry about it. We all make mistakes. Just don't do it again, eh?'

'I definitely won't,' Anna said.

'I'm in no position to talk, am I?' Molly said, reaching over and rubbing the top of Alfie's head. 'At least you didn't shag anyone's dad.'

Alfie groaned.

'Too soon?' Molly said, grinning.

Chapter 41

Alfie was the first to join Anna on the terrace. He set the pizza in the centre of the table, opened beers for himself and Anna, and put the other bottles in a bucket of ice that was already starting to melt in the unseasonably hot weather they'd been having for the last couple of days. Anna turned on the fairy lights – it wasn't dark yet, but it soon would be.

Once everything was set up, Alfie leaned over and kissed Anna on the side of her neck. She slid one hand up his back, feeling the muscles move under his T-shirt and turned to kiss him on the mouth. She still couldn't quite believe she got to kiss him whenever she wanted to. And she wanted to a lot.

'I had a meeting with Malc today,' he told her, as he sat down on the other side of the picnic table.

'Yeah?'

'He's met someone who's interested in backing Coffee Cafe.' He turned his beer bottle between his fingers.

'That's great news!' Anna said.

'I think it might be my dad,' Alfie said.

'And you're all right with that?' Anna asked.

Alfie shrugged again. 'If he wants to help then that's a start, right?'

Anna nodded. 'I think it's brilliant.'

'Did you talk to Lola?'

'Yep. It's an internship at The Riverside. Just six weeks and unpaid, but it'll be good experience. And Tony said I can work evenings.'

'Are you going to do it?'

Anna nodded. 'If they'll have me.'

'They'd be mad not to,' Alfie said and Anna reached over and stroked the back of his hand with her thumb. He lifted her hand to his mouth and kissed the underside of her wrist.

'I watched today's vlog,' he said from behind her hand.

'Oh, my God,' Anna said. 'Why would you do that?'

'Why wouldn't I?' Alfie said. 'It was really good. And it's had thousands of views already.'

'I know,' Anna said. 'I can't believe it.'

She'd recorded the vlog as herself, without the usual AnnaSparks make-up, but still with her hair down, because she'd started to like it better like that. She liked how Alfie couldn't resist running his hands through it; it made her shiver just thinking about it. She'd talked about what had happened, and apologised for making such a stupid mistake. And she'd vowed that she would be herself in future. Her usual commenters had been lovely and supportive, but she'd had lots of other comments too and private messages from much more famous YouTubers. She'd even been invited to a convention and a couple of journalists had been in touch, wanting to write a feature. But she was steering well clear of anything like that.

'My mum watched it. My friend Eleanor's mum told her about it at Slimming World, apparently. She said she was proud of me.' Anna still couldn't quite believe it.

'I'm proud of you too,' Alfie said.

Anna stood up and leaned across the table to kiss him.

'No PDAs,' Molly said, coming through the patio doors. 'First rule of terrace club.'

'What the hell's "terrace club"?' Alfie said, turning to smile at her.

'A thing I just made up to stop you two snogging every five minutes. Keep it in your room. Or your room.' She pointed at Anna.

Nina came out too and sat down next to Anna. 'Do not let me get drunk,' she said, as she opened a beer. 'I've got my audition tomorrow and I will not blow it.'

'You won't blow it,' Anna said. 'You'll be brilliant.'

'We'll see,' Nina said. 'And did I tell you I've got dinner with my parents after? So I won't be back until late?'

'You didn't,' Alfie said. 'But duly noted.'

Nina had resigned from the hotel after telling them about the stolen wallet and then she'd told her parents that she hadn't been at the Academy for the past two terms. And then she'd arranged a meeting with the Academy, told them everything that had happened and begged – or so she'd said – for an audition.

'The audition's just a formality,' Molly said. 'They'd be mad not to take you back.'

'I doubt that,' Nina said. 'But they were much nicer than I thought they'd be.'

'How did it feel to be back there again?' Alfie asked.

'It felt good,' Nina said, smiling. 'It felt really good.'

'I can't believe you've started without me,' Sean said, joining them and pulling one of the wrought-iron chairs over to the end of the picnic table.

'We had to,' Nina said. 'You were doing the "no, you hang up" thing with Charlie.'

'I absolutely was not,' he said. 'He was telling me about Roman. Lucas.'

'We know which Roman you mean,' Molly said.

'He's playing gay in his next film and he's given an interview about being bi.'

'Seriously?' Anna asked.

Sean nodded. 'The studio probably dealt with your journalist.' He smiled at Anna.

'Thank God,' Anna said.

'I was probably just research,' Sean said, shrugging. 'I think he learned a lot.'

He had a pile of envelopes in his hand and he opened the first one, before shoving the envelope under his beer bottle to act as a makeshift coaster.

'Why do all the condolence cards have lilies on?' he asked, holding the card up to show them. 'Why lilies?'

'Saddest of the flowers,' Molly said.

'It's from my dad's best mate from school,' Sean said. 'They were friends for fifty years. Imagine that.'

Anna looked around the table at Alfie and Molly and Nina and Sean. She couldn't quite imagine it. But she'd like to try.

Sean opened the next envelope, stared for a bit and then said, 'Fuck me.'

'What?' Molly asked, leaning over to look.

Sean looked up at his friends, but then couldn't seem to speak. He pushed the contents of the envelope across the table to Alfie.

'Bloody hell,' Alfie said.

It was a cheque. For thirty-five grand. From Sean's dad.

'There's a note,' Molly said. 'Do you want me to read it?'

Sean rubbed his face with both hands and nodded.

'It's from an insurance policy,' Molly said. 'That he had for your mum. He said he meant to give it to you before now.'

'He kept saying he was going to give me money,' Sean said. 'He bloody knew. He knew he was dying, the bastard.'

They all sat in silence, staring at the cheque in the centre of the wooden table.

'I can pay for that fucking Furby now,' Sean said.

The pizza was gone and almost all of the beer. The sky was dark and the terrace was lit by the fairy lights and the light from the lounge.

'We should go on holiday,' Sean said. 'I'll pay.'

'Where will we go?' Molly said. She was sitting sideways on the bench seat, one foot up across Anna's lap.

'Somewhere hot,' Alfie said, pulling his hoodie over his head with one hand and reaching for Anna's hand with the other.

'Somewhere we can swim in the sea,' Nina said from the cushions on the floor.

Anna looked around the terrace at her friends and then tipped her head back and looked up at the indigo sky.

'Somewhere where we can see the stars,' she said.

Acknowledgements

This is the longest book I've written so far and it was probably the hardest to write. So I've got quite a few people to thank . . .

Firstly, a massive slice of pug cake to my wonderful agent Hannah Sheppard – thank you for everything you do for me and for (virtually) introducing me to the other lovely authors you represent. We just need a team name now . . .

Huge thanks to Emily Thomas for suggesting I write this book in the first place and being excited about my extremely vague idea ('Maybe a group of friends in Liverpool and . . . stuff happens . . .') and to Naomi Colthurst and Jenny Jacoby for really getting what I was trying to do and pushing me to actually do it. And thank you to Jan Bielecki for the gorgeous cover.

Thank you to Corinne Lewis and Charli McCann for letting me come and look round LIPA, to Genevieve Clark and Paige Meehan for showing me round and answering so many questions and to Christina McMc for putting me in touch with Corinne. (The Academy bears no resemblance to LIPA and no former Beatles were involved in its formation!)

I was thrilled and honoured to be awarded a Grant for the Arts by Arts Council England to support me in writing this book – it's one of the highlights of my writing career, so thank you doesn't really seem like enough, but . . . thank you. (And thank you to Zoe Marriott for guiding me through the application form!)

Thank you to the Sisterhood and YA Thinkers for cheerleading and hand-holding and pant-wetting laughter. Not to mention the goats.

To Stella, Keren and Sophia for fabulously encouraging feedback (even if you did all contradict each other!). And to Katy Walker for 'finger pie'.

To all the incredibly supportive bloggers – I appreciate everything you do for me, my books and the YA community in general. A special mention to Michelle Toy for being awesome and sending me many Harry Styles gifs.

On the subject of Harry Styles gifs . . . writing this book coincided with me suddenly falling for One Direction (finger on the pulse, me) so I have to thank them for inspiration and constant distraction. I'd also like to thank Amy, Lindsay, Alicia, Rachael, Brigid and Georgie for always being happy to tweet-flail about all things 1D.

To my fellow former residents of St Mary's Street, Ealing, for inspiration and memories, particularly Byron and Sam (I may have nicked a couple of your stories . . . but don't worry, I probably remembered them wrong).

Finally, to David, for all the times I said I was going to Liverpool 'for research' and then spent most of the day in Central Perk watching *Friends*. And for, you know, the meals and teas and laughs and love. And to Harry and Joe for being funny and clever and not minding when I ignore them to write (as long as they can go and play Minecraft). You can't read this book until you're eighteen.

Keris Stainton

Keris Stainton was born in Winnipeg, Manitoba, which, by all accounts, is very cold. And also hot. But when she was four months old, her parents moved back to the UK, and now she lives in Lancashire with a fellow northerner, their two ridiculously gorgeous sons and a pug. Okay, they haven't got a pug, but Keris hopes if she writes it here it will come true. If you write it, pugs will come.

Keris has been writing stories for as long as she can remember, but she didn't write a novel until 2004 when she took part in National Novel Writing Month. She hasn't quite finished that one yet, but she has finished a few others, including *Jessie Hearts NYC, Della Says: OMG!, Emma Hearts LA, Starring Kitty* and *Spotlight on Sunny*. She has also written for the Hot Key Books Unlocked list under the pseudonym Esme Taylor. Find out more about Keris at www.keris-stainton.com or follow her on Twitter: @Keris

HOT
KEY
BOOKS